Words Can Kill

A Ghostwriter Mystery
(Book 5)

C. A. LARMER

Larmer Media
ISBN: 978-0-9924743-0-0
Cover design: Stuart Eadie

To the good friends in my life
(you know who you are)

ALSO BY C.A. LARMER

The Ghostwriter Mystery series:
Killer Twist (Book 1)
A Plot to Die For (Book 2)
Last Writes (Book 3)
Dying Words (Book 4)
A Note Before Dying (Book 6)
Without a Word (Book 7)

The Murder Mystery Book Club series:
The Murder Mystery Book Club (Book 1)
Danger On the SS Orient (Book 2)
Death Under the Stars (Book 3)
When There Were 9 (Book 4)
The Widow on the Honeymoon Cruise (Book 5)
Gone Guest (Book 6)

The Posthumous Mystery series:
Do Not Go Gentle
Do Not Go Alone

The Sleuths of Last Resort:
Blind Men Don't Dial Zero
Smart Girls Don't Trust Strangers
Good Girls Don't Drink Vodka

PLUS
*After the Ferry: A Gripping
Psychological Novel*

An Island Lost

CONTENTS

ACKNOWLEDGEMENTS

This book is all about the power of friendship and I have to acknowledge the good friends in my life who have lived and laughed beside me, through travel adventures, career changes, relationship dilemmas and many, many writers festivals. My life, and work, is the richer for it.

PROLOGUE

The woman's limbs flailed in all directions, one Nike trainer flying off as she plummeted from the edge of the cliff down towards the cerulean Mediterranean Sea. She must have screamed (how could she not?) but whatever sound she made was swallowed by the screeching of the train that was hurtling at the same time, through the mountain tunnel, towards the tiny village of Manarola, its happy day-trippers oblivious to her horror, seeing only a stunning view through their raised cameras and iPads.

"Isn't it peaceful?" one sightseer ventured to another just as the woman's body smashed against the jagged rocks at the bottom and was promptly collected by a wave and washed out to sea.

A metre below the fence line, her shoe was caught by a prickly pear cactus and settled into its spikes, the only evidence she had come before, while the tourists continued happily snapping away.

CHAPTER 1

"Max is missing."

They were three simple words, spoken casually by a woman young enough and pretty enough to still believe she was the centre of the universe and therefore her missing brother a minor inconvenience that she was hoping to palm off (preferably to Roxy Parker), but they still managed to send a sliver of ice through Roxy's heart.

She froze for a second, the warm glass of Merlot almost at her lips.

"Missing?" she said, then tried a little humour to dislodge the chill. "Like, missing his brain? Missing me desperately? What do you mean, *missing*?"

Caroline raised one spaghetti-strapped shoulder into the air and shrugged. It was late Thursday evening and unseasonably cold, but that didn't stop her from donning a sexy slip of a dress that showed off her golden brown tan and the intricate rose tattoo on the back of her right shoulder. Her long, lean legs were wedged into stilettos as high as the Harbour Bridge and were poking out now from beneath the table.

"I don't know, sweetie. Personally? I think it's all a false alarm." She scooped some lemongrass chicken onto her fork. "I nearly didn't call you but, well, it's got Mum and Dad in a bit of a tizz which is bizarre because they *never* get in a tizz. Unless somebody chops down a tree, of course, or mentions the letters CSG." She rolled her big brown eyes and plunged the fork into her mouth, talking while she chewed. "Anyway, they haven't heard from him in a few days and seem to think that's a big deal—something he said freaked them out, apparently." She offered her "go figure" look.

The two women were seated at a rickety table in an overcrowded Thai restaurant just a few blocks from Roxy's inner-city Sydney apartment. When Caroline had called her, keen to "discuss something important", Roxy had expected little more than boyfriend trouble or a change of career. God knows there'd been enough of both. This, however, was out of the blue.

She took a settling gulp of her wine and returned the glass safely to the table. "A few days is hardly a problem, is it?"

"My sentiments exactly but, well, Mum's being all loopy on this one so ..." She hesitated. "He hasn't called *you*, has he?"

The sudden crinkle in Caroline's otherwise flawless forehead was not without basis. The last time Roxy had spoken to her supposed "boyfriend" Max, a few months ago, it had all turned very sour, very fast. They had been dating for almost a year and things were going swimmingly (albeit more treading water than doing laps) until Max mentioned a sudden job offer with Mercedes-Benz in Germany. Roxy had reacted badly, a little "Caroline-like" in fact, and had not managed to find her maturity in the meantime. She was still feeling raw from the rejection and had been hoping Max would do as he always did and make the first move: call with apologies, send her a surprise airline ticket to Berlin, *something*. But of course he hadn't done that and so the silence had ensued.

Now it felt deafening.

"Anyhoo," Caroline was saying, oblivious to Roxy's internal discomfort, "I normally call Max when I have a problem; he cleans it up for me quick smart. Problem is, well, *Max* is my problem." She laughed. "Then I remembered that you're kind of good at looking into 'mysteries'"—she used the two finger quotation mark symbol that Roxy abhorred—"so was wondering if you want to track him down for me and tell him to call his bloody parents so I can get them off my back."

She raised one hand again to a waiter who had been tracking her from the moment she'd walked in and he scurried across, delighted to be at the stunning blonde's beck and call. She ordered another glass of wine.

"You want?" she asked Roxy, almost as an afterthought, and Roxy tapped her glass.

"Merlot, please." Then to Caroline, "Can we just back up a little? I still don't understand why your mother thinks he's vanished."

"Oh she's being so melodramatic, darling. I'm sure he's just run off with some German flooz—" she caught herself and had the decency to blush. "Oops."

Roxy shrugged her off. "I don't care if he has a girlfriend, Caroline."

"Sure you don't. Anyway, I'm not saying he *does* have a girlfriend, I'm just saying—"

"So why is your mum so worried?" Roxy cut her off. "What did Max say when they last spoke?"

Caroline leaned forward, one dress strap dropping provocatively from her shoulder. "That's the thing, he didn't say very much and what he did say made absolutely no sense. Mum reckons he said he was heading to Brazil for a few days."

"Brazil? For a few days? From Germany? Really?"

"I know! How bizarre is that? Mum *must* have heard him wrong. I mean, her hearing's not what it used to be and Max *was* calling on his mobile phone, from the road apparently.

Anyway, it's not so much what he said, it was the *way* he said it."

The waiter appeared with the wines and Caroline refitted her strap and then took her glass with barely a glance, causing the poor man's shoulders to deflate considerably as he turned away. She swallowed a generous mouthful and said, "He sounded kind of strange."

"How do you mean *strange*?"

"Mum says he sounded worried, stressed even, but you have to remember, Mum's a hippie. She thinks she can read people's cosmic energy down the phone line." Again with the eye roll. "She says Max's energy was 'as black as a witch's breath'. She rang me in a panic this morning when she couldn't get him on his mobile. He hasn't been answering his home phone or his e-mails either. I told her to chillax."

"And you haven't heard from him yourself?"

Caroline shook her long, glossy locks. "We rarely *talk* on the phone, darling, that's sooo twentieth century! We usually just swap texts, tweets, that kind of thing. But only about once a week, if that. I've since sent two texts and poked him on Facebook, but no response." Her eyes squinted. "He did post some rather strange shots earlier this week now I think of it." She reached for her stiff, lurid orange Prada handbag that had been wedged under the table and pulled out a smartphone, which was also encased in a bright orange cover. "Kind of like mountain shots, with snow and stuff. I don't think they're of Brazil. Isn't Brazil, like, hot?"

After scrolling through the iPhone for some minutes, she located the relevant Facebook pictures and thrust the phone towards Roxy. They looked harmless enough. Boring, even. They were simple landscape shots of a jagged mountainside, some dusted white with snow, the others an ugly greyish brown colour. Dark clouds hung above one shot, another showed glimpses of green valleys and a blue lake below. Max had shared them on his Facebook site with only the words, "Up in heaven" beside them. There was no indication of where they had been taken.

"You want more chook?" Caroline asked, indicating the lemongrass chicken dish, and Roxy shook her head no.

She glanced at the date below the pictures. "So he put these mountain pix up last Monday, nothing to explain where he is, and then called your mum on, what, Tuesday to say he's heading to Brazil?"

She held a long, manicured fingernail in the air. "Rio de Janeiro to be precise, and he called very early Wednesday morning, actually. Woke Mum up."

Roxy felt the ice dislodge a little. "Caroline, that was *yesterday*. He's been 'missing',"—now it was her turn to do the curly finger thing—"about a day and a half, what's the big panic?"

"As I told you, it's not what he said so much as they way he said it. Mum felt these really dark—"

"Vibes, yeah, yeah." She sipped her wine. "You know what it sounds like to me?" Caroline didn't answer. "Sounds like he's on a photo shoot for Mercedes, maybe one he doesn't particularly want to do, hence the dark vibes. Has anyone thought to ring his office in Berlin, ask them?"

Caroline held her palms out. "Now *this* is why I came to you! Of course Mum didn't call his office, it didn't even occur to her. I love the woman but she's hardly the sharpest peg in the shed."

"Tool," Roxy corrected and Caroline looked at her blankly.

"Anyway, that's a brilliant idea. Can you do it?"

Roxy sighed. "Yes, fine. Do you have the office number? Name of his boss? Anything?"

"Nope."

"What about his flatmate? Isn't he living with someone in Berlin?"

"Yeah, some American muso called Jake. Mum and I have both tried him. We're not completely useless you know."

"And?"

She took a final mouthful of rice then pushed her plate

away. "And nothing. He wasn't answering. I guess he's away, too."

"You haven't got his mobile number?"

"Why would I? Don't even know the guy." She took her iPhone back. "So you can see why we're all a little flustered." Roxy stared at her; she didn't look flustered at all. "But as I say, I'm sure it will all make perfect sense in a day or two." She glanced at the phone clock. "Shit, I've got to get going. You sure you don't want to come to this party?" She glanced down at Roxy's demure vintage black dress and strand of white pearls. "You can dash home and get changed first. It'll be worth it! They've got DJ Prawn on the bill."

Roxy couldn't think of anything worse, and that was before she'd discovered her estranged boyfriend was AWOL. She told Caroline as much. "Plus it's a school night," she said. "I've got a book to deliver tomorrow."

"Pfft! You'll never get over Max with that attitude," she replied and Roxy ignored this as she would identical comments from her mother and watched as Max's baby sister polished off the last of her wine, grabbed her lipstick from her bag and swiped a strip of bright red across both lips.

She jumped up then leaned down and air-kissed Roxy. "You got this one? I'll get the next. Sorry to love you and leave you, sweetie, but there's dancing to be done. Call me on my mobile the minute you find him, okay? I have *got* to get Mum off my back. If I hear one more loony story from her about dark auras I will kill someone." She smiled lightly. "Too do loo!"

And with that Caroline dashed out of the restaurant leaving Roxy—and at least one waiter—sighing in her wake.

CHAPTER 2

"**Max** is missing?" Oliver Horowitz said, his beady little eyes as wide as they could get, and Roxy quickly shook her head. Caroline had already put her heart through the ringer, she didn't need to alarm anyone else unnecessarily.

"Not for long," she assured him, leaning back on the bright red sofa in her agent's Kings Cross apartment.

It was now late on Friday night, twenty-four hours since her dinner date with Caroline and still no word from Max. Despite her gallant promises, Roxy hadn't found the time to call Max's Berlin office, partly because she was presenting the final draft of a book she'd just completed on the life and times of Edward Stray, an ex-politician from the 1960s who had plenty of opinions but very little worth saying.

Roxy usually enjoyed ghostwriting other people's autobiographies and was never really fazed when her name was left off the cover so they could pinch all the glory—such were the pitfalls of her profession—but this book had been a chore, and she was glad her moniker was nowhere to be seen. The man was both boring and banal and it had been a real struggle to find any glimmers of colour between his monologues on all that was wrong with the youth of today.

Luckily, she didn't have to like a client to write his life story, but gee it helped. And so it was with great relief she had finished the final draft and signed it over to her agent that evening, hence the celebratory drink in Oliver's apartment.

The other reason Roxy hadn't moved on finding Max was because she wanted to believe they were all overreacting. Big time. It had to be said, Roxy was usually the first to suspect foul play in any situation, any at all, but this time she didn't want to play ball. This time they were talking about Max Farrell and she wouldn't let her mind go there. Not yet.

"Sounds to me like he's on location for Merc, doing some fabulous photo shoot, but his mum is worried which has got Caroline worried—well, as worried as Caroline can get—so I'm just going to confirm where he is and we can all go back to our boring, mundane lives."

"Oi, speak for yourself," Oliver said and she glanced around the apartment, at the empty beer bottles on the coffee table, the TV which was now on mute, and the pile of gossip magazines that she'd clearly interrupted him reading before she'd arrived.

He followed her gaze and said, "Hey, there is nothing boring or mundane about Miley Cyrus's descent into hell. Sort of like watching a train wreck in slow motion."

Roxy stared at him with deadpan eyes. "Right, well, speaking of boring, you did wax lyrical about your fabulous phone plan the other day. Went on and on about how all your international calls are capped so ..."

"So you want to use and abuse me, yet again?"

"Something like that." She bat her emerald green eyes at him playfully now. "Mind if I make a few calls to Germany?"

"Germany! Jesus, woman!"

She continued batting away and he finally relented, plucking his hands-free phone from its cradle and flinging it towards her. "You know, I get a bonus if I sign friends and family up to the aforementioned phone plan, we just have to do it by—"

"Oliver! I kind of have to call now if I want to get

through to Berlin before they all head off to lunch. I've just looked up the time difference." She glanced at her watch. "It's late Friday evening here, which, if my calculations are correct, makes it midmorning on Friday over there, so I have to act fast. If I wait until tomorrow, it'll be the weekend. I'll sign anything you want after that. I promise."

Oliver pretended to zip his lips shut while Roxy called the number for international directories and after a few seconds said slowly and clearly, "Mercedes. Benz. Headquarters. Berlin. Germany."

It still took several frustrating minutes and a conversation with an actual human being before she was finally put through. As the dial tone began to ring, she held her breath and crossed her fingers metaphorically.

"Guten Tag, herzlich willkommen auf Mercedes-Benz, wie kann ich helfen?" came a gush of German on the other end and Roxy looked startled for a few seconds before her high school language class kicked in.

"Oh, um, guten tag! Um ... Sprechen Sie English?"

Oliver raised his eyebrows at her, impressed, and she gave him a smarmy smile.

"Yes, madam, this is Mercedes-Benz Head Office, how can I help you?"

"I'm trying to track down someone in your marketing department. Max Farrell. Do you know if he's in?"

"Just one moment please."

About twenty seconds later, a singsong, German accent came on the line. "Hello, ziz is Britt Gelsing in Marketing. You are looking for Max?"

"Yes, yes, I am. You know him?"

"Of course I know him!"

She felt her shoulders relax. "Great. Is he around today, do you know?"

There was a pause. "No, he is not here today. Can I take zee message?"

She deflated a little. *That would have been too easy.* "No, you see I need to track him down, for his family. We've tried his home and he's not answering. Do you know if he's on location at the moment?"

"Location?"

"Out on a photo shoot somewhere." She scrunched her eyes and said, "Like Brazil?"

There was a slight pause then a burst of laughter on the other end of the phone before the woman said something in German to someone nearby and there was a second burst of laughter. "In Max's dreams!" she told Roxy. "No Brazilian shoots for him. He has been working in zee factory, taking zee stills." Another pause. "Who is zis, please? Are you his sister?"

"No, I'm …" Now it was her time to pause. "A family friend. We haven't heard off him, that's all, and the family is getting a bit worried."

"Oooh okay, yes. I talk to Max's boss. You wait?"

Roxy told her she would and stared at Oliver hopefully. A few minutes later a man came on the other end. His voice was deeper and more guttural.

"Hallo. My name is Gunter Heidleburg, who is this, please?"

"Hello, I'm Roxy Parker. A good family friend of Max's."

"Oh, Roxy Parker, hallo! Max has told us all about you."

She gulped. "He has?"

"Oooh yes. How are you over there in kangaroo country?"

"Not so many kangaroos here in Sydney, Gunter."

He chuckled. "I just teasing you. How can I help?"

"I'm trying to track Max down, for his sister, Caroline. She hasn't heard from him in a few days and is worried." When she said it like that it sounded quite ridiculous.

"Oh, not to worry. Max is away, but not for us. He is on holidays."

Roxy felt a sliver of relief. "Okay, that makes sense. Do you know where he went? For how long?"

"Of course. He was heading for Mt Pilatus, just for the week. We loaned him a car for his trip, he very excited."

"I bet. So he's due back soon then?"

"Oh yes, we expect him back on Monday, can I get him to call you then?"

She didn't want to wait. "Mt Pilatus, you say?"

"That is right. It is a holiday place, in Switzerland. You don't know Mt Pilatus?"

"No, never heard of it. But thank you, that explains why he's out of touch." Perhaps there was no mobile phone reception up there. "You don't happen to know where he was staying at Mt Pilatus, do you?"

"Sorry, no I do not."

"Okay, no worries, I'll look into it. In the meantime, if you do speak to him before me, could you ask him to call his family ASAP? Just let them know he's okay."

"Of course! I am sure he is okay."

"I'm sure he is too." She didn't sound quite as convincing.

"Okay, well you enjoy the kangaroos," he said, laughing as he hung up.

Roxy repeated the conversation to Oliver and as he mulled it over, she reached into her handbag for her iPhone and started tapping away at Google.

"What are you doing now?"

"Looking up Mt Pilatus. If Max is there, I'm going to track him down, tell him off, and then get back to my life."

"Your boring, mundane life?"

"That'd be the one."

Ten minutes and several exasperating phone calls later, Roxy was having a very stilted conversation with a receptionist at a hotel on Mt Pilatus. She had lucked out. There were only two hotels on top of the Swiss mountain and one of them, the Hotel Pilatus-Kulm, had already assured her they had never heard of a Max Farrell and had promptly hung up.

With her fingers crossed, literally this time, Roxy had called the second hotel, the Hotel Bellevue, and waited. It answered with a flurry of what sounded like French and Roxy didn't bother with the niceties this time. She'd already worked out that most good receptionists spoke the universal language of English and so she'd simply said, "Hello, I'd like to be put through to Max Farrell's room please."

"Of course," the woman said and then she heard tapping in the background. "Can you repeat the name, please?"

"Yes, Max Farrell. F-A-R-R-E-L-L."

Another pause, longer this time. "Sorry, there is no Max Farrell staying with us."

That unsettling feeling lodged in Roxy's spine again. "Oh, right. I ... we were told he was booked in with you guys this week."

"Sorry, he is no longer here."

"But he *was*, right?"

There was hesitation again. "I am sorry, madam, we do not normally divulge information about past or current guests. Who is speaking please?"

Roxy took a punt. "This is Max Farrell's sister, Caroline. I'm calling from Australia on behalf of the family. We need to get in touch. Urgently. Family emergency."

Oliver's eyes widened again and she glanced away. She didn't normally impersonate others, it went against her journalistic code of ethics, but it was late and she was tired and that icy chill was moving in fast.

The hotel receptionist hesitated only briefly. "Okay, I look through the computer." Two minutes and many taps later she was back. "Max Farrell, Berlin address?"

"Yes."

"He was here."

"Was?"

"Yes, you are too late. He has checked out."

Damn it. "When did he check out?"

More tapping. "Wednesday morning, madam."

"Wednesday? But we were under the impression he was staying the full week."

"He was due to stay until Saturday but he checked out

early."

"Really? Do you know why?"

"No, I did not ask him this, madam." There was a slight sense of outrage in her tone.

"Did he say where he was going? Leave a forwarding address by any chance?"

"No, this is not usual. We assume he has gone back to Berlin."

Well you assumed wrong, she wanted to scream at her but said politely enough, "He didn't mention anything about Brazil or Rio De Janeiro, did he?"

"No, he did not."

"Thanks anyway." Roxy was about to hang up when something Caroline had said got her thinking. "He wasn't checked in with anyone was he? A woman, maybe?"

This time the outrage was obvious: "We can not give you that information, madam. Not even to family."

"Fine," she said less politely this time and they hung up.

Oliver was just getting up to fetch more beers and Roxy followed him into the kitchen as she spoke.

"I'm not sure whether I should be panicking or telling Mrs Farrell to 'chillax' as Caroline puts it."

He turned his stubbled jowls back to her. "Oh God, is she *still* using that term? I was hoping that would disappear from the lexicon by now."

"Oliver, you're not helping!"

"Okay, okay, *chillax.*" He reached into the fridge, fetched two bottles of Crown Lager and handed one over. "Get a bit of that in ya, then let's go through the facts and see what's what. Come on."

Oliver led her back to the sofa and dropped down again, spilling beer all over his faded green and yellow Hawaiian-print shirt but he didn't seem to notice or care. Roxy shook her head at him and took a few good gulps of her own beer before speaking.

"Right, so here's what I know: Sunday just past, Max takes a week off work and heads to the Swiss Alps where he's supposed to stay until Saturday, which means he should still be there. Instead, he checks out three days early, on Wednesday, tells his mum he's heading to Rio de Janeiro, of all places, and vanishes."

"That's it?"

"That's all I've got."

"Okay, I can work with that." Oliver slurped another sip from his bottle and smacked his lips together. "Right, so, maybe this Mt Pilatus place is boring as bat-dung so he skips out early and heads somewhere else. Maybe he took a detour on his way back to Berlin."

"Like Brazil? That's one hell of a detour."

"Yeah, that bit's bloody odd. Max's mum must have got that wrong. Why did you ask the hotel if he'd checked in with anyone else?"

"Dunno, something Caroline said got me wondering." She shook that off. "Listen, there's two more overseas calls I need to make. Do you mind?"

He sighed his consent and she picked up the receiver again. The first was to Max's mobile phone, which seemed to ring forever before it suddenly picked up. Roxy's heart somersaulted when she heard his voice and then settled again when she realised it was just the voice mail clicking in.

She took a deep breath, trying to swallow her guilt in the process, and said, "Max! Hi. It's Roxy. Umm ... Could you give us a call? Caroline's hassling me to find you. You've got your mum a little worried; you know what mums are like." She tried to laugh but couldn't manage it. "Anyway, just call as soon as you get this message. Let us know you're okay." She paused, wanting to tell him she was sorry, that she missed him, but she didn't want to scare him off so she simply hung up.

Next, she reached for her smartphone and began scrolling through for Max's Berlin apartment. Caroline had e-mailed the number a few months ago and while she had gone to the trouble of logging it into her speed dial, she had never quite found the courage to use it. She tapped the number into Oliver's home phone and pressed dial as she dumped her iPhone back into her bag. After many seconds, an automated English voice came on the line informing her she'd reached the apartment for Max Farrell and Jake Conway and was to leave a message.

Roxy growled and hung up, then stared forlornly at Oliver who was now flicking through a copy of *People* magazine. There was a creeping feeling settling into Roxy's bones again. Max had always accused her of being a drama queen but now she wondered whether she wasn't being dramatic enough.

A sudden beeping sound caught Roxy off guard and she jumped, startled, before realising it was coming from her handbag. She leapt upon it, retrieving her iPhone and clicking it back to life. She looked up at Oliver's eyes and smiled.

"It's a text message, from Max!"

He scoffed. "See, I told you it'd be all right. What does he say?"

She tapped on the in-box and then stared at the screen for a few seconds, attempting to scroll down.

"What?"

Still staring at the phone, Roxy held it out for him to see. There were only three letters on the screen and they didn't make any sense: PMP

"PMP? What the hell does that mean?" Oliver said.

She stared at it again. "I'm not very savvy with texting jargon, could it be an acronym like LOL—Laugh Out Loud?"

He thought about it. "I don't think so. I mean, I'm a jargon junkie and I've never heard of it. Here, give me the phone for a sec."

She handed it over and he stared at the screen for several minutes. Eventually he said, "Pre Menstrual Princess? Piss-off Miss Parker?"

Roxy glared at him. "That's four letters, Olie."

He laughed. "Sorry, it's probably just a mistake or maybe

he's trying to tell you he doesn't speak your language anymore. I know, maybe it stands for something in German."

He laughed again but Roxy wasn't laughing as she chewed on her lower lip trying to think. It had to mean something, surely? Max hadn't been in touch in months, why send this message now, unless it meant *something*? She waved two fingers at Oliver and he placed the phone back in her outstretched hand, then she stared at the screen for many minutes, her brain working overtime, her teeth doing their best to chew through her lower lip.

Just as Oliver was returning to the Miley Cyrus crisis, Roxy looked up and said, "It couldn't be."

"What?"

"Could it?"

"What?!"

She scooted across to where he was sitting and held the phone closer so he could see. "Okay, I don't want to be alarming or anything but—"

"But you're Roxy Parker and you can't help yourself?"

She whacked him across the shoulder. "Just look at those letters on my iPhone key pad: PMP. What else do you see?"

Oliver stared at each letter in turn and then back at Roxy. "Er, gobbledygook?"

"Look again." She began tapping on each key. "See, the key for P is also the key for Q, R and S. And the key for M is also the key for N and O."

He sighed. "Roxy, it's late, I've got important gossip to read, get on with it."

"Okay, okay. What if Max was in a hurry for some reason, and didn't have much time so just pushed the first letters but really meant to push the other letters connected to those keys?"

"Huh?"

"Look again: He pressed PQRS then MNO then PQRS: maybe he meant to say SOS."

"SOS? As in the universal distress sign for 'I'm in deep

shit'?"

She scrunched her face to one side. "Maybe this is a cry for help."

He looked at her like she'd finally flipped. "Rox, that's a big stretch, even for you. He's probably just playin' with ya, knowing how your mind works. I reckon he's teaching you a lesson for ignoring him for three months, probably laughing his head off right now knowing exactly how your crazy mind works."

Roxy thought about that. Max wasn't rude nor was he into playing games; that was her territory, it was one of the many reasons he had lost patience with her.

"Just text him back. Tell him off."

"Nope, I'm calling again." She pressed Max's mobile phone number. This time it didn't have a chance to ring. Instead the automated voice message came straight on telling her that the phone number she had called was "currently switched off or disconnected".

"Switched off or disconnected? It can't be! I just called him, you idiot! He just sent me a text message!"

"What's going on?"

Roxy shook her head, confounded, and then tapped in a quick text reply: "Hey Max. Got message. V. worried. Pls explain! xo R"

They both then sat staring at the phone, silently willing it to ring or beep or give some indication that Max really was okay. After ten excruciating minutes, Roxy could stand it no longer. She grabbed her smartphone and began to tap away again.

"*Now* what are you doing?"

"I'm booking a flight to Berlin."

"Seriously?" Oliver's eyebrows were knitted together like a big, bushy V. "By the time you get there, Rox, it'll be Monday morning and he'll be sitting at his desk wondering what all the fuss is about."

"Good. Then I'll have the pleasure of telling him off, FTBF."

"FTBF?"
"Face To Bloody Face!"

****

Max's face was not working. It was as though it had been rendered in fast-drying cement. He couldn't move his lips, could barely open his eyes. The ringing sound had woken him from his haze and he had tried to answer it, knew he had to answer it, but his fingers, too, were stiff and immobile.

He took several desperate breaths and tried again. He pulled the phone closer, pressed "reply" then tapped in a letter, then another, then one more before the cement started to solidify. He only had the chance to press "send" before he dropped into the darkness again.

CHAPTER 3

It had been many years since Roxy Parker had taken an international flight on a large jumbo jet and she would have been impressed were she not so strung out with a sickening mixture of worry and dread. Worry that Max really was in trouble, and dread that Oliver was right, and they were flying 16,000 kilometres for nothing.

"My God, there's over a thousand entertainment channels, would you believe?" squealed Caroline beside her, jabbing at the small screen in front of her seat. "And look, it says there's 150 movies! How on earth could you ever watch that many?"

Roxy tried to feign enthusiasm but couldn't manage it, nor was she too enthusiastic about Caroline joining her on the journey to Berlin, but then she was Max's flesh and blood. Plus, she was paying for the flights.

"I absolutely insist," Caroline had said when she'd broken the news to her later that Friday night.

Roxy had tracked her down at yet another dance party and, to her credit, Caroline had deserted "the hottest event of the year" to join her at Oliver's place to start planning. She wasn't at all convinced they should be heading for Berlin but a late call to her mother had put paid to that.

"She's now in a complete lather and says I simply can not let you go alone. She's convinced that text message Max sent really is a cry for help." She had stopped then and stared at Roxy with a strange mixture of awe and alarm. "Your mind really does work in strange ways, doesn't it? I mean, SOS? Who else would've picked that up? Anyway, thanks to Mum it looks like you've got company."

"Really, that's not necessary—"

Caroline held a finger up to stop her. "It's not a biggie. Besides, I've always wanted to visit Berlin, I hear it's the place *du jour*."

"Seriously, Caroline, there's no point both of us going. I can look for him myself."

"I beg to differ! Four eyes are better than two."

Oliver opened his mouth to say something and Roxy glared at him. "Don't even try," she said, pushing her thick glossy black Ray-Ban spectacles into place.

He shrugged, disappointed by the lost opportunity to make fun of his favourite client.

"Anyway, like Mum says, you shouldn't have to do this alone, Rox. Nor should you have to pay for any of it. He is *my* brother after all and, unlike you, I am earning obscene amounts of money on my stocks at the moment. I can help."

Roxy wasn't convinced Caroline would be any help at all, but she appreciated the company and could do with the financial assistance. Caroline was right. Ghostwriting other people's stories wasn't exactly a road to riches. She made a decent income, managed to meet the mortgage repayments on her tiny inner-city pad, but with the Edward Stray bio now complete, her diary was terrifyingly empty. There wasn't even a vacuous freelance article waiting in the wings.

"You do have some spare time at the moment," Oliver mentioned, clearly reading her mind and looking as guilty as he could manage. As her agent, he should have lined up another book by now but he was finding it increasingly difficult to convince people to employ a professional to write their life story. These days everybody had a blog, website and their own Facebook page, and considered themselves a budding author just waiting to be discovered, a la Elizabeth Gilbert or David Sedaris. Roxy's particular skill had become devalued and it would cost them both dearly, but that was a conversation for another day.

And so the two women had booked themselves on the first available flight to Berlin that Saturday morning, Roxy turning up in comfy black leggings and red and white striped top with a small suitcase and red leather handbag, Caroline in quite the opposite. She was dressed to kill in skinny, baby blue jeans, a spangly silver top and strappy creamy wedges that looked about as comfortable as a smack in the head. Her Burberry designer suitcase was large enough to clothe a family of four and God knows what she was hauling around in that enormous matching handbag, although Roxy did spot several glossy magazines, a large makeup case and a full-sized iPad.

Caroline was tapping away at it now as they slowly worked their way through a tasteless yellow blob the flight attendant had euphemistically referred to as "omelette".

"I got an e-mail from Mum and she says to thank you big time for doing this, Rox. She still hasn't heard anything from Max, or from the bloody flatmate for that matter. Says she's left something like ten messages on his home phone. How hard is it to call back?"

Roxy thought of her own mother then and felt the familiar twinge of guilt. She had called her very early that morning, giving her as brief an appraisal of the situation as was possible before the hysteria had kicked in.

Why was she going? What on earth was she thinking? How could that Max Man ask this of her? How dare he, for that matter?!

Roxy shuddered and pushed her mother's shrill voice from her mind and said, "What about your dad? Does he think we're overreacting?"

"Maybe a little, but as he says, it's one thing for Max to

ignore *his* messages, or mine for that matter, but he'd never ignore Mum's." She delicately peeled the lid off her juice packet. "I can't help thinking that maybe his phone has just run out of power, you know? He might have left his charger at home and doesn't realise we've been trying to get in touch."

"So how does that explain the weird text I got last night? Plus, hasn't he got another gadget? Like an iPad or something? Surely he would have responded to your e-mails or Facebook messages by now."

"Yeah, he's got the iPad mini I gave him for his last birthday, but maybe he left that in Berlin."

"Then how did he post those mountain pictures on Facebook last Monday? They're obviously of Mt Pilatus."

Caroline rolled her eyes at Roxy. "You sound like my inept parents. You can do that on any smartphone these days, Rox."

She eye-rolled her back. "Hey, I'm no Luddite. I've got the latest iPhone, don't you know!" She reached for the seat pocket in front of her and pulled it out, Max's face dancing to life on the screen.

"Max is your screensaver?"

Roxy blushed. "Well, we need a picture of him, just in case."

"Sure, *that's* the reason he's your screensaver."

Roxy ignored this and stared at the image of Max for a few moments. It was a closely cropped photo, his brown fringe flopping down, almost covering one eye, his smile wide and wolfish and tugging at her heartstrings as it always did. She pushed her so-called breakfast away.

"Did you talk to your folks about the Consulate-General in Berlin? Getting them to check with the airports?"

"Dad says no way; too early to call in the Big Guns. Max isn't officially a missing person yet, is he? He's due at work on Monday. He may show up, darling, making fools of us all."

"Well, if he does, brilliant. But if he doesn't then your

dad has to call the Australian Embassy. We need to check with passport control in Berlin and Brazil, find out if he ever arrived there."

"Hopefully it won't come to that. Oh, and did I tell you I tried Max's flatmate again, before we left?"

"Anything?"

"Zip."

Roxy considered this. "I wonder where he's been all this time. What do we know about this guy, anyway?"

"Not a whole lot. Max found him through some online classifieds when he was looking for a flatmate. He has a great apartment, apparently, but it's large and pricey and he needed someone to help out with the rent. So he took Jake in."

"Musician, right?"

"Yes," Caroline replied just as the flight attendant appeared with the coffee pot. They both held their cups out to be filled, Roxy grabbing a few extra sugar satchels at the same time. "In fact," continued Caroline, "*because* he's a muso, I think he's been pretty slack with the rent. Last I heard Max was thinking of booting him out. I guess he hadn't got round to it."

"Or maybe he had," Roxy said.

"Oh, right, you think that's why Jake's not answering? He's moved out?"

Roxy's thoughts were actually a lot darker than that and she couldn't help wondering whether Max's disappearance had something to do with unpaid rent. Caroline had clearly cottoned by now because a tiny worry line appeared above Caroline's eyes.

"You don't honestly think this flatmate has done something to Max?"

"No, of course not. I'm just chucking theories out into the universe. Ignore me."

The worry line turned into a scowl. "For goodness sake, Roxy, people don't go around killing people over unpaid rent, you know."

"Hey, settle down. Nobody's killing anybody, okay? Max is okay. No one is dead."

Little did she know, as she sipped her sweet, murky coffee 30,000 feet above the earth, those words would soon come back to haunt her.

CHAPTER 4

Twenty-eight hours, two stops and endless cups of appalling coffee later, Roxy and Caroline arrived at Berlin's Tegel airport, piled their luggage into the back of the first available taxi, and made their way straight to Max's apartment in the grungy inner city suburb of Kreuzberg.

It was just after 11:00 a.m. and Roxy was weary to the core. She'd barely managed an hour's sleep the whole flight. Caroline, on the other hand, had slept like a baby, her head propped against Roxy's shoulder most of the way, a velvet mask over her eyes, little yellow ear plugs firmly in place. She'd swallowed a Valium halfway along and that, coupled with several gin and tonics, had helped knock her out for the rest of the flight. Roxy had refused all medication, she'd wanted a clear head, but she realised now she had done herself a disservice. Her head just felt fat and foggy and she tried to shake it into shape as she anticipated meeting Jake and getting some clear answers about where Max might be.

En route from the airport, Caroline checked her iPhone for messages and yelped when she found one from Jake. At last! Roxy was thrilled, too, and they both listened to it several times as the taxi zoomed across the freeway and towards the city centre. It was a voice message that had come through to Caroline's mobile sometime while they were over the Indian Ocean, and he seemed both upbeat and blasé. He had a chilled out American accent and sounded younger than they expected, a little like Keanu Reeves in a bad surfie flick.

"Hey, Max's sister! Call off the hounds, babe. There's a stack of messages from you guys, you clogged up the message bank. Max is cool, man, he's got it all under control, I've just seen him, he's A-O-K."

The message then stopped abruptly, not so much as a friendly good-bye, but that was typical of Americans, they decided, having seen their fair share of US TV dramas.

"Anyway, I'm relieved," Roxy said, slumping into her seat. "But I do wonder what he means by 'he's got it all under control'? What's he talking about?"

Caroline raised a shoulder. "Who knows. Jake can explain it all when we see him." She smirked at Roxy, giving her a playful tap across the shoulder. "I *told* you everything was fine! Still, now we get to have a glorious holiday. I'm looking forward to checking out some of these famous Berlin nightclubs."

Roxy smiled at her but couldn't quite muster the same enthusiasm. She wouldn't relax until she saw Jake and heard it all for herself. She wanted to know where Max was and why he hadn't been responding to their messages, and she couldn't get to his apartment fast enough. Yet when they arrived at the relevant street, the taxi was blocked from entering by a flashing police patrol car that was parked across both lanes. Roxy's stomach clenched.

"Is everything okay?" she said to the cabbie.

He looked over his shoulder at her. "You out here. No can go."

Roxy glanced worriedly at Caroline who was dabbing some gloss on her lips and checking her reflection in a small hand mirror. "You've got the right street, yeah?"

Caroline flung her makeup back into her handbag and

glanced down at her iPhone where she must have tapped in the address.

"Yep, this is it. Come on, let's do it!"

They had managed to change some cash at the airport and Caroline pulled out some euros and handed them over before gathering her things and hopping out. As the poor cabbie wrestled to free Caroline's suitcase from the boot, Roxy continued scrutinizing Max's street, wondering if his sister had noticed the strong police presence. Apart from patrol cars at either end, there was an oversized white van in the middle of the road and several other cars that looked suspiciously "official" with radio antennae sticking out and dark glass on every window. Both entrances to the street had been cordoned off with police tape, yet another universal sign that shit had officially happened and, with the taxi now backing away, Roxy headed straight for a tall, thick-set police officer who was manning the tape at their end, chatting to a man holding what looked like a TV news camera by his side.

"Um, hello, *Sprechen Sie English?*"

He raised his eyebrows but said nothing. She wasn't sure what that meant but tried her luck anyway. "We need to get down this street." She pointed. "Um, her brother lives here." This time Roxy pointed back to Caroline who was standing behind her, leaning on her suitcase.

The officer glanced towards Caroline and back to Roxy, nudging his eyebrows mutely again.

"Can we?" Roxy waved a hand back down the street.

He sighed, stepped away from the cameraman, and said in very stiff, slow English, "Vot number?"

"Sorry?"

"Vot number you vant?"

"Oh ... um ..." Roxy turned back to Caroline, calling out, "What's the building number, Caro?"

Caroline looked almost bored as she glanced down at her iPhone and yelled back, "Seventy-eight!"

That's when the officer's laissez-faire attitude changed and Roxy shrank back. She didn't want his attitude to change, she wanted him to brush her off, tell her to come back later when the street reopened. But he didn't do that. He now had an alarmingly invigorated sparkle in his eyes.

"Come! Follow!"

He called something out to a younger officer at the other end of the tape and the man's jaw dropped and he nodded. The cameraman also looked excited, thrusting his camera up to his shoulder, and Roxy put her head down and kept walking.

They were led down the street, past several more flashing police cars, a group of curious onlookers and the big white van, and towards a crumbling grey building with ominous gargoyles on each corner and even more ominous police officers standing to attention at the entrance to the building. Its doors had been propped open and there was a small plaque with the number 78 etched into it. Through the doorway Roxy could see several more people milling about, some in civilian clothes, some in police uniform.

A wave of nausea hit her then and her legs felt wobbly but a quick glance back at Caroline's blank features gave her strength. If Caroline wasn't getting worried, why should she? She looked at her again. She seemed to be in a kind of daze, detached almost, and Roxy wondered whether she was thinking positively or was simply in denial, and if that was better or worse than the fear that was now coursing through her veins. In any case, she reached back and grabbed her friend's hand.

"It'll be fine," she said, more to console herself than anything.

"'Course it will," Caroline replied. Then, to the officer, she asked almost breezily, "So what's going on?"

He held a hand up to stall her then called out to someone inside the foyer of building 78. A man in a dull brown suit turned to stare at them for a second before saying something to the others and making his way outside.

"American," the first cop said, nudging his head at the women, and Roxy bristled.

"Australian. Actually."

The plainclothes cop nodded. "You are Australian. Okay. Vot is your name?"

Roxy waited for Caroline to answer but when she didn't, she said, "I'm Roxy Parker, this is Caroline Farrell. Her brother Max lives here."

Oh, God, she thought, *please let him still live here.*

"Apartment number?"

Roxy nudged Caroline who slowly consulted her phone. "Ahh ... 3B?"

Without missing a beat, the man said, "Come."

He waved them up the stone stairs and into the building, which was swirling with activity. Roxy spotted another police officer at the lifts, and what looked like two forensic pathologists dressed in plastic green smocks and plastic covered shoes, standing, wide briefcases in hand, waiting for the lift to arrive. One was laughing, another holding a takeaway sandwich.

There was a wall of letterboxes on one side and a young man with a bald head appeared to be brushing them for fingerprints, and on the other wall were two shabby black leather sofas. The plainclothes officer led them across and asked them to take a seat, then returned to the group near the entrance who were still deep in conversation.

Very soon a short, stocky woman in a tight black suit stepped out from the group and strode towards them. She smiled warmly as she took a seat beside Roxy and for a few seconds didn't speak.

Roxy rushed to fill the silence. "What's going on? Is Max okay?"

The woman held a short finger in the air. "First things first, madam. I am Inspector Gruen. Your names please."

Caroline sighed irritably and Roxy quickly told her the information, adding, "Caroline is Max Farrell's sister. He lives ..."—*please let him live, please let him live*—"in unit 3B."

Gruen nodded and her smile dropped slightly. "And where have you come from?"

Roxy could feel her own patience waning. "Straight from the airport. We've just flown in from Sydney, Australia. We're trying to hunt down Max Farrell. Is he ... is he okay?"

The woman was no longer smiling. She had turned to look at Caroline who was now scrolling through her mobile phone as though she didn't have a care in the world.

"I have some bad news," she said. "We have found a body. In Unit 3B."

"A body?" Roxy managed, the colour draining from her face. "What are you trying to say?"

The policewoman cleared her throat. "I am trying to tell you that someone has been murdered."

CHAPTER 5

Roxy had heard of the expression "time slowing down" but had never really experienced it before, at least, not to this extent. She suddenly felt numb, dislocated, outside of her body. There was a whooshing sound in her ears and the walls seemed to be circling around her head yet everything was on slow-motion.

She saw a petite, black-haired woman talking to an officer by the stairwell. She was covered in body piercings and clutching a packet of cigarettes, waving them about as she spoke. She looked shaken but not alarmed. By the front doors an elderly man in a bike helmet and dazzling yellow Lycra was also talking to a police officer, who was clearly giving him the brush off. And the green-clad forensics officers had now vanished, the elevator making its way skyward.

Level 1 ...

Level 2 ...

Level 3 ...

Ping!

Roxy must have snapped out of it then because time sped up again and the whooshing sound stopped. She shook her head and heard herself speaking calmly, sounding almost aloof: "Does the body belong to Max?"

The detective answered briskly, "We do not know, yet. There has been one identification but it is not official." She hesitated, glancing at Caroline who was still staring at her iPhone as if her eyes were literally glued to it, and back to Roxy. "We need a positive identification. Can you do this, please? It would help."

Roxy turned to Caroline. "Do you ...?"

"Oh, you do it, darling," Caroline said, her eyes still not leaving the screen. "I'm just checking Facebook. See if he's been in touch. Mum's also sent a few messages so I'd better get back to her, too."

Detective Gruen caught Roxy's eyes and the two women exchanged worried frowns before the detective said, "Looks like it's you. Are you ready?"

No, Roxy thought, *no I am not!* But she realised Caroline was in no condition to do it. She was obviously in a serious state of denial, either that or she was more self-centred than Roxy realised, so she took a deep breath and somehow managed to drag herself back to her feet and follow the detective through the foyer and towards the elevator. It seemed like a lifetime before it arrived, another lifetime before it reached floor three, but the whole time she kept telling herself, "It's not Max. It's not Max. It's not Max."

Wishful thinking was all she had left.

As the elevator doors cranked open, another swirl of activity could be seen down the corridor. A forensic officer was talking loudly in German to someone in a cheap grey suit, and a man with a camera was focusing it on the handle of an open door. There was no number on the door, but it had to be Max's apartment. The only other door Roxy could see was farther down, and it was firmly shut. She spotted the same fingerprint guy brushing several spots along one wall, or was it a different guy? She could not tell.

"Just one moment, please," Gruen said firmly, stalling her

just beyond the elevator, and Roxy nodded, watching as she disappeared inside the open apartment.

A minute later she was back. "Follow me."

Roxy followed, heart pounding, nausea kicking in again, but they walked past the unit and around the corner where a man wearing green plastic was standing beside a wheeled stretcher, zipping something up. Roxy flung a hand to her mouth. She had seen enough *CSI* to know it was a body bag, a lightweight, white bag with a full-length zipper down the middle.

Detective Gruen spoke softly in German to the man and he looked at Roxy, said something to Gruen, and then began to unzip the bag.

"You must not touch anything, not a thing. Okay?" Roxy must have nodded because she said, "Thank you, it is necessary we do not contaminate."

Gruen stepped back and Roxy somehow stepped forward, towards the body bag that was now being slowly reopened by Mr Forensics. A putrid, rotting egg-like odour slapped her in the face first, followed by a gush of relief.

"It's not him," she said with a rush, staring at the waxy grey features, the open jaw, the puffy, closed eyelids. "It's not Max."

Oh, thank God. It's not Max.

Detective Gruen sighed. She sounded disappointed; perhaps it would have been easier for her if it had been Max. The man that now lay exposed on the gurney was unfamiliar to Roxy. He was bare-chested, his black jeans gaping open slightly to reveal a tuft of curly hair at his painfully thin navel. A tattoo was spiralling up from beneath the jeans and there was another large, smudged tattoo across his right shoulder. It looked a little like a serpent. It was the man's head, though, that would haunt Roxy's dreams for years to come. It had been split open on the right side of his temple, parts of yellowy white matter protruding through the skull, his black hair matted where the blood had congealed around it.

"Do you know this man?" Gruen asked, perhaps for the second time and Roxy dropped the hand she had wedged hard against her nose and lips and took a few necessary breaths.

"No," she said eventually before it occurred to her and she felt nausea strike again. "Oh, God, maybe. Max lived with a flatmate. Jake someone or other. It could be him, but I don't know for sure." She felt deep sadness now, followed swiftly by disappointment but she couldn't yet articulate why.

"Yes, Jake Conway," Gruen was saying. She spoke again in German and Mr Forensics stepped forward and began zipping the bag back up.

"What happened to him?" Roxy asked as Gruen led her away and back down the corridor towards Max's apartment.

"Blunt trauma. We will know more in a day or so. Do you want to sit down?"

"I'm okay. When did this happen?"

"Very late Friday night or early Saturday morning is our best guestimate as this stage."

"But why? Why would anyone ...?"

She didn't answer. "Can you wait one more minute?"

As the detective spoke to an officer who had been hovering close by, Roxy glanced into the open apartment, into Max's Berlin life. The unit was large, larger than she was expecting, and decorated with a creamy collection of very modern, very chic furniture. Roxy wondered if it had come pre-furnished or if Max had selected each piece on his own, padding out his new life in Germany. The walls were covered with half a dozen framed, black and white photographs, mostly of historic monuments, but there was one on the back wall, behind a plush cream lounge that stood out. She stared at it and choked back a sob.

It was a large, A4-sized photograph of Roxy, bright eyed and smiling provocatively into the lens. She was wearing a dark T-shirt and her hair was shorter, cut into her trademark bob, but several strands were blowing about in an unseen wind. Roxy couldn't even remember when Max had taken that shot, but she looked happy, she looked in love. Now it just left her feeling cold.

The officer with the camera brushed past her and into the unit, then straight to the lounge where he started snapping away again. At first Roxy couldn't see what he was photographing but then he nudged the sofa out of the way and she spotted it and recoiled. There was a guitar lying upside down just beyond the sofa, on a fluffy, cream rug. Next to it was a large deep brown stain that looked a lot like blood.

"Are you okay, Miss Parker?" Gruen said beside her and Roxy nearly jumped a foot.

She patted her heart and turned to face her. "Yes. I think so. Can you tell me, do you have any idea where Max is?"

Gruen looked at her surprised. "We were hoping you could tell us this."

Roxy shook her head. "We've just arrived from Australia. We've been trying to find him."

"Is he lost?"

"We're not sure. We left a stack of messages but he never got back to us."

"You left messages?"

Roxy nodded. "Stacks of them, on his answering machine." She nodded her head inside the apartment. "Just check, you'll see."

Gruen looked at her strangely. "We have checked the answering machine. There are no messages. Not one."

Roxy felt a chill run through her. *How could that be?* She took a deep breath then proceeded to fill the detective in on the family's concerns. She explained how Max had gone on holidays to Mt Pilatus but had checked out early and disappeared. How the family had left dozens of messages on the Internet and at home.

"When did you last speak with Mr Farrell?"

She tried to think. "Um ... late Friday night. No, well, we didn't actually speak. I got a text from his mobile. It said ..." She hesitated, wondering how to play it. "It just had the letters PMP, but we wondered whether he meant, SOS.”

She paused, expecting the detective to call her on it but when she didn't say a word, Roxy continued. “In any case, Max did speak to his mother before that. She lives back in Australia, in Northern NSW.”

“When was this?”

“Um, very early last Wednesday morning, I think it was, which would have been late Tuesday your time, I suppose. Max said he was ...” she hesitated again, knowing how strange it all sounded. “He said he was heading to Rio de Janeiro.” She wanted this to be true now more than ever before.

Detective Gruen pulled out a notebook and began writing something down when Roxy had a thought.

“When did you say Jake died?”

Gruen looked up from her pad. “We are not sure, probably late on Friday night. Why?”

“But that's when he left us a message.”

“Who? Mr Conway?”

“Yes.”

Gruen looked more interested now. “What exactly did it say?”

Roxy tried to think. “You'll have to double-check with Caroline, it came through on her mobile phone.”

Roxy explained about the voice mail message Jake must have left some time in the past twenty-eight hours while they were en route to Berlin, and Gruen looked suddenly invigorated and began madly scribbling away again.

Eventually, she looked around and caught the eye of the officer who had been lurking nearby. She waved him over and spoke for several minutes in German to him before turning back to Roxy. “This is Officer Hann. He will take you down to the station now.”

“Station?”

“Yes, we need to ask you some more questions. I would also like to get a recording of that last message from the deceased to Miss Farrell.” She must have repeated that request in German to the officer because he nodded. She turned back to Roxy. "That message should give us a better indication of the time of death."

Roxy felt a little startled—had Jake left that message just before he was murdered? Had the murderer been in the room when he left it?—but she was also weary to the core. "Do we have to go right now?" she asked. "It's been a stressful twenty-four hours." Or at least it had been for her. She wasn't sure what frame of mind Caroline was in.

The detective gave her an apologetic smile. "It will not take long, but it is imperative. Most importantly, we need your help to find Mr Farrell. We need to talk to him about this. It is most urgent."

The way she spoke set off alarm bells in Roxy's head. She wondered now if they suspected Max had something to do with Jake's murder. It sent a trickle of anxiety racing through her.

CHAPTER 6

When Roxy returned to the ground floor with Officer Hann, she noticed that Caroline was no longer on the sofa, and she looked around, finally spotting her just outside the front doors, dragging on a cigarette, the only indication that she was at all nervous or concerned. Roxy turned back to the officer.

"Can you give me a few minutes, please? I need to talk to my friend and prepare her."

He looked sceptical but nodded anyway and she stepped outside and towards Caroline who was leaning against the metal banister at the top of the stairs. Beside her, on a lower step, was the petite, black-haired woman Roxy had seen earlier, talking to an officer. She was dressed completely in black and had several nose rings, multiple earrings and a small stud through one eyebrow.

"Oh, Roxy darling, this is Holly, Max's next-door neighbour."

Holly was dragging on a matching cigarette and waved it at Roxy. "Hey."

Roxy nodded at her and then turned to Caroline. "So, it wasn't Max, in case you were wondering."

Caroline half laughed. "Of course not, darling, I knew it wouldn't be."

"How? How did you know?! Weren't you at all worried?"

Caroline took another deep drag. "Oh calm down, Rox. There was no point in both of us stressing out, was there? Besides, Holly's already filled me in. She's the one who found the body. Says it's the flatmate, Jake."

Roxy glanced at Holly and back to Caroline. "So if they knew it wasn't Max, why'd they just put me through that?! It was horrendous!"

Holly gave a kind of Elvis Presley sneer. "Cops never take my word for anything. It's probably all the piercings." She sighed. "Yep, that's Jake all right. Poor git." Her accent was pure cockney, straight from the working class suburbs of London. "I mean, he could be a right tosser when he wanted to be, but he didn't deserve that, did he?"

"How did you find him?" Roxy asked.

"Oh, I was feeding Max's cat."

"Max has a cat?" both women said at the same time and she nodded.

"Pinky. It's just a stray that took to sleeping under Max's bed. He asked me to check his food every couple of days while he was away, since he couldn't trust Jake to keep it topped up, could he? He'd given me his key so I let meself in this morning and ..." She shivered and wrapped her arms around her torso. "No wonder he didn't show up at his gig last night."

"You mean Jake?" Roxy asked and Holly nodded, dragging deeply on her cigarette again. "Do you know what happened to him?"

"Copper says he was smacked over the head with his own guitar. Poor bugger." Holly squinted a little at Roxy. "I've seen your face before. Are you another sister of Max's?"

"No, I'm just a friend." Caroline snorted beside her but Roxy let that go and said, "So how long have you known Jake and Max?"

"Errr, let me think ... I've been in 3A, that's just across the corridor, for, I don't know, about two months? The guys are always so sweet, they helped me move in and all. Well, Max did. Jake just stood around smoking pot most of the time." She pulled some invisible tobacco from her tongue. "You do know Max is away at the moment, right? In Austria, I think he said."

"Wasn't it Switzerland?"

She shrugged. "Something like that. Cold, high up, not my cup of tea. You Aussies are funny. The only place I'd go on holidays is a warm beach somewhere. Preferably Spain."

"He could be in Brazil," Caroline offered and Holly's pierced eyebrow shot up.

"So Max never mentioned Brazil to you?" Roxy asked and she shook her black locks, no. "Did he tell you when he was coming back?"

Holly took a final drag on her cigarette and then dropped it to the ground, quickly stepping on it, squishing it into the cement like that was going to get rid of it. "Not really, but I assumed he'd be back yesterd'y 'cause Jake was supposed to be playing Brewsters last night, wasn't he, and Max said he'd catch the gig so ..."

"Brewsters?"

"Yeah, divey bar a few streets back. We go most Sat'dy nights. Jake has a regular gig there with his band, the Angry Euros." Her top lip curled again. "Crap name, hey? Anyways, we go and support him when we can. As you do. He gets paid about sixty quid a pop so I wonder why he bothers, but he says it's better than nothing, idn't it? A paid rehearsal, so he says, and it's not that bad." She gulped. "At least he used to say that ... He's gone now, 'idn't he?"

Caroline placed a hand on her arm. "Yeah, sorry."

"Can't get me head around it. Anyway, it's a good thing Max didn't zoom back for the gig because, as I say, Jake never showed. I stood around for an hour before I got sick of batting off sleazy Germans and left."

Officer Hann appeared then and looked at Roxy

expectantly but she shook her head. "Please, just let Caroline finish her cigarette?"

He frowned then walked down the stairs to the street and pulled out a packet of his own and lit up. Roxy turned back to Holly. She had so many questions, so little time.

"So Max was definitely expected back last night? And he never showed."

"That's what he said. God, he's going to be so cut up when he finds out about Jake. I mean, they had their moments, but still."

"Moments?"

"You know, the odd barney."

Roxy felt her skin prickle. She hoped that Holly hadn't mentioned these "barnies" to the police. "What did they fight about?"

"Oh, nothing, honestly, don't worry yourself about it."

"Did you hear them fight recently?"

"They just had a few words the last time I saw them at Brewsters, that's all. Jake was late with the rent again, Max was *livid*. Threatened to kick him out, but Jake just laughed. Said Max always said that. They weren't really fighting, were they? It was just boring, everyday flatmate stuff, you know the type." *Not really,* thought Roxy. It was one of the perks of living alone. "By the end of the night they were best buds again. I told the cops all this, honestly, I wouldn't worry."

Roxy felt her anger rising. "They don't really think Max had anything to do with that ...?" She glanced back into the building, towards the scene of the crime.

Holly shrugged, non-committal.

"Of course they don't!" Caroline spat. "That's ridiculous." She gave Roxy another indignant glare as she finished off her cigarette.

"When did you last see Jake?" Roxy asked Holly.

"Same time as Max, at Brewsters, 'bout a week ago. Oh, but I *heard* him, very late Frid'y night."

"What, the night they think he was murdered?"

"Yep, it was definitely late Frid'y night, which is why I

was surprised when he didn't show for the gig on Sund'y. Band were expecting him so they were pissed off, too, I can tell you that. Not happy campers. Bass player had to step up and sing." She thought about this. "He wasn't that bad actually. Anyway, I told the coppers this already."

"Hang on, what do you mean, 'heard'?"

"Sorry?"

"You said you heard Jake on Friday night."

"Oh yeah, right, well, I didn't see him as such. But I heard him, speaking Italian like. I didn't even know he could. He's from LA, you know." She caught herself again. "*Was* …"

"Italian?" This mollified Roxy a little. Max didn't speak any languages. She hoped the cops knew that, too.

"Yep, heard him say the word '*benvenuto*' which I know is Italian for 'welcome' 'cause I went out with an Italian once. He was a tosser."

"Did you see who he was speaking to? Jake?"

"No such luck, but he must've been speaking as he came in along the corridor 'cause you can't hear much when the apartment doors are shut. Nice thick walls these ones. Old building, that's why. Wasn't bombed during the war, apparently. That's also why it ain't got any cameras, that kinda stuff that would've helped the coppers. All the new buildings have that kinda shite. Me? I'm happy without the invasion of my privacy, thanks very much."

"Come please," Officer Hann called out from the road. "We must go now."

Roxy sighed and turned back to Holly. "Listen, I don't have a local SIM card yet, but can I get your number, call you later maybe? See if you've heard from Max or remembered anything?"

"Sure," she said, and then held her cigarette packet out to Caroline. "You better have these. From the way those cops are talking, I think you're gonna need them."

CHAPTER 7

The bushy-faced German detective was asking a lot of questions they simply could not answer, although Roxy wished to God she could.

"Where is Max?"

"How can we speak to him?"

"Why has he not come back?"

Roxy was seated beside Caroline at a large table in a small conference room at the Kreuzberg police station. Officer Hann sat across from them but it was this older man with the bushy brown beard and a name they could not pronounce who was doing all of the interrogating, leaning across the table towards them. It was clear to Roxy that Mr Beard Man was playing with the idea that Max was somehow involved in Jake's death and she could hear her tone turning surly as she retold the story and insisted Max was nowhere near his apartment when Jake was murdered.

"But how can you say zees?!" Beard Face demanded. "You do not know where he is. Or *do you?*"

Roxy slumped. "No, we do not."

"We think he might be in Brazil," Caroline offered and the look she got from everyone in the room showed that nobody, not even Roxy, believed that anymore.

"Let us go back to zee message you got from Mr Conway," Beard Man said. "We now know this was left just after midnight on Friday, Berlin time, which was while you were on zee airplane, correct?"

They both nodded and he pulled out his chair and sat down, then opened a file and began to read from it, Jake's Californian twang completely lost as the German spoke:

"'Hey, Max's sister. Call off zee hounds, baby. There is a stack of messages from you guys. You clogged up zee message bank. Max is cool. Man. He has got it all under control. I have just seen him. He is ...'" He stared hard at the file, looking confused.

"A-O-K?" Roxy offered.

"What is AOK?"

"It just means everything's fine. Everything's okay."

He looked at her uncertainly then turned his bushy face back to Caroline and said in a very slow, deliberate voice, as though he were dealing with a textbook "dumb blonde": "Zees tells me that Mr Conway has just seen your brother. In person. So he could not have seen him in Brazil and be back in Berlin in zat time frame. Do you agree with zis, Miss Farrell?"

Caroline shrugged. She was holding onto that scenario and they could all go to hell.

After several more questions along the same vein, the detective changed tack and asked them if Max spoke Italian.

That's more like it, Roxy thought, remembering what Holly had said about hearing Italian spilling through the corridor outside Jake's apartment not long before he died.

"No, he absolutely does not," Caroline said. "We both learnt a little French at school. Not a word of Italian. Not one."

"So he would not know zis word, '*benvenuto*'?"

Caroline hesitated, glancing at Roxy and back. "Well, I don't know for sure, I mean, maybe." She glanced uncertainly at Roxy again. "Australians are more likely to say '*ciao*'. That's kind of better known, you know?"

He stared at her like she had finally flipped then changed tack again, asking questions related to Max's belongings: Did he own anything precious? Was he in the habit of keeping large amounts of cash at home? Clearly they were now on the burglary track and this relaxed Roxy even further.

"Don't know about any cash," Caroline was telling him, "but he owns some decent cameras: a pretty fancy Nikon, and a video camera, I think." She glanced at Roxy again, as if for confirmation, and Roxy squished her lips to one side and shrugged.

She couldn't provide any more details than that and felt a surge of guilt. How little did she really know about the man she professed to love?

Eventually, after realising the two jetlagged Aussie women could be of no more assistance, Beard Man finally let them depart, but not before ordering Officer Hann to photocopy their passports and organise a local SIM card for Roxy's mobile phone. This wasn't charity, he explained. "We need to know how to reach you. Just in case."

In case of what, she didn't dare ask, and they eventually made their way back through the station and out into a gloomy Berlin afternoon. All around them traffic was roaring, cyclists were zipping past, and pedestrians had their heads down, going about their business as if someone had not just had the life beaten out of him by his 1920s Gibson guitar.

"Where the hell are we going to go now?" asked Caroline, looking blankly around.

Roxy pointed to a café across the road with a black and white awning and a set of tables on the pavement. "Let's start there. I need to wake up the brain cells."

They made their way across with some difficulty. The cyclists here seemed to have right of way and a death wish, flying past with lightning speed, while Caroline struggled to wheel her suitcase across, watching it topple over several times in the process.

"Really, Caro, did you need to bring quite so much crap?"

"Oh zip it, woman. I'm not travelling all the way to one of the coolest cities in the world without a few decent outfits." Her eyes fixed pointedly at Roxy's black leggings.

She sighed and made her way to an outdoor table, collapsing into a chair with relief. A waitress promptly arrived and they ordered what they hoped were two lattés, then Caroline leaned back in her chair, folded her arms and said, "So what happens now?"

"God knows," Roxy said.

She had not thought much beyond arriving in Berlin and heading straight to Max's flat. She had mentally prepared a list of questions to ask Jake, had determined that he was the key to this and would know exactly what Max was up to. But he was no longer talking and she was stumped. She felt that twinge of disappointment again and then another flash of guilt. The poor guy was dead and all she was thinking about was a lost contact for Max.

Caroline pulled out the packet of cigarettes Holly had given her and Roxy must have frowned because she said, "Oh lighten up. We're not in a nanny state anymore. You're *allowed* to smoke at cafés here, you know."

"That wasn't what I was worried about. Didn't you give up those death sticks?"

Caroline cocked her head to one side, the cigarette unlit in her mouth. "You really aren't going to lecture me about smoking at a time like this, are you, Rox?"

She looked away. No, it didn't seem to matter so much anymore.

"Miss Emo didn't think to give me her lighter, though, did she?"

Caroline glanced around as if a match would miraculously appear and, oddly enough, it did. An older, blonde man, who had been watching them from a nearby table leapt up to produce a lighter, and leaned down to light her cigarette. Caroline inhaled deeply than rewarded him with a glowing smile and he smiled back, almost falling over the waitress as he returned to his table. Roxy watched it all with mild amusement. Caroline's charm clearly had global appeal.

The waitress handed over their coffees and they sat silently for a few minutes, Caroline blowing smoke straight into Roxy's face, Roxy pretending to ignore her as she dumped several spoonfuls of sugar into her cup. She wondered again why she'd let Caroline come along. It felt like she was escorting a child half the time. She wondered, too, how Caroline could continue to be so blasé. Perhaps she was doing it for her own sanity but it only left Roxy feeling more rattled, as though she had to do the worrying for both of them.

"Oh, I suppose I should check Facebook again," Caroline said, reaching into her bag for her iPad then looking around. She caught the waitress's eye and waved her over. "I'll see if they've got Wi-Fi."

As she spoke to the waitress, Roxy pulled her mobile phone out and realised it was now all in German. She found her way to the settings and changed the language back to English then sent a quick text message to Max's neighbour Holly, just giving her their new local number should anything crop up. Next, she scrolled through her phone book for a number she had logged in before leaving Sydney. It was for Max's boss, Gunter, at Mercedes' Berlin office. She knew it was Sunday, she knew he was unlikely to be in, but she wanted to try.

A few minutes later, she was being put through to the marketing department and the voice of Britt Gelsing came on.

"Oh, Roxy Parker, hallo! Gunter eez not in today. He only works Monday to Friday."

"I was afraid of that."

"You still looking for Max?"

"Yes. I'm now in Berlin, with Max's sister."

"You have come all ziss way! My goodness, *now* I am getting worried."

"You obviously haven't heard anything from him?"

"No." There was a slight pause. "Zee police have been calling, too, looking for Max. Do you know what is going on?"

Roxy shut her eyes, felt her shoulders slump. "Yes. Max's flatmate is dead."

"Dead? Did you say dead?"

"I'm afraid so, he was found murdered this morning, in their apartment."

"Oh my, my. Is Max okay?"

"We don't know. He's not back, which is why I'm calling. We're still trying to find him."

"Oh my goodness me." There was another long pause in which time Roxy glanced across at Caroline who was shaking her head, indicating that she could find no messages from her brother. "Oh my goodness," Britt said again. "Zis is no good. No good at all. I think, perhaps, you should call Gunter at home. Do you have zee number?"

"No."

"Wait a second." A blast of elevator music came through the phone line for a few minutes and then Britt was back rattling off a series of numbers, which Roxy repeated aloud indicating for Caroline to tap them into her iPad. She did as instructed and then Roxy thanked Britt and hung up.

"The cops have been calling Max's office and they suggest I try and get in touch with his boss. What was the home number I just read out?"

Caroline read it back to her and Roxy placed the call, waiting a few rings before it picked up.

"*Guten Tag*," came Gunter's deep voice and Roxy identified herself, telling him what she had just told Britt. "Apparently the police have been calling your office, also looking for Max."

There was a deep intake of breath at the other end. "This is bad news, Roxy. We have to try to find him."

"I couldn't agree more."

"After you called, I sent him an e-mail but he has not replied to me either. He is due back at work tomorrow, we could wait until then."

"We could," Roxy agreed, closing her eyes wearily. "But I'm starting to get more and more worried."

"Yes, me too. What can I do? How can I help?"

Roxy opened her eyes. She knew now exactly what she had to do. "You could get us a car, Gunter, if that's at all possible."

"A car?"

"Yes," she said, glancing at Caroline's look of confusion. "I think it's time to head for the hills."

CHAPTER 8

The hills were certainly alive with music but none that either woman wanted to hear.

"They have dodgy radio stations over here!" Caroline announced after many minutes trying to find a decent station on the car stereo system. In the end she gave up and settled on an Usher song as she stared out the car window in a huff.

The road from Berlin towards Switzerland was also not as picturesque as Roxy had expected, but it was fast. They were on the infamous German autobahn where speed limits were generally open, and while Roxy stuck to 130 kilometres per hour in the middle lane, she was flabbergasted as other cars went whizzing past her at such break-neck speeds she never saw them coming and barely saw them pass.

"They have to be going 200!" Caroline cried, her eyes wide as she watched them disappear up the freeway.

"Crazy," Roxy said, wondering quietly about the accident toll. Even if she'd wanted to, she wasn't sure Mercedes-Benz would be too thrilled with her flogging the shiny new compact SUV they had loaned her for the drive. She wondered, too, if it was the same car they had loaned to Max.

Soon after telling Gunter of her intentions, he had rung back, not only confirming the car loan, but offering to put them up for the night at a Berlin hotel, a very plush one just a block from Max's apartment. "We feel bad," he told her. "We lose Max on our watch."

"Well, he was on holidays when he vanished," she reminded him. "You guys can't really take any blame."

"Still, you enjoy our guilt, you get nice hotel room and car, so take it. We will get the car to you this afternoon, and you can have as long as you need. Make the most of it I say!"

Roxy intended to, but first she needed a good night's sleep. She'd already used *Google Maps* to find Mt Pilatus and discovered that they had a long drive ahead of them. No matter how fast they sped up that autobahn, they were never going to make it in time to catch the last train to the top from the Swiss village of Alpnachstad at the base of the mountain. Plus there was the small matter of being severely jetlagged. Caroline might be fresh as a daisy, but Roxy was the designated driver and in dire need of a good night's kip.

"In that case," Caroline had suggested as they made their way to the hotel, "how about we check out the Chemical Club?"

"The what?"

"The hottest bar in Berlin, darling! They have these drinks there that come in test tubes and are bright blue with, like, little bubbles that sort of pop out or something. That's what my friend Lexy told me. Says they are to die for!"

Roxy stared at her. *Could she hear herself?* "Caroline, we're not here to party. We're here to find your brother."

She blinked back at her. "And we can't do both?"

"No! Well, at least I can't. You do whatever you like."

Caroline had slipped into a sulky silence then and by the time they'd checked into their room and freshened up, she'd forgotten all about the Chemical Club, or had at least given up on the idea, and they simply ordered room service and then headed for bed.

By 6:00 the next morning, the two women were looking and feeling brighter as they checked out of the hotel and into their swanky silver Mercedes. The car already had a Satellite Navigation system installed and someone had kindly keyed in directions to Alpnachstad in English. All Roxy had to do was remember to stick to the right-hand side of the road and they'd be there in roughly nine hours. They intended to do it in one hit, having already booked a room at the Hotel Bellevue for Monday night, and been informed that the last train to the top was at 5:10 p.m.

"We're making it, if it kills us!" Caroline had announced, not aware of how her cavalier language pulled at Roxy's heartstrings.

Still, as she watched the maniacal European drivers whizz past, Roxy felt her spirits lift, and it wasn't just because the autobahn was smooth and the jetlag now easing. They were on their way; they were doing something to find Max. Better yet, with each passing hour, they were putting good distance behind Jake's gruesome murder.

Before they left Berlin, they sent messages to their respective families and called Inspector Hann, explaining where they were going and why. Only Roxy's mum, Lorraine, had tried to dissuade her, and Roxy tried not to think about her now as she focused on the road ahead.

The journey itself was fairly uneventful with endless fields of corn, solar panels and wind farms to keep them entertained, but both women's minds rarely strayed from the task at hand.

"What are we hoping to find up there?" Caroline ventured at one point and Roxy squished her lips to one side.

"Good question. I don't know but it was the last place Max was seen, so I feel like it's the best place to start. Maybe somebody spoke to him, saw something, has some idea where he might have gone."

She knew she was grasping at straws, Caroline knew it, too, but it felt good to be grasping at anything at this stage.

Staying in Berlin and waiting for Max to show while the police circled asking pointed questions was not on her itinerary.

At 10:05 a.m. Berlin time, they received a text message from Gunter letting them know that Max had not yet turned up at work. *"He was due an hour ago,"* Gunter had written. *"This is not like Max."*

At midday there was another text, this one sounding more alarmed: *"Max still not here! Pls find and bring him home."*

"And what if we don't find him, or anything for that matter?" Caroline persisted, flicking through the radio channels in another futile attempt to locate something worth listening to.

"That won't happen," Roxy replied. "In my experience, there's always something to find."

And Roxy's experience in this area was extensive. In her work as a ghostwriter and investigative journalist, she had helped crack several baffling mysteries, largely thanks to her dogged determination and gut instinct. Just a year ago, she had saved her agent, Oliver, from the proverbial gallows, and she was not going to accept failure this time, either. She knew that the more you dug about, asking questions and opening cans of worms, the more questions were answered and the more worms were uncovered. Secrets and information had a way of oozing out, and Roxy had a way of making sure they did.

The women stopped just twice on their journey, once to grab a strong coffee and some croissants (and cough up 70 cents for the privilege of using the service station restrooms) and a few hours later to fill up the tank and their stomachs again to fuel them on.

As they reached Switzerland, the endless fields turned to placid lakes and vibrant green hills with fairy-tale-like villages tucked into the folds, and Roxy made a promise to herself that she would come back one day under different circumstances. She would stop and idle about without a murder hanging over her head. Better yet, she would have

Max by her side instead of his incorrigible sister and they would laugh and they would sing along to the truly terrible Top 40 tunes that were now blaring out from the radio. And they would reminisce about this time and how lucky it was that everything had worked out fine.

She felt a lump settle in her throat and choked back a tear just as the SatNav broke through a Lady Gaga tune: "*In 2.2 kilometres, at the next exit, bear left.*"

"That's Alp-nack-stard!" Caroline announced clumsily as she peered at the small screen. "We're almost there."

Roxy checked the car clock. It was 5:01 p.m. They had made it by the skin of their teeth. Her tears evaporated and she felt a wave of joy.

The joy didn't last long. After parking the car in the first available spot and making a frantic dash for that last train to the top, a bleak mood settled over Roxy again. The train ride was almost as hairy as the autobahn, heading straight up the cliff at an average gradient of around 40 degrees. As the steepest cogwheel railway in the world, Caroline found the trip exhilarating yet Roxy could not relax and enjoy the stunning view that dropped away below them as they chugged up the final stretch of the mountain, which stood over 2,000 metres above sea level. She just wanted to get there and get some answers.

While she nodded and murmured in response to Caroline's cries of delight, her heart was simply not in it, and she chided herself yet again that she had behaved so appallingly with Max. If she had been less immature and selfish, she might have been living with him in Berlin instead of that poor American musician whose freeloading had come to a brutal halt. If she had congratulated Max on his great German job, she might have been the one to travel to Mt Pilatus with him, they might have held hands on this journey and gasped happily together.

Instead, she was now blind to its beauty and all she could see were hair-raising cliffs and unforgiving terrain. It was the perfect backdrop to a mystery, she thought morosely, especially when the Hotel Bellevue came into sight, perched at the very top, like an elaborate eagle's nest, circular in shape and made entirely of gleaming silvery concrete and glass.

"God, it's like something from a James Bond movie!" Caroline said, and she was right.

It looked just like the setting of the 1970s' film *On Her Majesty's Secret Service*, apt, really, because that was the only Bond movie to star Australian actor George Lazenby. Roxy recalled the plot now as the train chugged closer, remembering the baddie, Blofeld, and his bevy of glazy eyed beauties, the "Angels of Death". She shuddered a little as the train finally screeched into the station and the doors swung open. She just hoped the inhabitants were a little more welcoming.

"Welcome to Mt Pilatus!" came the cheerful tones of the train conductor as he helped them carry their bags to the lobby and Roxy felt a little better. It was a good start.

They were soon standing in a cavernous room with a low ceiling and a rocky wall at one end, which served as the reception area for both the Hotel Bellevue and the Hotel Pilatus-Kulm. That hotel was more traditional in style, a rectangular building made of stone and brick yet Roxy was not surprised Max had chosen the circular Bellevue. It looked a lot quirkier, certainly more intriguing, and she wondered now as they stepped past the ogling sightseers towards the reception, what secrets it would give up.

Beyond them was a large "tourist centre" with a bar and shop, and enormous windows that faced out to a terrace with stunning, panoramic views.

"Hello, *Bonjour, Guten Tag, Benvenuto*," the smartly dressed woman behind the counter said, and Roxy was impressed.

"You speak a few languages," she said and the woman smiled wider.

"Oh yes, we all do here in Switzerland, we border so

many countries, you see. But our main ones are French, German and Italian."

Italian, thought Roxy, a small bell going off in her head.

"Well, G'day in Australian," said Caroline, clearly wanting to speed things up. "I made a booking last night. I'm Caroline Farrell, this is Roxy Parker."

The woman began to tap into her computer then stopped and glanced back at them with a flicker of recognition. "Ah, yes, Miss Farrell, we have been expecting you. Our General Manager, Mr Leon Schelling, would like to meet with you, but has asked me to check you in and get you settled first."

"Oh, right, great."

The receptionist continued tapping away, collecting both their passports and entering the details into her computer. She also took an imprint of their Visa cards and asked them to sign some forms, then produced two keycards and handed them over.

"Your room is on the second floor, you take the lift to our right." She waved a hand towards it. "There are complimentary drinks in the main foyer at 6:30 p.m." She pointed out to the spacious tourist area behind them. "Just under the stairs, there is a bar. Mr Schelling will meet you there. We serve a three-course dinner at 7:30 p.m. in the Restaurant Queen Victoria. That's at the Hotel Pilatus-Kulm—"

"We can't eat in your restaurant?" Roxy interrupted. She wanted to replicate Max's visit and speak to anyone who might have seen him, including restaurant staff.

"Ours is only open for breakfast, madam. You can access the restaurant through the main building, past the bar, or take the external walkway." Her eyes rested on their flimsy jackets. It was not yet winter in this part of the world but it was still very brisk and Roxy's padded denim jacket was no match for the arctic wind outside. Caroline was wearing a fluffy white, faux fur jacket that looked a little better but the receptionist was taking no chances. "You should use the indoor access way, it will suit you better. You have luggage?"

"Do we have *luggage!*" Roxy said, smirking down at Caroline's oversized suitcase.

"Oh, it's nothing we can't handle," Caroline snapped back, picking the bag up and tottering off towards the elevator.

Roxy thanked the receptionist and followed her to the lift and up to the second floor where they were soon gasping all over again. The view from their room was breathtaking. Large, thick glass windows looked out over an outdoor café, not surprisingly devoid of patrons on this chilly evening, and across to the craggy, snow-dipped cliffs on the mountain and down to wispy white clouds below.

"This is really familiar," Caroline was saying as she dropped onto the prime bed beside the window. "Max took a stack of pictures almost exactly from this angle."

"We should check out those pictures again."

Caroline shook her head firmly. "No way, Miss Marple, put your magnifying glass away. We need to do as instructed and settle in first, then hit the bar." She unzipped her bag and pulled out a bathbag. "I've got first dibs on the shower!"

As she disappeared into the bathroom, Roxy stepped across to the window and unlatched it, a blast of frigid air rushing inside. To Roxy, it was a welcome tonic, waking her up and blowing away the melancholy—she had always preferred the cold to the warmth, after all—and she leaned out to inhale the fresh oxygen and soak up the magnificent view. She spotted several people standing near the edge of a high ridge, rugged up and taking photos. Several more appeared from what looked like a series of caves at one end, another man was lumbering down some steep, stone stairs, fresh from a nearby lookout. Roxy guessed that most of the day-trippers had caught the last train back to Alpnachstad by now and she was glad of it. She liked her solitude just as much as she liked the cold.

She was just closing the window and fastening the lock when something on a distant peak caught her eye. She pulled her glasses off, wiped them clean, and then looked again.

There was a thin, winding path that led away from the main drag and up towards a peak and what looked like two large satellite dishes and at least half a dozen antennae. Did they require all that to get a radio signal up here? she wondered. It seemed like overload, but it also dismissed her early theory that Max couldn't have called because there was no mobile phone reception. She pulled her own phone out of her handbag and watched as several tiny bars appeared at the top of the screen.

Yep, there goes that excuse.

Before she could give it more thought, Caroline was out of the shower and shuffling through her luggage, tossing clothes out as she went.

"You go on about my suitcase but I haven't got a thing to wear!" she was whining. "I wasn't expecting this place to be quite so classy." She looked up at Roxy who was still mesmerised by the view and threw a rolled up scarf at her. "Come on, Missy! We've got ten minutes till drinks, and I don't know about you, but I need a very large glass of something!"

CHAPTER 9

Half an hour later the two women stepped out of the lift and back into the hotel foyer looking a lot more refreshed than when they'd arrived. Roxy had changed into black skinny jeans and a creamy, oversized jumper with dangly silver beads hanging across the front, and hoop earrings at her ears. Her jagged black locks had been swept back into a short ponytail and she was devoid of makeup, except for a dab of glossy plum lipstick. She had brought her handbag into which she'd placed Caroline's iPad and her own smartphone, not because she expected to receive any calls, but because she had the photo of Max on the screen saver, and she was hoping to flash it in front of the hotel staff.

Beside her, Caroline was wearing swirly, multicoloured skinny trousers, a black top and the same faux fur jacket. She'd changed into high-heeled, black boots and added a little blush and eyeliner to liven up her face. Yet again, heads turned as they made their way towards the bar below the staircase but Roxy was under no illusion they were looking at her.

There were various couples milling about, all with drinks in hand, and Roxy made a beeline for a basket of cheese that was sitting on the bar, untouched. She thrust two cubes into her mouth just as a young barman appeared, a bottle of Moet in his right hand.

"Good evening, ma'am. Some champagne?"

"You don't happen to have any Merlot, do you?"

"Of course."

He went to place the bottle down when Caroline stepped forward. "Don't even think about it. I'll have one of those."

He bowed his head and poured her a glass before fetching Roxy's wine. When he returned with it he saw Roxy thrusting more cheese into her mouth and he contained his smile. "You are hungry tonight."

"Starving. This is really tasty."

"It is our finest Swiss cheese," came a smooth voice behind them and Roxy swung around to find a meticulously dressed man standing there, a small smile on his lips. He was tall and lean in a navy blue suit with a silver tie, crisp white shirt and gleaming silver cuff links. Roxy noticed an oversized Tag Heuer on his right wrist which he was holding out now towards her.

"I am Leon Schelling, General Manager, you must be Caroline Farrell?"

"Actually, that would be me," Caroline said and he glanced across at her. "That's my friend Roxy Parker."

"My apologies, Ms Farrell. Ms Parker."

He shook both their hands and then said something in Italian to the hovering waiter who promptly turned away.

"Shall we take a seat?"

Leon led them to a set of chairs at one end of the bar, which faced away from the other patrons and out towards the alpine view. Roxy noticed that the sun was dropping fast and the mountain was beginning to glow gold.

The waiter appeared again, this time with a fresh bowl of cheese and a glass of soda water for Leon.

"Please, help yourself," he said to Roxy, adding, "but I warn you, dinner will be very delicious, so you do not want to destroy all your appetite."

"No chance," she replied, dropping another cube into her mouth.

Leon took a dainty sip of his drink then brushed a hand across his slicked back hair and turned to face Caroline. "Now, shall we proceed? I believe you are here making enquiries about your brother, Ms Farrell?"

"Yes, I am. Max was due back in Berlin two days ago and has not shown up."

He blinked at her momentarily. "I see. And this is a problem, why?"

"Well ... because we thought he'd be back by now."

"Back in Berlin?"

"Yes."

He blinked a few times. "May I ask, how old is your brother?"

"He's ... er ..." She glanced unapologetically at Roxy.

"Thirty-five in December," Roxy said, giving her a withering look. How could she not know that?

"Right, that's what I was about to say."

The general manager smiled. "A big boy then. Surely, he can look after himself?"

"Of course he can," said Caroline. "It's just that none of us have heard from him, and well, he did check out of here early so we wondered whether something had, you know, happened?"

The way she said it sounded lame and he dipped his head to one side.

"I am sorry, I do not mean to sound flippant, but aren't you being a little—how do you say?—premature? Maybe your brother has taken an extended holiday, enjoying the Swiss scenery some more. Surely you can not be worried at this early stage."

Caroline glanced from Leon to Roxy and back. "It's just ... you know, it's not like him."

He almost snickered. "Ah, boys, they can be unpredictable, yes?"

"I guess so," stammered Caroline.

"Er, no," interjected Roxy, fast growing annoyed by the general manager's patronising attitude and the way the conversation was progressing. "I don't think you understand the urgency." She dropped her cube of cheese back down, her appetite now gone. "We're not being premature at all. It's not just that Max has disappeared."

Lazily, patiently, his eyes moved from Caroline to Roxy. "Oh?"

"Max's flatmate, an American man called Jake Conway, has been found murdered in their Berlin apartment. He was killed late Friday night or Saturday morning." Leon's eyes had widened and he wasn't snickering anymore. "We have no idea what's happened to him but we believe he saw Max just before he died. So, we don't really care whether Max is being an 'unpredictable boy' on some extended holiday enjoying your lovely Swiss scenery." She knew her voice was dripping with sarcasm and she tried to straighten her tone. "That's not really the issue, Leon. We just need to find him and make sure he's okay. The Berlin police would also like to confirm he's alive and well."

She didn't mention the small matter of Max being a potential suspect in Jake's death, nor did she have to. Leon was now nodding his head in earnest, his long fingers together, prayer-like at his lips.

"That is different, yes, yes, I can see that now. But..." He frowned. "Surely you do not think this has anything to do with the Bellevue?"

"We don't know what to think," Roxy said. "We don't know why Max's flatmate was killed or even if it has anything to do with Max, for that matter." She glanced around. "All we know is that Max is missing and this was the last place he was seen. That's why we're here and that's why we need your help to find him."

"Of course, of course, anything at all. But what can I do?"

Roxy took a settling gulp of wine and watched as he signalled to the waiter to refill Caroline's now empty champagne glass.

"We need to fill in some blanks," she said. "We believe that Max was booked to stay here last week for the whole week, but checked out early, is that correct?"

The manager nodded. "Yes. I have studied the booking. Mr Farrell arrived Sunday evening, on the last train, and was settled into room 202."

"Oh, that's our room," said Caroline and he nodded again.

"He was expected to stay until Saturday morning but departed early, on Wednesday morning."

"Did he say *why* he had to leave early?" Caroline asked now. "Where he was going?"

"I am sorry, no. I explained to him that he would have to pay for the full six days as he had made a non-transferrable booking and he said this is fine. He had no choice but to go."

"No choice?"

"This is what he said." He paused. "He seemed to be in a hurry, I have to tell you this. He kept looking around as he checked out. He was very keen to make the next train down to Alpnachstad."

"Did he say why he was in such a hurry?"

He shook his head. "I did not ask, I am sorry. We do not question our patrons. You understand?"

"Of course," said Caroline but Roxy quietly bristled.

A young man forfeits an expensive booking and checks out early, looks anxious and tells them he is in a hurry, and they don't bother to ask why. *Was she the only nosy Parker on the planet?*

"Was Max with anyone?" Roxy asked and Caroline suddenly coughed, sending a spray of champagne across her lap.

"Oh, Jesus, I'm such a klutz, sorry!" She grabbed a cocktail napkin from the table and began patting her jeans while Roxy flickered a curious glance at her then repeated the question to Leon.

"If you mean, was he booked into the room with anyone, then no, he was not."

Roxy stared at him. *What kind of an answer was that?* "He wasn't booked in with anyone?" Leon shook his head, began to stare intently at his glass. "But ..." she felt her weary brain turn over a few cogs, "he was *with* someone? Was it a man? It could have been his flatmate, Jake—"

"He was not with another man." The hotel manager said this while still staring at his soda glass and Roxy felt herself bristle further.

"Please, Mr Schelling," she said, leaning towards him, trying to catch his eyes. "We need to know all the details. No matter what."

He placed his hands back in at his lips and looked up at her. "We are not in the habit of discussing our guests' er, how shall we say, *liaisons*."

The way he said that word sent a small shiver through Roxy's heart. *So he was talking about a woman, then?* "Please," she repeated. "It's important. This could be a matter of life and death. Max's privacy is secondary at this point. I think his sister, at least, has a right to know."

Roxy turned to Caroline who was also deeply engrossed in her glass, and her frown deepened. *What was going on?* Before she could prod further, the manager sighed.

"Very well. I will tell you this: Mr Farrell did strike up a, how you say, *friendship* with someone while he was here. I believe."

The shiver intensified and she said, "Oh?"

"I did witness him talking at the bar with one of our female guests at one point."

"Oh," Roxy managed again.

Caroline cleared her throat and asked, "Do you know who this woman is?"

He shook his head, smiled apologetically. "You must understand we had a full house that night. A large Austrian tour group, a military contingent, several American couples. I would not like to say."

"Not like to say?!" Roxy began but Caroline cut her off.

"But you think Max and this woman were friendly, right?"

Leon appeared to stiffen a little. Was he just uncomfortable discussing his clientele or was there something deeper, darker at play? "Again, I would not like to insinuate. I only saw them having a drink together. On the Monday night. That is all."

He's hiding something, Roxy thought, glancing across at Caroline who was now chewing on her champagne flute. And that's when it hit her. Caroline wasn't surprised by this news at all.

She was hiding something, too.

Roxy's head began to spin. Was this the "German floozie" Caroline had joked about back at the Thai restaurant in Sydney? Was there something she was keeping from Roxy?

"This is all I can tell you, I am sorry," Leon was saying as he got to his feet. "I must now see to my other guests, but please, do let me know if there is any way I can help you. Any way at all."

You can start by telling me the truth! she wanted to say but she simply watched him walk away, then she rounded on Caroline. "Okay, spit it out!"

Caroline blinked innocently back at her. "Sorry?"

"You *should* be bloody sorry! You've been keeping something from me. Max was with some woman while he was here, wasn't he? You obviously know that already, you didn't bother to tell me!"

Caroline slumped back into her seat, her shoulders hunched over defensively. "Okay, okay, don't get all stressy. I don't know anything for sure but, yes, I did see pictures of some woman."

"Pictures?"

"On his Facebook page." She sighed, sat forward and grabbed Roxy's handbag, pulling her iPad out. She tapped away for a few minutes then sighed again. "Just give me a sec, I'll see if the barman has a password for the Wi-Fi."

"Grab me another Merlot while you're there," Roxy snapped. "I think I'm gonna need it."

As Caroline walked across to the bar, Roxy drained her glass and tried not to think the worst. So, Max was chatting with some woman at a bar. Big deal. In fact, maybe this was a *good* thing. Maybe he told said woman all about his plans, his fears, whatever was going through his mind. Maybe she was a passing acquaintance, nothing to worry about. In fact, maybe she was still here and they could question her, tonight!

Caroline reappeared holding her device out for Roxy to see. "Okay, here's his Facebook page."

She appeared to shrink back a little as she handed it over and Roxy flashed her a scowl. "I've already seen these shots. You showed me in Sydney."

"No, I just showed you the ones I wanted you to see. Scroll up a bit, there's a second lot he posted, the next day, on the Tuesday. She's in those."

Roxy scowled at Caroline again and did as instructed, bracing herself for God knows what. Within seconds she saw her, a chirpy looking blonde, thirty-something, with tanned, chiselled features and a hot pink visor on. She was smiling widely, her arms spread out as she stood before the stunning mountain view, the same view that was now forgotten through the window beyond. There were three more images of the woman on the site. One showed her standing by a cave entrance, beaming like a Christmas tree, another showed her in profile, looking wistfully down the cliff face, and the final shot was the most gut-wrenching of all. It showed the blonde and Max standing side by side. Max had one arm slung across her shoulder, the other on his hip. The same mountain view was behind them and while the woman was still smiling like a crazed idiot, Max had a strange look on his face. Was that worry in his eyes? Anxiety?

Either way it didn't matter. The shiver in Roxy's heart had turned into a tremor and she was quaking with feelings of jealousy, anger and betrayal. *Who was this woman?* She didn't seem like Max's type at all. She was way too blonde, way too perky, way too Little Miss Princess-like.

"This doesn't mean he's with her," Caroline was saying. "As in with, with. Maybe they just struck up a friendship and that was it. No biggie."

She stared at her coldly. "So why didn't you show me then? Back in Sydney?"

"Because I knew you'd react like this."

"Like what?"

"Like all weird and jealous and crazy."

Roxy growled. "Do I look weird and jealous and crazy?"

"Uh, yeah!"

She growled again. "I'm 'crazy' because you kept these from me. This could be important, Caroline. Maybe this woman knows where he is. Maybe he's with her now. I mean, you can't keep this stuff from me."

She held her palms out. "I'm sorry. I know. I've been meaning to tell you, I just couldn't find the right time."

"The right time?! We just spent twenty-eight hours stuck in a tincan over the Indian bloody Ocean! Another ten hours in a car together. You couldn't find one lousy minute to tell me?"

Caroline shrank further. "Sorry. Jeeze. I was trying to spare your feelings, that's all. I know you're still hooked on Max ..."

Roxy couldn't believe what she was hearing and she swiped angrily at the iPad, scrolling through the pictures again. "Anything else you haven't bothered to show me?"

"That's it, I promise."

Roxy stopped swiping and took a few sips of her wine. She closed her eyes for a moment and tried to calm down. She couldn't believe Caroline had kept such vital information from her. It put everything in a different light. Perhaps if she'd known about this "other woman" she might not have jumped on the first plane to Europe.

As if reading her mind, Caroline said softly, "I was afraid

if I showed you those pictures you wouldn't care so much."

Roxy's eyes flew open. "Care?"

"I was afraid you'd be even angrier with Max and then you wouldn't help me try to find him."

Roxy sighed. Caroline was right, of course. If she thought about it, if she were truly honest with herself, she'd admit she was just as angry with Caroline for denying her this clue as she was with Max for teaming up with a perky blonde on a romantic Swiss mountain.

In a more conciliatory tone, she said, "Listen, I appreciate you trying to protect my feelings, but you can't do that. This is not about me. We need to find Max. If he's run off with some *German floozie*"—Caroline winced as she said it—"then great, he's alive. Better than the alternative. Doesn't matter where he is or who he's with, we've got to be honest with each other if we're going to find him. Okay?"

Caroline nodded. "I promise. No more secrets."

"Good." Roxy went to turn the iPad off when something caught her eye. "What's this shot?"

Caroline leaned across to have a look. "Dunno. Looks like the caves around here. It's dark, pretty crappy handiwork for Max."

"Who's the guy?"

"What guy?"

"In the back there, right-hand corner."

Caroline looked again. "Oh, I didn't notice him. I don't know. Does it matter?"

At that moment, a waiter appeared at their side. "Ladies, dinner is ready in the Restaurant Queen Victoria, if you would like to make your way over now, you can beat the tour group."

Caroline jumped to her feet, grateful for the distraction, but Roxy kept staring at the photo on Max's Facebook page. It was a very dark shot, clearly taken at night and she was sure the man who stood off to one side, his face cloaked in darkness, had a rifle at his side.

Now why would a man be standing near the hotel with a gun late at night?

CHAPTER 10

The pretty French waitress was staring at Roxy like she had rocks in her head.

"You want a Milo?" she said. "*Chocolat* drink, *oui?*"

"Er, no. Definitely do not want a chocolate drink." Roxy looked to Caroline who was studying the menu oblivious to everything but her stomach. "Merlot—mer-low."

The woman kept batting her eyelids blankly and then held a finger up. "*Un moment.*"

As she dashed off towards the front of the restaurant, Roxy glanced around the room. It was actually a very beautiful space, probably once a ballroom by the look of it, with polished wooden floors and soaring marble pillars and elaborate crystal chandeliers. It was only just starting to fill up, the first of the large tour group wandering around their tables as though looking for the prime position. Another long table at the other end of the room was already filled with men, about twelve of them, all in military uniform, and Roxy was about to point them out to Caroline when another waiter appeared at her side. This one was tall and handsome, with two small plates in his hands and a wide, white-toothed smile on his face.

"Here you go, ladies," he said in an accent that was part American. "Courtesy of the chef, a smoked salmon roulade."

"Thank you," Caroline almost purred, dropping the menu to give the gorgeous waiter her full attention.

He smiled at her then turned to Roxy. "Now, my French friend's English is not so good. Was it a Merlot you were after, ma'am?" Roxy nodded. "We have 2008 French. Cool?" She nodded again. "Merlot for you, too, miss?" He turned back to Caroline, his smile widening further, and this clearly pleased her. She smiled back then fake shuddered.

"God no, I actually have taste! I'll stick with champagne, if that's all right."

"Perfectly. Enjoy your *hors d'oeuvres*." He bowed and walked away.

"Yummy," Caroline said and Roxy nodded.

"Mmm, it looks delicious."

Caroline laughed. "I wasn't referring to the food!"

Roxy rolled her eyes. "Try not to lose focus, Caroline."

"Oh lighten up, Missy. Max would want me to have fun. Besides, maybe I can *lure* some information out of our hunky black waiter."

"Or maybe we could just ask."

When the waiter returned with their drinks, removing their first course at the same time, Roxy produced her iPhone and said, "We're wondering if we can ask you a couple of quick questions."

"Sure, shoot."

She tapped the screen to life, revealing the mugshot of Max. "Do you remember this guy at all? He was a guest here last week, and—"

"An Aussie guy, yeah, sure I remember him."

"Great, did you speak to him?"

"Not really. Klaus served him."

"Klaus?"

"German waiter. He's not on duty tonight. But I remember he said that Max was a lot of fun."

"That's my brother," Caroline said and he smiled at her

anew.

"He's a photographer, right?"

"That's right. How did you know?"

The waiter glanced about the room then leaned into them, his voice considerably softer. "Well, according to Klaus, your brother got in a bit of trouble, shooting up at the peak. I think they asked him to delete some of his images. He wasn't happy." He stopped. "That happens a bit, though. Why you askin' anyway? He okay?"

"We don't know," Roxy said. "Do you know why he had to delete those photos?"

He held a hand up. "Oh, it ain't nothin' to worry about. They just don't like people gettin' too close, you know?"

"Too close?"

Before he could answer, a tinkly bell rang out from the back of the restaurant and he stepped back. "Sorry, got to get back to it. Second course awaits."

They watched as he returned to the kitchen then Caroline turned to Roxy with her eyes squinted. "That's really interesting. Why would they make him delete his shots?"

"And what's he talking about—'getting too close'? Too close to what?"

Caroline shrugged and Roxy recalled the satellite dishes she'd spotted earlier, and the picture of the man with the rifle. Was that all part of it, and did Max see something he shouldn't have?

"Were there any other strange pictures on his page, of people with guns or ...?"

"Not that I noticed, but then I wouldn't, would I, if he had to delete them. We should ask Leon."

"Speak of the devil," Roxy said and Caroline followed her eyes to where Leon was standing at the front of the restaurant, deep in conversation with their waiter. The waiter had his head low and appeared to be shaking it ruefully then he nodded and returned to the kitchen. Leon glanced around at the women and Roxy waved at him, batting her eyelids innocently.

Between a clenched smile she said, "He's hiding something. I don't know what. But I'll bet my second course he's just told our waiter to keep his big mouth shut."

"You think?"

"Yep. Be cool, Leon's on his way over."

A minute later the hotel manager was smiling down at them.

"Hello again, are we enjoying our meal?"

"Delicious!" Caroline gushed.

"Good, good," He hesitated before saying, "Please forgive me, but if you could refrain from questioning the restaurant staff. They are extremely busy tonight, we have a full house so they really must not be interrupted. I am sure if you have any further questions, you could speak to me directly."

"Well, actually, I do have some—"

He held a thin finger up to stall her. "I am most sorry, I can not speak at this moment. Please, make an appointment in the morning, after breakfast? Yes?"

The two women nodded silently and watched as he walked away, making a detour to the table of uniformed officers and glancing back at them several times.

"Oh yes," said Caroline. "He's definitely hiding something."

At the end of the meal, Roxy had every intention of ignoring Leon's instructions and tracking the waiter down to question him further, but her body had other ideas and by the time she'd finished her dessert—a tasty chocolate-apricot mousse tartlet served with raspberry jelly—she could barely keep her eyes opened. And so, against her better judgement, she held up the white flag and followed Caroline back to the hotel room to bed. It would all just have to wait until morning.

At 4:14 a.m., Roxy was wide awake. She lay staring at the ceiling for some time, the soft sighing of Caroline's breath in sync with the eerie whistling of the wind outside. After half an hour attempting to get back to sleep, she gave up and slipped out of bed and across to the window, looking out at the dark, swirling sky.

She felt deeply melancholy. Clutching her arms to her chest, she wondered where Max was, why he wasn't the one snoring in the bed beside her, and if she'd ever get a decent night's sleep again. She thought of her mother, too, and how she had not been at all surprised by Roxy's failed relationship. Had expected it, in fact.

"You're destined for spinsterhood," Lorraine had said matter-of-factly only the month before and Roxy had tried not to rise to the bait. "I used to wish you'd find Mr Right. Now I just wish you'd find Mr Anyone'll-do."

"Thanks for the vote of confidence, Mum."

"Well, I'm sorry, Roxanne, but you've only got yourself to blame. I mean, Max was never my favourite, you know that, but he would have done. Don't you see? He was perfectly adequate."

Oh God, she had thought then as she did now. Her mother was wrong on so many levels, but most of all, she was wrong about Max. He was more than adequate, he was her best friend, and she had not only managed to lose him, she might never find him again.

She allowed a fat tear to roll down one cheek, then swiped at it impatiently and was about to return to bed when something outside caught her eye. There was a figure moving in the distance, across one edge of the far rock face. Roxy wiped her eyes dry and kept watching. It moved again. A man. Now another. Then two more.

They couldn't be tourists out and about this early, could they?

She kept watching as the men moved out of the darkness and under a light. They were wearing camouflage, like soldiers. Two of them appeared to be talking, heads held closely together, while the other two turned in a circular motion around them as though on some kind of look out. All four had long sticks in their hands. Rifles.

Roxy stepped back behind the curtain quickly, her breath

catching in her throat. She was sure they couldn't see her here in the darkened room, but she still felt a surge of apprehension as she watched them, then she thought of Max's photos, the ones that were confiscated. Had he spotted the soldiers, too? Had he taken photographs and ended up witnessing more than he should have? Was that why he had checked out in such a hurry and disappeared from their lives?

CHAPTER 11

By 7:00 Tuesday morning, Roxy was up and dressed and eager to get going. Caroline, however, was still snoring away in bed, one arm flung across her face, the other tangled up in the sheets below her neck, her blonde hair strewn like cooked spaghetti across the pillowcase. She had her eyepatch on again and Roxy noticed an opened box of paracetamol by the bed. She reconsidered waking her, simply scribbled a quick note on hotel letterhead, left it by her pillow and tiptoed out.

Down in the main foyer, the receptionists were already at work, checking out early departures and tagging luggage for the train ride. Roxy strode up to the one she met yesterday and smiled.

"Good morning."

"Oh good morning, madam. Breakfast is served in the—"

"Actually I wanted to see if Leon is about. I wanted a quick word."

"Of course. I will check if Mr Schelling is available."

She said something in French to the man beside her and he took over at reception while she stood and disappeared behind a circular shaped wall. A few minutes later she returned, Leon at her heels.

He had a stiff smile on his lips. "Good morning, Ms Parker, you are up bright and early." He waved a hand to the sofa on the side. "How can I help?"

"I wanted to take you up on your offer last night. I have some more questions."

His brow wrinkled but he said nothing as they sat down.

Roxy took a deep breath. She didn't want to get the waiter into any trouble, but she had to ask. "Is there some kind of military base up here on the mountain?"

Leon looked surprised. "Yes, the Swiss army have a patrol base and they carry out exercises up here, but nothing for you to worry about."

"Didn't you also mention there was a 'military contingent' staying in the hotel when Max was here?"

"Yes, there was, still is in fact. They were at dinner last night, in case you didn't see them. But I fail to see what this has to do with your friend."

"I know that Max took some photos while he was here and was asked to delete them. Can you tell me why?"

He blinked several times and took a moment before he answered. "I don't think it's relevant to his disappearance."

"Well, I'll be the judge of that. What did he photograph, Leon? I need to know."

The manager appeared to wrestle with his thoughts for a few more seconds then he sighed heavily. "He took some pictures of a military exercise. It is top secret, of course. We explained this to him, asked him to remove the images and he was happy to oblige."

"Happy?"

"Yes, this was a matter of national security. He understood."

"What kind of military exercise?"

He smiled at her like she was a naughty child. "As I say, top secret."

Roxy considered this and then tried a different tack.

"Does the Swiss army own this mountain, this hotel?"

"No, no they do not. The railway owns it. They lease the land to the army. This is public knowledge."

"Not top secret then?" she said and he offered her a wry smile. "How do I know that Max didn't see something he shouldn't have seen and ... well ..."

Leon's smile deepened. "And, what, got 'bumped off'?" She blushed and he leaned back in his chair, looking more relaxed. "Ms Parker, we often have guests asking us if this is the hotel used in one of the James Bond movies, yes?"

She nodded. They had wondered the same thing themselves.

"We may look like a 007 location, but there are no licenses to kill here. Your Max simply violated our confidentiality clause."

"What confidentiality clause?"

"You signed it when you checked in."

"I did?"

"It was on the reservation form." He waved a few skinny fingers in the air. "It is no big deal. It simply stipulates that you will not trespass on military property—which when you walk around the site today you will see signs are well posted at various intervals. It says you will not photograph said sites as well. It is not that we think Mr Farrell had photographed anything of any interest. It is just protocol. All military bases around the world have such protocol. I think, even those in your country, Ms Parker."

"I didn't think the Swiss got involved in military type behaviour," she replied, thinking of their fence-sitting during both World Wars. "Don't you guys prefer to stay neutral?"

"We do not fight other people's wars, this is true, but we do take part in peace-keeping missions. We have a very proud military tradition in this country. In fact, unlike yours, or even America for that matter, it is compulsory for all Swiss men of a certain age to do periodic military training. I can assure you, we take our armed forces very seriously. After all, we are the ones who invented the Swiss Army

Knife, yes?" He thought that was quite amusing but Roxy wasn't laughing.

"So, the soldiers that I've seen around here ...?"

"They are in training."

"And the satellite dishes?"

"All part of the base. I think you will find such things at any base anywhere on the planet." He sighed again. "I am sorry to disappoint you, really I am. I know you are looking for answers, trying to find your dear friend. But I do believe you are looking in all the wrong places."

"Well, where do you think I should be looking?"

He stood up. "That is not for me to say. Perhaps this is less to do with war and more to do with love."

Before she could question him further, he said, "Ah, here is Ms Farrell now." Leon waved towards Caroline who was just stepping out of the elevator staring about. "Will you allow me to escort you to breakfast?"

Roxy stood up. "No thank you, Leon. I'm sure we can find our own way there."

She flashed him a "this ain't finished yet" look then made her way across to Caroline who had her stunned mullet face on, along with last night's trousers and a crumpled black T-shirt.

"You okay?" Roxy asked and Caroline groaned.

"Jetlag. I think it's finally hit. Feel like my brain's been hijacked and replaced with a bowl of mashed potato."

"Couldn't have anything to do with the six glasses of champagne you put away last night?"

Caroline scoffed. "Oh that's small fry for me." She scowled at Roxy. "How come you're so sprightly?"

Roxy shrugged. "My brain's suddenly working overtime. Come on, let's see if the Swiss know how to make a decent cup of coffee."

The breakfast coffee was not only delicious, the buffet was mouthwatering, and the two women overloaded their plates with fresh fruit and pastries, yogurt and pancakes before taking a seat to one side. They were making their way through their second helping when a waitress with bright red hair and cat's-eye glasses appeared with a fresh pot of coffee.

"Some more, please?"

"That'd be great," said Roxy, digging her spoon into a bowl of traditional Swiss Birchermüesli.

"Oh you are Australian," the woman said and Roxy looked up this time, nodding. "We get lots of Australians here."

Roxy smiled. "Really?" She glanced around then reached for her iPhone, producing the image of Max. "Do you remember meeting an Australian man called Max here last week. He was—"

"Of course, Mr Farrell. Very nice man."

"He's my brother," Caroline chirped and Roxy stared at her.

Did she never get bored with that line? "Did you serve him breakfast or—"

"Oh yes, miss. Max and his girlfriend."

Roxy's heart nosedived. She tried to speak, to ask the obvious question, but she'd lost her tongue. Her worst fears were materialising. She'd wanted to ask the waitress about the confiscated photos, about the military base, but this "other woman" kept popping up. *Like a bloated, rotting corpse.*

Fortunately, the coffee had now worked wonders on Caroline's mashed brain and, recognising Roxy's sudden distress, she took over. "I'm Caroline. We're trying to track down my brother. He hasn't been seen in almost a week. Can you tell me a little bit about this woman he was with?"

Sensing something was amiss, the waitress seemed to backpedal. "Oh, he was only with her the one morning."

"When was that?"

"Oh, um, I think it was last Tuesday. I don't know." She looked nervous now.

"Tuesday morning. So they came to breakfast together?"

"Yes. Well ..." She shook her head, the coffee pot almost spilling over. "They sat together, you see, but your brother came in first. She joined him soon after. I felt sad because," she blushed, "well, he is a good-looking brother you have there! Do you think he is okay?"

"We're not sure, that's why we're asking." Caroline glanced at Roxy who was still in a stupor. "So what happened then? They had breakfast and ...?"

She considered this. "Then I did not see them again." She stopped. "Oh, but I think maybe they go hiking."

"Hiking? Really, why do you say that?"

"Because they both wearing the hiking shoes and caps, and the woman, she has the .... I don't know what you call them, like hiking sticks?"

"Trekking poles?" Caroline suggested and Roxy snorted. *Trekking poles indeed! They were for the elderly and infirm!*

Caroline gave her a worried glance before asking the waitress, "Do you know the name of this woman?"

She shook her head firmly, stared at the coffee pot and backed away. "I must go, I am sorry, I have to keep working."

Caroline watched her slip away and then looked at Roxy. "You okay?"

She folded her arms in front of her and mimicked a smile. "Yes, I'm fine."

"Really?"

The smile deflated. "Jesus, Caroline, it's not about me, how many times do I have to tell you that."

"Sheesh, okay, chill out. So, what do you reckon? This the same woman Max was chatting to at the bar?"

"Either that or he's a bigger slut than I realised." Roxy regretted the words instantly but Caroline didn't seem to take offence.

"Do you think they—and don't get cross—do you think they might have, you know, hooked up? I mean, having *breakfast* together is usually a dead giveaway."

"Thank you, Caroline, I had joined those dots already."

"I asked you not to get cranky."

"I'm not cranky!" Roxy hissed and then caught herself.

She unfolded her arms and took some calming breaths. "Sorry. I'm ... I'm just confused, that's all."

Roxy was angry with herself again. If, as she had told Caroline, it was not about her or her feelings, why was she taking it all so damn personally?

Focus, Roxy, focus!

They sat in silence for a few seconds, sipping their coffee, their breakfast now forgotten in front of them.

Eventually Roxy sat forward. "Do you have your iPad with you?" Caroline nodded. "Good. We need to get those pictures of the woman up and show Leon. I need to know who she is, and what the hell she was doing with Max."

"So what about all this military talk?"

"Don't know about that stuff. But I do know a way we can use it to our advantage. Come on."

CHAPTER 12

Leon Schelling was looking more uncomfortable by the minute and all Roxy's questions about the military base were beginning to ruffle his otherwise immaculate feathers, so when she produced a picture of the perky blonde for him to identify, he was grateful for the diversion, and she was counting on that.

"Come on," she said to Leon. "You tell me who this woman is and I'll stop asking so many nosey questions about the base."

He sighed and glanced around his office as if checking for hidden cameras or the like. Caroline had made her way back to their room in search of more headache tablets, so Roxy decided to tackle the hotelier alone. Enough with the word games, she'd decided. It was time for some answers.

Sensing her mood, he had quickly ushered her into the privacy of his office telling the receptionist to hold all calls. Now he was staring at her like she was a toy he'd grown weary of. "We do not normally reveal our guest's names to the public, Ms Parker, I have already told you that."

"And do your guests 'normally' just vanish soon after they've had military photos ripped out of their camera?"

His jaw clenched. "What do you want, Ms Parker?"

"I want to know if this is the woman you saw Max having drinks with on Monday night." He hesitated before glancing again at the Facebook pictures and giving a quick, curt nod. "Hallelujah!" she said. "We're finally getting somewhere. We believe Max was also seen with this woman the following morning, at breakfast. It looks like they were heading off on a hike together." Roxy softened her tone, mustered her warmest smile. "Please, Leon. I know you're trying to do the right thing by your guests, and I respect that, I really do. But I need to know her name. A life may be at stake. Two lives. Please."

He straightened his hair behind his ears and glanced around the room again. Eventually he said, "It is another Australian. Mrs Candace Marlow. Candy, I believe they called her." His wrinkled nose showed Roxy exactly what he thought of that and she would have frowned along with him if she wasn't so perplexed.

"Did you say *Mrs* Marlow?"

"Yes. She was here with her husband, Donald."

Roxy sat back with a thud. "Oh ... right. But ... but where was the husband in all of this?"

Leon gave Roxy a look that spoke volumes and she finally understood his reservations. It all made sense now. The hotel manager suspected Max had had an affair with a married woman, at his hotel, under the unsuspecting husband's nose. No wonder they were all clamming up. It had everything to do with secrecy but not of the military kind.

She scrambled to get her thoughts together. "Were Max and this Candy woman"—*what kind of a name was that?*—"were they, you know, *together*? Did you see them being ... *intimate*." She didn't want to know but she needed to nonetheless.

He crossed his arms. "I saw nothing of the kind, Ms Parker. But if, as you say, they were having breakfast together, well, one can draw their own conclusions."

She silently groaned. "And did they leave together? Max and *Candy*." She could barely say the name without gagging.

Leon was shaking his head. "All I can tell you is what is in my files. The Marlows left together as planned, on the gondola at 8:15 a.m. Wednesday."

"The gondola?"

"Yes, it is another way down the mountain. It takes you to a place called Kriens. Mr Farrell left an hour later, via the train for Alpnachstad. What happened after that, after they all left my mountain, is none of my concern. Now, please, I can tell you no more."

He stood up and went to show Roxy the door but she didn't budge. "Please, Leon. Is there any chance of getting a contact number for the Marlows? An address?"

"No, Ms Parker," he said wearily. "Not a chance in hell."

Back in the hotel room, Roxy had become despondent, lounging on the bed and flicking through the TV channels, and Caroline was getting worried.

"Come on, Rox, let's try and track down that cute waiter from last night. See if he knows where the Marlows might be. Or we could take a stroll around the mountain. We haven't even checked out those caves yet. Maybe there's some secrets lurking in there?" Still Roxy said nothing. "Come on, sweetie, we've got to do something!"

Roxy turned to her. "Okay, sure, I know what we can do!" Caroline looked hopeful. "How about we go down to the gift shop and get ourselves two Swiss Army knives. Then we could use them to stab your bastard brother when we find him, in the arms of a married bloody woman!"

She turned back to the TV and continued bashing at the remote control buttons as channels flew by. Caroline sighed and sat down next to Roxy.

"I'm sorry, Rox."

She shook her head, couldn't look at her again. "My mother was right. I am such a bloody fool. Here I am in Switzerland, for God's sake." She waved the remote control at the view. "I flew all the way from Australia, with some ridiculous idea that my boyf—" She caught herself, "my *ex*-boyfriend was in mortal danger. Turns out, the only danger he's in, is getting a bop on the nose from a jealous husband."

"He could also get a really nasty sexually transmitted disease if we're lucky," Caroline offered but Roxy didn't even register a smile. "So you honestly think that's all this is about? Max following some chick around Europe like a love-sick puppy?"

Roxy shrugged. She didn't care anymore, or at least she wished she didn't. Caroline was shaking her head.

"It just doesn't fit."

"Don't try and make me feel better."

"I'm not. But it's just not Max's MO. It's not the way he does things."

"Really?" snorted Roxy. "We're talking about the same guy who followed me all the way to a tiny country town out the back of nowhere to tell me he loved me. Not his style, huh?"

"Well, you're different. He's only just met this woman."

"How do you know that? How do you know they didn't plan this rendezvous beneath the unsuspecting husband's nose? Leon did say she's Australian. Maybe they'd been having an affair in Berlin for the past month." She stopped, dread creeping through her bones. "Maybe he'd been seeing her longer than that. Maybe *she's* the reason why he took the Berlin job."

"Oh no you don't!" Caroline eyes fired up. "Max never cheated on you, you know that as well as I do. Nope, none of this is his style and you'd see that for yourself if you weren't so preoccupied with your little Pity Party."

Roxy ignored this and kept stabbing at the remote control.

"Anyway," Caroline added, looking suddenly triumphant, "how does any of this explain Jake? Huh?"

"Jake?" She'd forgotten about him.

"Yes, Jake! Think about it. Max disappears and then

suddenly his flatmate shows up murdered. What's *that* about?"

"Coincidence." Roxy dropped the remote and got up from the bed. "Good try but I'm just not buying it. I'm usually the first to dismiss coincidences, Caroline, but I'm sorry to say, that's all this is. Maybe Jake was killed by a burglar or had a run-in with someone completely unrelated. Who knows? It's likely all just a big, sad coincidence."

"Still, we have to find Max! That's the *whole* reason we came over here. Let's just find him and then we'll know for sure that everything's hunky-dory. Well, apart from the early midlife crisis he's obviously going through. I mean, did you get a look at that woman?" She mock shuddered. "Soooo cira-1985."

"You know what? If this is a midlife crisis then we should just let Max get on with it." Roxy grabbed her empty suitcase from the bench by the wall and began pulling her things out of the closet.

"What's happening here?" Caroline said.

"I'm packing up. It's time to head home."

"Shhh, not you! I mean, *here*?" She was staring at the television screen, her eyes as wide as saucers, then flung herself across the bed to grab the remote control and zoomed the volume up. Roxy went to say something but Caroline held a hand up to silence her as the reporter broke in. She was speaking in Italian, standing with a microphone on a windy rock ledge, and Roxy was wondering what on earth the woman was saying that so intrigued Caroline until a picture of another woman flashed up on the screen. Roxy and Caroline both gasped.

"Oh my God," said Caroline. "That's ... that's ..."

"*Candy*?" Roxy pulled her glasses off, gave them a quick wipe.

"What's the reporter saying?" Caroline was almost screaming. "What is this about?"

Roxy snatched the remote off her and turned the volume up further, but it didn't make any difference. They still couldn't understand a word of it. They continued staring, mesmerised for another few seconds before the reporter handed back to the anchorwoman who promptly moved on to a story about a frisky Italian politician, or at least that's what it looked like. Roxy turned the volume back down and began flicking through channels, trying to find another news broadcast.

"That was Candy Marlow, right? I wasn't seeing things?" asked Caroline.

"Yep, looked like it to me. I don't speak a word of Italian. Did you catch any of it?"

"No! Why would Max's mistress be on the news?"

Roxy gave up on the TV and grabbed Caroline's iPad. "Let's look it up. Maybe there's some info on the Internet." She stopped. "Damn it, what's the bloody Wi-Fi password?"

Caroline snatched the iPad from her and got busy with Google while Roxy tried to clear her head. Maybe they had got it wrong. Maybe they were so preoccupied with Max's mystery woman they were seeing her face everywhere.

Yet it definitely *looked* like Candy Marlow, a slightly younger version granted, but she had the same blonde perkiness, the same tanned, chiselled cheeks, and the same little cap, this one in white. It was a combination that made Roxy's skin crawl.

Why would she be on the Italian news?

"I can't find anything," Caroline was saying. "I don't know where to look. It's not on my usual news sites."

"Try typing in her full name, Candace Marlow. Or try Candace and Donald Marlow."

Caroline tried various combinations and eventually turned to stare at Roxy, her eyebrows sky high, her red lips open wide.

"What?!" Roxy screamed at her. "What does it say?"

"You won't believe it."

"Try me!"

Caroline shook her head. She didn't believe it herself. "According to this CNN report, Candy Marlow's husband reported her missing five days ago. She's vanished from the face of the earth."

CHAPTER 13

Candace Eloise Marlow was a confident hiker. Passionate, too, and took every opportunity she could find to haul on the boots, grab the trekking poles and head off into rocky terrain, and the rockier the better. She'd been hiking since she was a young girl living in spitting distance of the Blue Mountains, just north of Sydney, and was considered a seasoned hiker, so it was a surprise for all when she disappeared on a walk around the relatively easy coastline of the Italian Riviera.

Everyone, that is, except her husband, Donald. He loathed hiking, always had, and rarely accompanied his wife on her walks, usually sending her off with a warning of the dangers that lay ahead. He'd only ever walked with her a few times, he told the police as they sat questioning him in the police station in the tiny Italian fishing village of Riomaggiore, and the last time he had slipped badly on the way home and twisted an ankle. That was the final straw, and from then on he always sent his wife off alone, albeit "with great reluctance".

Except for the day she disappeared, he quickly added. There was a man with her that day, he'd insisted, he just didn't know who it was.

The police had raised their eyebrows sceptically so he rushed to explain himself. "That's all she told me, I swear to God. She said, 'I don't need you, anyway, I have my own escort!'"

Was the escort young? Old? Local? Tourist? To all of these questions, Donald had no reply. His wife occasionally found herself an escort, he said, somehow managed to con some poor bugger into accompanying her. For although she loved hiking, Candy loathed hiking alone.

The police wondered about this. Did it mean there were now two hikers missing? Or did it mean one of them had blood on his hands? After all, Candy had now been lost for almost five days and no one had come forward claiming to know a thing. The police had already dismissed a theory that she had run off with this so-called "escort" because they had found a Nike shoe clinging to a protruding cactus, just metres from the cliff top. Donald had already identified it as belonging to his wife. What's more, her personal items were still in their apartment, including her purse and handbag.

Oh no, they feared the worst for Mrs Marlow, and now Mr Marlow, too, was also in full panic mode. Or, at least, that's how he came across, his hands madly twisting at his handkerchief, his eyes fluttering about like a crazy man, his naturally pale skin red and splotchy. Still, one of the detectives, a large, barrel of a man called Mario Rossi, had his suspicions. He wondered whether they could believe a word that came out of the middle-aged Australian's mouth.

Rossi's partner, Carmela Constantini, was smaller, prettier and had no such qualms. "Pfft! The cliffs are steep, the pathways shabby," Carmela had hissed at him in Italian later. "We have been expecting something like this for years. Finally, it has happened. Why do you need to see a crime when the only crime I can see is with the council for not repairing the pathways?"

"He is dodgy," Rossi had retorted. "He is hiding something. I can tell."

"So what do we do?"

"We keep looking, of course, but we keep one eye on Mr Marlow. Just in case."

Meanwhile, 500 kilometres way, Roxy and Caroline were also keen to clap eyes on Donald Marlow. They had already tried and convicted him in their own minds and decided he had to be guilty of something. They just weren't sure what.

Soon after recognising Candy on the TV screen in their hotel room, they had swiftly got to work, tracking down information and finding out all they could. So far the details were sketchy and unsubstantiated but what they learned sent shivers down their spines. According to news reports and what they already knew, the Marlows must have driven directly from Mt Pilatus last Wednesday to the Italian Riviera where Candy supposedly owned a holiday apartment. Two days after arriving, on the Friday, Candy had set off on a five-hour hike and never returned.

"According to Italian police," Caroline said, reading directly from the latest Internet report, "'Mrs Marlow disappeared on the nine-kilometre *Sentiero Azzurro*, or Blue Trail, a magnificent stretch of coastline that links the ...'" She hesitated, unsure how to pronounce the next words. "Sinky Teary?"

She spelt out the word Cinque Terre and Roxy said, "I think it's pronounced Chinkwa Tare."

"Yeah, whatever, so she went missing on this Blue Trail, apparently, not far from some town called Manarola, wherever the hell that is." She shrugged. "Anyway, it says here that the coast guard is currently combing the waters off Manarola but believe there is little chance of finding her alive. 'They hold grave fears for the Australian national's safety, blah, blah, blah.' Oh, oh, listen to this bit! 'According to unsubstantiated reports, Candace Marlow may have been accompanied by an unidentified man.'"

Caroline looked up at Roxy, her lips forming a perfect O. They were both thinking the same thing, both had an idea who that unidentified man might be, but neither was willing to articulate it.

Caroline returned her attention to the news feed. "It also says here that Mr Donald Marlow is 'currently assisting police with their enquiries'. Yeah sure he is," she spat. "He *knows* what happened to his wife. He's probably the man she was spotted with before she vanished." She started clicking her fingers frantically. "I know! He must have found out about his wife's affair, it probably wasn't the first time, and he tossed her over the edge in a fit of rage. Maybe it was the final straw!"

"So where does all this leave Max?" Roxy asked softly. His name was nowhere to be seen in any of the articles, his face nowhere to be found on the TV channels or in the background to photographs.

Caroline looked at her again, her brow knotted together. "Max can look after himself. He'll be fine. Plus we don't even know Max is anywhere near this Motorola place."

"Manorola," corrected Roxy.

"Whatever, sounds like a mobile phone company to me. We keep making this assumption that Max is with Candy, that he followed her down the mountain. But what if that was just a quick fling, it meant nothing, and he headed off— *as he told my mum he would*—to Rio de Janeiro? Maybe he's there right now, happily basking in the sun quaffing Caipirinhas as we speak."

"Still doesn't explain how Jake managed to see Max over the weekend before he died," Roxy pointed out, adding, "and what the hell is a Caipirinha?"

"Brazilian national drink, darling. Made with cachaça, sugar and lime juice. Quite delicious."

"What are you? A walking cocktail encyclopedia?"

She bat her eyelashes. "I've had more than my share of Latin men, I'll have you know."

Roxy didn't doubt it. She grabbed Caroline's iPad and began tapping away.

"Now what are you looking for?"

"Manorola, I want to find out where it is, exactly."

The younger woman stretched her long arms into the air then walked across to the window, looking out at the view. It was midmorning and the mountain was fast disappearing under a shroud of mist. It looked almost eerie, matching the mood that permeated their room. Caroline folded her arms, lost in her thoughts until Roxy gasped audibly behind her. She swung around.

"What?"

"Tell me again, *exactly* what Max said to your mum the morning that he called."

"I already told you, he was heading to Brazil for a few days."

"Did he say Brazil?"

"Yes. Well, not exactly, no. He said he was heading to Rio de Janeiro, which is the same thing—"

"No, no it's not!" Roxy cried. "It all makes sense now."

"It does?"

She joined Caroline by the window and showed her the iPad screen. "Here's the *Wikipedia* page on Manarola, right?"

"Riiight."

"It says here that it's part of a popular tourist area called Cinque Terre or, in English, the Five Lands—'a rugged portion of coast on the Italian Riviera that is comprised of five towns'."

"So?" Caroline's eyes were starting to glaze over again.

"Bear with me. So, Manarola is one town, there are four others that all border each other along the coast." Roxy produced five fingers and began to count them off. "There's Manarola, Monterosso al Mare, Vernazza, Corniglia and, wait for it, *Riomaggiore*." She gave Caroline a "ta-dah!" look but the younger woman's expression remained unchanged and Roxy scowled impatiently. "Riomaggiore! Doesn't that sound a lot like *Rio de Janeiro* to you?"

"So?" Caroline repeated and Roxy felt like swiping her across the head with the iPad.

"So, I think your mum got it wrong. I think your brother

rang her early last Wednesday and said he was heading to Riomaggiore, not Rio de Janeiro. She heard wrong. He's not in Brazil. He's in Italy, on the Cinque Terre!"

Now Caroline was catching on. Her eyes widened, her lips gaped. "Gee, that does make more sense and they do sound very similar ... So you think this proves Max is really there, in Italy, with this Candy woman?"

"Well, yes. The problem is, 'this Candy Woman' has vanished and so has Max." Roxy gave her a pointed "Are you with me yet?" look.

Caroline was shaking her head. "It doesn't mean anything, Roxy. You don't honestly think Max went over the cliff with her, do you?" Tiny traces of fear flickered into Caroline's eyes and she was shaking her head from side to side, as if that would somehow push it away.

Roxy turned her attention back to the iPad and continued tapping.

"What are you doing now?" Caroline demanded, hands on her hips.

"I'm looking up *Google Maps*. It's time to visit the Five Towns and hope to God Max is still in one of them."

CHAPTER 14

Seaside villages don't come much more picturesque than Riomaggiore, one of the most popular of the Cinque Terre, its shell-coloured buildings tumbling like broken crockery towards the azure bay below. The farthest of the five villages from Mt Pilatus, Riomaggiore was a good five-hour drive through the Swiss countryside into Italy, down past Milan and along a jaw-dropping, winding road west of the port city of La Spezia, and it was almost dark by the time the women arrived.

They had checked out of the Hotel Bellevue at record speed, just making the 11:00 a.m. train back down the mountain, Leon Schelling looking relieved to see the back end of them. By midday they were on the road, their purpose renewed, their brains on overload. Once again, the surrounding beauty went largely unnoticed as they imagined a hundred different reasons why Max hadn't phoned.

Caroline tried out her old theory that Max's phone was simply flat and he was blissfully unaware of all the fuss, but Roxy was feeling typically pessimistic. Logically, the whole thing made a kind of terrifying sense: Max starts an affair with a married woman in a romantic Swiss hotel. He checks out of his room early and follows her to the Italian coast. Perhaps he's still smarting at Roxy's rejection, perhaps he's just lonely or needs this distraction, or maybe he really has fallen in love. Roxy tried not to settle on this last conclusion but she knew only too well how all-consuming Max's heart could be. Isn't that what forced her to push a wedge between them in the first place? Max had declared his love first, he'd wanted her to move in, and she had found it all too suffocating. Perhaps in Candy Marlow he'd found a kindred spirit, someone who liked his puppy dog act, encouraged it even?

Roxy shook the miserable thought away and refocused. Okay, so for whatever reason, Max hooks up with Candy and decides to follow her down the mountain to Italy. Perhaps they had prearranged a romantic rendezvous on a deserted cliff walk. The husband wasn't a hiker, that's what the press had said. Perhaps Max and Candy thought they would have more privacy that way. She *was* spotted with an unidentified companion, after all. Yet the husband gets wind of this, follows them on their walk. Perhaps he has a gun, perhaps an assailant? Either way, he somehow manages, by accident or design, to send poor Candy tumbling to her death. And Max ...

Roxy gulped back a tear. Perhaps Max fell, too—she couldn't bear to think of it—or perhaps he had made a run for it and was currently in hiding, terrified the husband would catch up with him. She shook her head again. Max wasn't a coward, she told herself, he wouldn't hide away, terrified of anyone.

Would he?

She gasped, remembering the text Max had sent while she was still in Sydney. The one she had decided meant, SOS.

Perhaps it really was a cry for help. She racked her brain now, trying to recall exactly when the text had come in. It was back in Sydney, she remembered now, late Friday night. That would have made it some time Friday morning in Italy.

The same morning Candy had disappeared.

So why didn't he finish that text? And why hasn't he been in touch since then? And what did any of this have to do with his dead flatmate, Jake?

"Oh my God," Roxy exclaimed, clutching the steering wheel.

"What?"

"Max's neighbour in Berlin, Holly, said that Jake was speaking to somebody in *Italian* before he died. Jake's murder has to be connected to all of this, it has to!"

Caroline thought about that. "You know, we are in Europe, Roxy. Half the continent probably speaks Italian. Unlike us uneducated Aussies, these guys are all multilingual. Hell, even the Roma gypsies speak four languages, they probably say 'benvenuto' before they rob you. I don't think it proves anything. Besides, Jake was in Berlin, remember. Not Italy."

Roxy groaned. "I know, I know, I'm grasping at straws." She pretended to bang her head against the wheel.

"Easy, tiger. One drama in the family is more than my mother could stand. Let's just try not to think about it too much, try to get there in one piece, okay?"

Roxy nodded. It was an impossible task. Her mind was already running away with a whole new string of theories.

Perhaps, perhaps, perhaps ...

****

"Psst! You look for room?"

Roxy broke out of her reverie to find an older man with a mop of white hair and a thick white moustache staring keenly at her. They had just parked their car at the top of Riomaggiore in the cramped and overpriced parking station, and were making their way slowly down the main road which was steep and cluttered with shops, restaurants and tourists at every glance.

As they walked down the cobbled road towards the

centre, Caroline struggling to keep her suitcase upright, Roxy studied every person they passed, hoping to spot Max amongst the faces. She scanned the cafés, too, wondering if he was nestled inside, sipping a cold beer, or strolling farther down, towards the train station and the sea.

Caroline was more preoccupied with her cumbersome suitcase and it wasn't until the Santa Claus look-alike caught their attention that they realised they were, indeed, in dire need of accommodation. Darkness was slowly descending and they hadn't even thought to book a hotel or look for a tourist information centre.

"You look for room?" the man said again, clearly used to repeating himself to tourists. He was standing outside what was clearly a hat shop, leaning against a banister overloaded with fisherman's caps, straw hats and sports caps, one hand on his hip, his bushy white eyebrows raised.

The women reset their course and wheeled their suitcases across.

"Yes we are," Roxy said and he waved them closer with one hand and reached for his mobile phone with the other.

"Two?" He was holding two fingers up. "How long-eh?"

"Oh, um, I'm not sure, a few nights, maybe."

His eyebrows wedged together. "You Australia?" They nodded and he smiled. "I like Australia." He then bashed some numbers into his phone, flashing the women quick glances as he made the call. "Ninety euro a night?" he said at one point and they nodded. He nodded along and kept talking. Eventually he hung up and smiled widely. "Hugo, he come-eh. He has good room. Clean room. Just here."

He pointed to the right of his shop, to a set of stone stairs that led up to a deep green wooden door. This in turn led into a three-story building right in the heart of the village.

"You wait-eh, over there." His head nodded towards a café across the road called The Marina, a strange name considering there were no boats or even water in sight.

They thanked the man profusely and Caroline tugged at her suitcase and began to make her way to the café when

Roxy said, "You really feel like coffee? At this hour?" It was almost 6:00 p.m.

"God no. I feel like a stiff drink, and they have free Wi-Fi here with purchase." She pointed at a sign near the front window.

"I knew there was a reason I brought you along."

Caroline scoffed. "I thought I was bringing *you* along."

"Whatever."

The women dumped their bags beside a cushioned sofa at a table outside and were promptly served by a tall, blue-eyed waitress. She looked Swedish and spoke almost no English but they managed to order drinks, a red wine for Roxy, a gin and tonic for Caroline, then asked for the Wi-Fi password. She had no trouble understanding that and as she went to fetch it, Roxy pulled out her smartphone and brought up the photo of Max. His all-encompassing smile gripped at her heart again. When the waitress returned, Roxy showed her the picture and asked if she had seen him, but the woman just looked confused.

"Cute," she said.

"Yes, but have you seen him?" Roxy tapped her eyes then waved a hand around the café. "Here?"

"Oh, no."

Roxy thanked her then took a very large swig of her wine. She normally preferred a good Merlot, but all they had was a cheap local Shiraz that could peel the paint off a wall, so it would have to do. She needed to settle her nerves. It had been a demanding drive along impossibly narrow, meandering roads and Roxy was not sure how she had managed to get them through in one piece. All that kept her going was the thought that with every passing kilometre they were edging closer to Max.

"Do you think he's here?" Caroline said, flitting her eyes around the still bustling streets.

Roxy shrugged. "God I hope so. I'm over this."

"Me too." Caroline keyed the password into her Wi-Fi settings. After scrolling through her e-mail in-box, Facebook and Twitter accounts, she exhaled heavily. "No word." They both visibly slumped. "I've got an e-mail from Mum, just a sec."

She began reading it, scrolling down the page with one manicured finger, before looking back at Roxy. "Mum says Dad's finally woken up to himself and has been in touch with the Australian consulate in Berlin. They've promised to look into flights in and out of Germany and Brazil."

Roxy scoffed. "Too little, too late."

"Yes, well, might as well let them. Just cross that one off for good."

Roxy knew it was a waste of time. Max had to be here, he must have meant Riomaggiore, not Rio de Janeiro, when he spoke to his mother. It was the only thing that made sense. This new woman in his life had gone missing close to its sister town Manarola. For whatever reason, he must have followed her to the Italian Riviera.

A distant chopping sound caught their attention and they both looked skywards as it grew louder, a helicopter whooshing into view, sending a gust of air through the street and squeals of delight from smaller children queuing for gelato.

"What's going on?" Roxy asked and the waitress waited until the helicopter moved away and the noise subsided.

"Tourist missing. Look for lady."

"Must be Candy," Caroline said and Roxy nodded, turning back to the waitress.

"No luck yet?"

"They no find." She said it as though it were the only possible outcome.

"She must've slipped, the poor darlin'," came a lazy, southern American drawl behind them and Roxy looked around to find a very large, very sweaty couple staring at them from another table. The woman looked a lot like Rosie O'Donnell, her chubby face dimpled by a warm smile and bright, vivacious eyes. Beside her, the man looked rather glum, his fat lips pursed shut, his eyes sad behind steel spectacles. He was dabbing at his dripping face with a serviette.

She glanced back at the woman. "Are you talking about Candy Marlow?"

"Yes, I am. You heard about that, then?"

"Just a little. What happened? Do you know?"

She nodded her head, her chin wobbling like loose dough. "Oooh yes, dear. The poor love, she went on that walk, you know, the five-hour hike between here and the other four towns. I says to Vern, I says, 'Those walks are dangerous. No way we're doin' that walk.' Nobody should be. One slip and you're a goner." She shook her double chin again. "Poor darlin'. Hubby's distraught of course. Now *he* was sensible."

"Oh?"

"Oh yes, he didn't go with her. Says he told her not to do it. But she wouldn't listen. *Determined,* he said. He used that word, didn't he, Vern? Determined." She tutt-tutted. "And now ... well, as I say, he's distraught."

"Is he still around?" Roxy tried to keep the eagerness out of her voice.

"I guess so, I mean he's gotta hang around 'til they find the poor soul, now don't he? Poor pumpkin was sittin' around dazed and confused this mornin', weren't he, Vern?" She slapped a hand at her husband's shoulder but he didn't so much as twitch, and so she rattled on. "The search party has been lookin' for days and days, that chopper's been goin' back and forth, and the poor man just sits around, waitin' for news, like it's gonna land in his lap. I mean, that's gotta be bad for the soul, now don't it? Anyways, I ain't seen him lately so ..." She paused. "Maybe he got his news."

She gave Roxy a pointed look.

"You think they found Candy?" Caroline asked now and the American woman shrugged.

"No, no, no, no, no!" said a thin, dapper-looking man who was just stepping into the café and overheard their conversation. "*Polizia* say still no find. But they did-eh find her shoe."

"Shoe?"

"*Nike* shoe." Like that was some kind of proof in itself.

"Was it hers?" asked Roxy and he gave her a look that indicated he, for one, thought it had to be.

She was about to question him further when someone called out to them from across the street. It was their white-haired guardian angel. He was smiling and pointing up the road towards another elderly man, this one with receding grey hair and stooped shoulders, who was hobbling towards him. It had to be Hugo, the one who owned the holiday rental.

The women drained their drinks and pulled out their purses to pay.

"So Monty Tedesco strikes again," the American woman said, shrugging her head towards their Santa-like saviour.

"You know him?" Roxy asked.

"Oh, everybody knows Monty. He's always at his hat perch, helpin' everyone, a real gentleman that one. Although, I have to say, when I did actually need him the other day, he was nowhere to be found, isn't that right, Vern? I got burnt somethin' terrible that day. My delicate skin ain't used to these harsh climes, although I can see at least one of you will have no problem with that."

She gave Caroline another pointed look and the Australian woman couldn't decide if she was being complimented or criticised. They paid for their drinks then fetched their bags and made their way towards Monty who was watching Hugo. He had stopped to talk to the man behind the gelato stand.

"Ahh, Hugo," Monty said, chuckling. "He take-eh his time, no?"

"That's okay," Roxy replied. "We're not in a hurry. So, Hugo owns this place and just rents it out for holidays?"

Monty nodded. "He has five apartment."

"Five, that's a lot."

"Yes, a lot-eh. I t'ink life is easy for Hugo. He just renteh the room, then he go and sleep all day." He chuckled again just as Hugo approached. They shook hands like old mates then Hugo turned to the women.

"*Benvenuto!*" he said. "You want a room?"

Without waiting for an answer, he proceeded to lead them up the stone stairs and towards the green door just beside the hat shop.

Hugo was not just stooped, he had a distinctive hunchback but it didn't seem to slow him down as he took the stairs swiftly, two at a time. His craggy face and knobbly limbs suggested old age but he had the energy of a young mountain goat.

"Lock-eh broken," he said unapologetically when he reached the front door and he pushed it open to reveal an extremely narrow, extremely steep staircase leading upwards. He located a light on the wall, showed the women where it was and continued bounding up the stairs. At the first level he stopped and pulled out a clump of keys. He chose one and plunged it into the door, taking some time to unlock it. When he did, he chuckled, and then pushed the door wide open.

The room was basic but clean, with homely furnishings and a small kitchenette. There were several windows facing the street, covered by green shutters, and he threw these open to let in the last of the day's light. Hugo then took them on a quick tour, showing them the double bed in one room—"Bags this one!" Caroline declared—and the single bed in the other, and Roxy noticed a small crucifix above each one. The bathroom was relatively modern, it must have been renovated recently, but the rest of the apartment looked like it hadn't been touched since the 1970s, and that was fine by Roxy. She wasn't going to fight Caroline for the best bed, either. All she needed was a place to rest her head and start her search for Max.

As Hugo handed over the spare key and prepared to leave, Roxy decided to try her luck again and showed him the photograph. Like the waitress before him, however, he simply looked confused and shrugged blankly at her before bounding back down the stairs.

Roxy closed the door behind him then slumped onto the cushioned sofa beside Caroline who was squeezing at her temples, her eyes shut, her brow crinkled painfully.

"You okay?"

"Oh, I've got a killer headache, Rox. Those long drives have been *exhausting*."

Roxy stared at her. She hadn't done any of the actual driving but she resisted the urge to point out that little fact, and pulled herself back up. "How about I go find us some food and you stay here, get some *well-earned* rest."

"Oh you're a darling," Caroline said, not catching her friend's sarcasm as she stifled a yawn and nestled further into the couch.

By the time Roxy had used the bathroom and pulled her denim jacket from her suitcase, Caroline was out for the count, her long body sprawled across the entire length of the sofa, her lips drooping open as she softly snored.

Roxy stared at her for a moment, awestruck. While Caroline's carefree attitude with its blatant narcissism was beginning to grate, she couldn't help admiring it at the same time and wishing she had just smidgin of it herself. Maybe then her nerves wouldn't be in such a tangle, her heart wouldn't feel so strung out. She sighed then closed the shutters to reduce the cooling breeze, switched a soft lamp on, and headed outdoors again, down the steep staircase to the street.

A slight movement caught Roxy's eye and she glanced around. Monty was pulling some caps off a high ledge just outside his shop, and as she watched him it occurred to her that if the American woman was right, this was the man to ask about Max. She stepped across to him.

"Thank you so much for your help," she said, pointing up towards the apartment.

"You welcome," he replied, beaming. "Where you from in Australia?"

"Sydney. I'm Roxy." She held a hand out to shake his.

"Monty," he said, shaking back. "I have family in Australia, they live Mel-borne. You know Mel-borne?"

"Yes, it's really beautiful."

He agreed. "I meet-eh lots of Australia this time of year."

That's what she was counting on. She pulled out her smartphone and presented the picture of Max. "What about this man. He's Australian. Did you meet him?"

Monty looked at the picture, giving it some thought. Eventually he said, "Oh yes-eh, I t'ink maybe I see this man."

His tone was casual but Roxy thought her heart would explode. "Really?!"

"Sure."

She took a deep breath trying to calm down. "Where did you see him? *When?*"

He shrugged lazily, no idea of the impact his words were having on her. "Two-eh, maybe three days ago."

"Here?"

"Yes-eh here. I t'ink he stay at Ola's place."

"Ola?"

He pointed down the hill, towards the coastline. "Near boat ramp, no? You go past-eh train station, down-eh steps to the left. Ola's Villas. You see."

Roxy wanted to grab the man and hug him to death but she decided on a less confronting smile instead.

"He boyfriend of you?"

Her smile faltered. "No, no, no. Just a friend."

Monty grinned like he did not believe a word of it but she was too excited to care. She thanked him again and tried not to run like a mad woman down towards the boat ramp.

Could it be this easy? she wondered. *Could Max be just metres away?*

CHAPTER 15

As Roxy found her way through the underground tunnel that led past the train station and towards the bay, her first instinct was to pull her hair out of its tight ponytail and adjust the strands around her face, brushing her black fringe down in the process. She wished now that she'd popped on a little lip gloss and maybe a fresh shirt before she'd set out. She was exhilarated by the thought that she might soon be face to face with the man she loved, and terrified at the same time.

What would he say?

How would he react?

Roxy's steps began to slow down. A sinking feeling settled in her stomach and she wondered if she was about to make a complete fool of herself. Perhaps she would find Max relaxing in his hotel and he would be both shocked and appalled by her presence, by the way that she and Caroline had reacted to his disappearance.

Suddenly all the doubts she felt up at Mt Pilatus came rushing back and she wondered now if they had jumped the gun. Maybe Caroline had been right all along. Maybe Max's mobile devices had simply run out of battery power and he had no idea his loved ones were frantically searching for him.

Would he laugh at her for that? Or be furious and disappointed?

She shook her head. *So why, then, did he send her that text message? SOS.*

As she strode through the underpass, riddled with doubt, something caught Roxy's eye and she stopped. It was a familiar face, staring out at her from the arched tunnel wall and she stepped towards it to take a closer look. A crudely designed Missing Poster showed Candy Marlow smiling widely above the line, "Help! Tourist missing!" There were a few lines urging people to contact the police if they had seen her and a phone number provided at the bottom. There was a similar poster beside it, this one in Italian with phone numbers at the bottom that you could tear off to call. Not one had been taken.

Roxy stared at the posters for a few minutes and didn't care suddenly whether she had overreacted or not. Two people Max had befriended in Europe were dead or missing. He hadn't returned any of their calls or e-mails in five days. Who wouldn't assume the worst?

Feeling emboldened, she turned away and continued quickly through the tunnel and up towards the jetty. There were a dozen brightly coloured wooden fishing boats piled on top of each other on the ramp, others secured by ropes and red buoys, bobbing about in the small bay which was now glistening gold from nearby lights. Two fishermen were enjoying a smoke on the side of one vessel while a small boy played in another, a toy gun pointing at an invisible enemy.

Nightfall had descended but the area was well illuminated thanks to the twinkling lights from several surrounding restaurants and bars, and the crowds were swelling again as they settled in for drinks and dinner. Bursts of laughter came from groups sitting at outdoor tables and there was the salty smell of fresh seafood in the air and a cool breeze that was not unwelcome. Roxy felt that pang of regret, of missed opportunity again.

She looked around but couldn't see any signs for Ola's Villas so stepped towards a trattoria called Ted's where an oily haired waiter in a brown velvet vest and multiple gold chains was ogling the crowd, and asked for directions. He squinted his dark eyes at her and offered her a leering smile.

"You want-eh table first?"

"No, thank you, I just need to know where Ola's Villas are."

"Why, you no hungry? I make-eh you hungry tonight, yes?"

"No," she said firmly. "I just want to find Ola's Villas."

He thought about this. "Okay, I tell you then you come back and eat-eh with me, maybe yes?"

She glared at him. "Maybe no."

He gave a half shrug that seemed to indicate a guy's got to try, and pointed her towards a narrow, darkened side street, which appeared to lead away from the jetty and into the rock face.

"Through there?"

"*Si*. Just keep-eh going, you find."

Roxy did as suggested and followed a labyrinth-like pathway, past several closed doors and shutters and up a steep, winding set of stone stairs until she found herself in front of a crumbling stone building with a freshly painted, lit-up sign that read: "Ola's Villas: No vacancy".

That's what she was hoping for.

Crossing her fingers, she knocked on the front door. There was no sound. She knocked again, then again. Feeling frustrated, she stepped back, peered up towards the closed windows and yelled out, "Maaaax!"

Her voice echoed up and down the street, a dog barked in response, but no one answered. She sighed and then stepped back towards the door about to start knocking again when a high window in a building directly across the path lurched open.

An elderly woman looked out. "You want Ola?!"

Roxy swung around, relieved, and yelled back, "Yes!"

The woman disappeared and a few minutes later her front door opened to reveal another woman, younger, prettier. She had long flowing hair that was bleached blonde and dark at the roots, and her voluptuous figure had been wedged into a tiny red dress. Just. She was chewing on some gum and batting eyelashes that were caked with mascara so chunky Roxy wondered how her eyelids didn't stick together.

"Ola?" she asked hopefully and the woman shook her head.

"Ola no here. I Sofia. Ola 'ave-eh no room tonight."

"Actually I don't need a room. I'm looking for my friend who is staying at Ola's." Roxy produced the photograph. "Max Farrell. Australian man."

The woman looked at the photo, then darted a quick look back at Roxy before giving her a shrug.

Well that was helpful. "Have you seen this man around?"

Again she shrugged, raising her fleshy shoulders high, her ample bosom almost lifting out of her dress.

Roxy tried not to scowl as she said, "Do you know where I can find Ola?"

"You come back tomorrow. She back tomorrow."

This was not what Roxy wanted to hear. Time was flying by and she felt so close now, just inches from Max.

"Is there a police station here?"

Sofia looked surprised by the change of tack and stepped back a little behind her front door. "It closed. You come back tomorrow. Ola here tomorrow."

"And Max?"

"I no see him." Her tone had turned irritable, and Roxy knew how she felt.

She looked around. Where could Ola be? Surely she had to be in Riomaggiore somewhere. It was a relatively isolated village, chances were Roxy had just passed her eating her dinner at a café or restaurant.

She thanked the woman, for what she didn't know, and threaded her way back down the path, Sofia standing by her door, chewing madly as she watched her go. Back on the main road, Roxy noticed that the sleazy waiter was now leering at a group of young, badly sunburnt women in insanely short shorts and tight tank tops. They looked like British backpackers and were making a beeline for a pizza bar at the other end of the jetty, much to his disappointment.

Roxy walked up to the waiter and asked about Ola. "I no see," he said. "You want-eh table now?"

"No thanks."

"We share one together, you and me. Not so lonely."

You had to give the man points for persistence, she thought, and in different circumstances she might have found him amusing, but not tonight. Barely able to crack a smile, she made her way back to the main drag, through the underpass, up the stairs and towards Monty who was just closing up shop when she got there.

"You find-eh you boyfriend?" he asked.

"Friend," she corrected, thinking, "What is it with these people?!" "Ola wasn't there either. Do you know where she might be?"

"No at hotel?"

"No."

He gave it some consideration. "One-eh minute." He dashed back inside his shop for a few seconds, then returned with a key and finished closing up, giving the front door a good rattle to check it was locked. Satisfied, he waved Roxy along and began striding with determination back down towards the bay.

For the next half hour the two of them went door-to-door, from bar to restaurant to café to bar again. At each venue, Monty stopped and chatted in fluent Italian to whomever was in charge and each time he shrugged his shoulders, stroked his moustache and kept walking. Eventually, he held his hands up and open, as though he had exhausted all possibilities.

"Ola no here. You try again, tomorrow, no?"

Roxy's heart sank. She did not want to try again tomorrow. She wanted to speak to Ola tonight. *Now*. This woman had seen Max Farrell, she was her closest link.

As they walked back to Roxy's apartment, a young local man stopped to say hello to Monty, greeting him like a long lost friend, and they spoke in Italian for a few minutes before Monty must have explained Roxy's quest. He turned to look at her then and suggested a few cafés they had already tried.

"What about parking station?" he said. "Maybe Ola go away. You ask there."

Monty was looking dubious but Roxy was determined. "I need to find out," she told him. "I won't get any sleep tonight if I don't."

"It's-eh big walk, no?"

"I'm happy to do it. Please, you get on with your night. I know how to find my way there."

Monty seemed to hesitate, as though wrestling with his conscience and, Roxy guessed, his hungry stomach, before he said, "Okay, I show you."

"No, no! Monty, really, you've done more than enough."

He wasn't listening, however, was already saying good-bye to his friend and heading back through town and up the hill towards the car park. Roxy had to race to keep up with him.

The parking station at the very top of the town was a busy place by day but at this hour was virtually deserted and for a moment Roxy wondered if she should have waited until tomorrow as everyone had suggested. Monty was certainly friendly but she couldn't help wondering if she should be letting a strange Italian man lead her away from the village, away from Caroline and the crowds.

Caroline! Roxy had forgotten all about her, but before she could give her another thought they had reached the top of the parking station and Monty was deep in conversation with a skinny, middle-aged man behind the toll booth out the front. He was nodding enthusiastically and it was the first positive sign all night so when Monty turned back, Roxy was surprised to hear him say, "He no see Ola. She still in town."

She stared at the man. "Really?"

He nodded.

"How do you know she's still around? Maybe she left without you seeing?"

They looked at each other and chuckled at that. Monty explained, "Everyone park-eh their car here. Henri see everyone who come and go. He say, she no go. She must-eh be in Riomaggiore."

Henri said, "Last Friday, she go away, I see." He put his fingers to his eyes. "This week, she no go, car still here. You want see?"

"No, I believe you. What about the train? Maybe she took the train somewhere?"

That made the men laugh even harder.

"Ola *never* use train," Monty explained, as though it were written in blood.

"You try piazza?" the parking attendant said then and Monty smacked a palm across his forehead.

"*Naturalmente!*" He turned to Roxy. "Come-eh!"

Before she could object, he was striding back towards town, all the way down towards the underpass. This time, however, he took a detour up a set of steps, which, Roxy guessed, led above the train tunnel. Just as Roxy's legs were beginning to buckle and she was second-guessing herself all over again, they stepped out into a wide, paved terrace that served as a playground for the local families. There were over a dozen children running about, dolls in hand, balls at their feet, several on scooters and skateboards, and to one side, a group of mostly black-clad women ignoring them completely, deep in conversation beneath bright streetlights. It seemed late for the kids to be out and about, but then what did Roxy know? They'd probably had a two-hour siesta in the middle of the day, which she'd always thought was a rather civilised thing to do.

"Ola!" Monty boomed and from amongst the crowd a large woman turned around, mono-brow raised expectantly. "You come-eh!"

Roxy caught her breath. *At last.*

Ola was an elderly woman with scratchy grey hair and the faint fuzz of a moustache above her top lip. She had a no-nonsense look about her and strode swiftly across the piazza towards them, checking Roxy out the entire way.

"*Che cos'è?*" she said to Monty, her tone cranky, her eyes still on Roxy.

He spoke to her in Italian and then she raised her hands as if saluting the sky.

"Ahhh, you come-eh for Max!"

Roxy felt the same rush of relief. "Yes! You know where he is?"

The woman dropped her hands. Her mono-brow dipped a little. "Me? No!"

Roxy stared at her and then at Monty. He also frowned, then proceeded to speak to the woman again who returned fire with loud bursts of Italian and much hand waving. After several mystifying minutes he turned back to Roxy.

"Okay, so Ola say Max-eh stay with her, then go away."

"Away? Where?"

He spoke to Ola again before saying, "She no know. He disappear-eh."

No, no, no, no, Roxy thought. *Not again!* "When?!"

There was another loud exchange between the two locals and then he said, "Last-eh Friday. He go away-eh and no come back."

This was more than Roxy could bear. She found her way to a low rock wall and dropped down, deflated again. Each time she got a little closer to Max, found someone who had seen him or knew something of him, he seemed to slip back out of her reach again. The two locals were talking in loud bursts, their hands gesticulating wildly as they spoke, and eventually Monty joined her on the rock wall. His eyes were downcast.

"Ola say, can you get-eh Max's things. Pay his bill, no?"

"His things? You mean luggage?"

"Yes-eh."

She felt a glimmer of hope. "Max's luggage is still at Ola's hotel?"

"Yes-eh, he go away, no pay, no take-eh the bag."

Roxy felt her heart lift. She knew, logically, this was a worrying development. Disappearing without your luggage was not a good sign, yet she was buoyed by the revelation. If Max's stuff was still in Ola's Villas, perhaps there was a clue in there, too. Perhaps there was something that would shed light on where he'd gone and why.

It was *something*.

It also indicated that this had to be Max's last stop. No matter where he was, what condition he was in—and she was not letting her mind go there—she knew that he had to be close. He had to be here, somewhere.

Encouraged, she stood up and pushed her glasses firmly into place. "Can you show me?" she said to Ola. "Now."

****

Muffled voices woke Max from his sleep and he swung his head around with a start.

Everything was dark, musty, dank. He felt his heart drop all over again as he realised his predicament, and then tried to move but his hands had been tied firmly behind his back, his eyes covered with something, an oily tasting rag in his mouth. He strained to hear what was being said but it was as though they were speaking through water.

He caught what sounded like "polizia" and "riskio", but that was all. Then, after a short silence, a loud creaking sound made his blood pressure spike as he realised someone was entering the room. He heard the crunch of boots approaching and felt his entire body stiffen, his nerves on edge as someone stopped and leaned in, a stale breath now hot against his face. The rag was suddenly ripped from his mouth.

"Come, eat." It was a man's voice, familiar yet not familiar. Gruff, impatient, angry.

Something was being shoved through his lips and he realised it was a piece of bread, dry and slightly stale. He wondered if it was poisoned but he was so famished he didn't care, opening his mouth wider as the man thrust the pieces in, then chewing like his life depended on it, which it probably did. After several mouthfuls, there was a slight pause before something hard and plastic was being shoved against his lips and he resisted at first until he realised it must be a water bottle, luscious drops of liquid dripping through. He opened his mouth again and swallowed eagerly, some of it gushing down his neck and across his sweat soaked shirt. It felt good.

"Come!" the man said again, yanking him by the arms and dragging him to his feet. His legs felt weak and wobbly and he struggled to keep up as the man pulled him roughly across the room before halting, creaking something open, and shoving him forward.

Suddenly someone else was grasping at his belt buckle, undoing his jeans, and he flinched, trying to back away.

"You stay!" the man growled. "Toilet!"

He stopped writhing and let them help him. It was demoralising and mortifying but he was glad of it, too, and not just because he was desperate to relieve himself. It also gave him a tiny shred of hope. Whoever these people were, whoever had tied him up and locked him away for what seemed like forever now, had a little heart, a little consideration. They wanted him to stay alive. Or they wouldn't bother with all this, would they?

It was enough for him to hold on to.

CHAPTER 16

The room that Max had booked in Riomaggiore was smaller and less luxurious than Roxy and Caroline's, and theirs was barely two-star. A tiny bedsit with a single bed against one wall and a sofa bed for a lounge, there was a makeshift kitchenette, a miniature dining table with two un-matching wooden chairs, and a bathroom befitting a jockey. The single bed had a sickly pink bedspread over it, incongruous in this dark and dreary room, but Roxy noted it was neat and tidy, and wondered when he'd last used it.

With Monty's help, she had learned from Ola that Max had arrived late Wednesday evening, six days ago, and had made a loose booking for the week. Ola was not a hundred percent sure when she'd last seen the Australian, but believed it was Friday morning when he was heading out for breakfast, to Ted's, she said, "around nine-eh". Or at least that's what she remembered. She hadn't really given it much thought, she explained unapologetically, probably wouldn't until he was due to book out tomorrow, except that the Australian woman went missing and now the police were enquiring of all visitors to the town. She had been asked to tell Max to contact the local police except she could not find him and was surprised to see his room had not been touched in days, the fresh towels exactly where she had left them on Friday morning, the sheets untouched as well.

She told Roxy all of this as they made their way back through the maze of streets to Ola's Villas, Monty helping to translate when language became a barrier and, despite Roxy's pleas, refusing to leave her side.

"I will help-eh you find you boyfriend, he will be okay!" he'd said and Roxy admired his optimism, she was starting to feel a little more buoyant herself. That is, until she saw Max's room, the untouched bed, his black duffle bag sitting unopened beside it.

"See!" Ola said after she'd unlocked the door and switched on the harsh lighting. "He bag still 'ere!" She pointed at it then stepped across to the bathroom. "And-eh 'ere!" Roxy caught a glimpse of a bathbag on the sink. "Other man, 'e go, but you friend, 'e stay."

Roxy's eyes widened. "Other man?"

Ola frowned at her. "Yes, 'e go. I no see 'e things. So why Max-eh stay?"

"Do you mean woman?"

Ola looked at Roxy like she was the dimmest tourist she'd ever met. "No! Man-eh."

"Max met up with another man here?"

Her patience was wearing thin. She glowered at Monty as if it was all his fault then turned back to Roxy and explained: "You friend-eh he book-eh room with other man, no? They check in together. I no say this?"

"No," Roxy said, prickles of confusion creeping up her back. "So where is this other man?"

Ola shrugged. "He stay-eh two night, then he go and Max-eh stay. But now he go and I no get pay." She rubbed her fingers together in the universal sign of cash.

"So this man was a friend of Max's?"

Again, her expression spoke volumes about Roxy's mental capacity. "Yes! Of course-eh!"

"Do you know who the man is? Where he ended up

going?"

"I don't know-eh. How I know this?" She glared at Monty again.

"What about a woman?" Roxy persisted. "Did you see him with a blonde Australian woman?"

Ola almost bared her teeth. "No! I tell polizia, he no with Australian woman, he with American man. I tell them. Why no one listen to me?!"

"*American* man?" Roxy's alarm bells were clanging to life.

Monty must have misread her expression because he put a hand on Ola's shoulder and said, "She no care about other man-eh, Ola. She want-eh find Max."

"No, no, I am interested," Roxy interjected. *Very much so.* "Can you describe the other man?"

Ola gave it some thought. "He tall-eh, skinny, *too* skinny. Loooots of tattoos." Her downturned lips and scrunched mono-brow told Roxy exactly what she thought of that.

"Did he have a large tattoo on his right shoulder? Like a serpent or a dragon or something?"

Ola considered this, weighed it up. "Hmmmm, maybe. Something big-eh there. Ugly." She tapped her shoulder, her lips drooping further. "He Americana." As if that explained everything.

The bells in Roxy's head had turned into a fully blown orchestra and she was struggling to get her thoughts together. She sat on the sofa and gave herself a little shake.

It couldn't be? Could it?

This "other man" had to be Max's flatmate, Jake. It sounded exactly like him. Yet ... yet what was he doing here, in Riomaggiore, a full forty-eight hours before he showed up dead in his Berlin apartment?

Roxy leapt to her feet again. "Oh God, I've got to call Caroline!"

She grappled for her phone as Ola and Monty watched, looks of bemusement across their faces. Ola said something in Italian to Monty who shook his head sadly.

It took several attempts for Roxy to key Caroline's

number into her phone, her fingers were trembling and her brain was racing. Unlike her, Caroline had not switched to a local SIM card when they arrived in Europe. She wanted Max to be able to reach her at her usual number, so Roxy was forced to call her on that, too. She knew the call would be re-routed and expensive, but she didn't care. She needed to speak to her, and quickly.

The phone picked up after just one ring. "Jesus, Roxy, where the hell have you been?! It's almost 9:30, I'm starving!"

"Sorry, Caroline."

"Where are you? If you're enjoying a Merlot somewhere without me, I'm going to kill—"

"Caroline, it's not that. I've found something."

"What?!"

Roxy sighed. "It's a long story. Why don't you put on a jacket and come and meet me. You need to see this."

CHAPTER 17

There's something particularly depressing about wading through a loved one's belongings when they're not there, sort of like peeking through their diary or ogling the bathroom cabinet. It just felt wrong. Both women knew they had to do this, to wade and peek and ogle, yet it still felt invasive, as if they were trampling all over Max.

It was now late on Tuesday night. Roxy had finally convinced a worried-looking Monty to head home to bed, thanking him profusely yet again, then arranged to meet Caroline on the main road, just near Ted's Trattoria, convinced the younger woman would never find her way to Ola's Villas in the dark. Many of the eateries were beginning to close and their fairy lights going out, but she did notice that the pizza bar was still open and managed to grab two slices before Caroline arrived.

Ola, who seemed more concerned with settling the bill than locating the missing tourist, had happily handed over a room key in exchange for some cash, and promptly disappeared, and this suited Roxy to no end. She wanted to get in and start hunting through Max's things. But first she needed to get Caroline up to speed and she did this as they ate their crispy basil and bocconcini pizza, perched on the edge of Max's bed, staring glumly around the room.

Caroline agreed this new player on the scene sounded a lot like Max's old flatmate.

"But why would Jake be *here*?" she said, winding a long strand of mozzarella around her fingers. "And how does he end up dead in Berlin two days later? And *why*?"

"All good questions," Roxy told her. "Makes no sense to me either, although it does explain why Jake said he'd just seen Max in that message he left you."

Caroline considered that message. "That's right. He said he'd seen Max and Max had it under control. Whatever the hell 'it' is."

They both glanced around the room, not convinced Max had anything under control. He was missing. His stuff was still here. It felt like utter chaos to them.

"Max has to be here still," Caroline said. "His bag's here. So he *has* to be here. In Riomaggiore, somewhere."

Roxy wished she were right. "But where?" Visions of the craggy coastline, of waves crashing hard against the rocks, flashed through her mind and she tried to push them away. She wondered if he was clinging onto a rock somewhere, but quickly dismissed this. Surely the coast guard or the helicopters would have spotted him by now.

"Did you find his wallet? His phone? His camera?"

"I haven't looked properly yet. Maybe they're in his bag, but I doubt it. Ola says she last saw Max heading off to breakfast, so at the very least he'd have his wallet on him."

"And his camera. He never went anywhere without his camera."

They looked around the room again. It felt so desolate, so lonely. What secrets did it hold? What had its walls been witness to?

Eventually, Roxy placed the final bit of crust in her mouth, wiped her hands together and pulled the duffle bag from the floor, placing it carefully on the bed. "Shall we?"

Caroline nodded and Roxy unzipped it slowly then

peered tentatively inside, afraid of what it might contain.

"Oh come *on*, let's just do this."

Caroline pushed Roxy aside and dug her hands in. Within minutes she had the contents laid out on the bed but there was not much to see: a few shirts, a jumper, a pair of black jeans, several sets of underwear and socks, some Converse sneakers, and two books—a Lonely Planet Guide to Switzerland and a battered copy of *The Book Thief* by Markus Zusak. A side pocket produced a tangle of black earphones, several pairs of dirty underwear, causing Caroline to recoil, and a phone charger, which she now held high.

"So much for that theory," Roxy said.

Nowhere in the room could they find Max's wallet, mobile phone, camera or any devices for that matter, nor was there a travel journal with his deepest, darkest thoughts scribbled inside. No such luck.

The two women then moved to the ridiculously tiny bathroom at the other end of the room and Max's bathbag, which was propped against the sink. Caroline went through it as Roxy watched from the door, spotting a raggedy toothbrush, some deodorant, two Band-Aids, a newish shaver and shaving cream and a tiny box of dental floss.

"Oh well, at least he had clean teeth when he vanished," Caroline said lamely and Roxy didn't even bother to laugh. "Oh, there's something else here, in the side pocket."

Caroline pulled it out and regretted it instantly. It was a set of condoms, three connected in a row. She glanced warily at Roxy whose face was now set in stone; she was wondering how many he had started with and who they were for. After a quick glance around, Roxy strode back into the main room and made a beeline for the cupboard beneath the sink.

"You're not?!" gasped Caroline as Roxy pulled out a small garbage bin.

"We have to know if he was here with her. Or with anyone for that matter. It's important."

Important to you, Caroline thought, her nose crinkled with disgust, but she kept that to herself. The look on Roxy's face was dark and foreboding.

As she rifled through the bin, Roxy tried to prepare herself for the worst, envisaging dozens of used condoms, maybe some dead roses and an empty box of chocolates, but its contents were fairly innocuous. She found some plastic wrapping that looked like it belonged to the floss, a used tea bag, a few serviettes, which may or may not have held pizza slices once, and a beer coaster for Ted's Trattoria & Music Bar.

Roxy pulled the coaster out and stared at it for a few moments, turning it over then back again. This place had come up a few times, she realised, then glanced across at Caroline who had returned to the bed and was placing Max's belongings back into his bag.

"For when he returns," she said softly and Roxy joined her there, holding the beer coaster out.

"What's that?"

"It's our next port of call. Come on."

Back on the street, Ted's was one of the few eateries still open, yet it, too, was starting to wind down. A long, cavernous room with a slanted, bare stone ceiling and white rendered walls, the restaurant had eight wooden tables squashed together inside and another six in a small, outdoor patio at one end, facing the street. The bar at the back had two chrome stools and a bright selection of spirit bottles that were illuminated by a neon light above and a mirrored wall behind. To the right of the bar was a long corridor, which led into what Roxy assumed were the restrooms and kitchen, and perhaps even a stairwell to the floors above.

It was now 10:15 p.m. and all of the indoor tables were empty, red wine spills on the tablecloths and crumpled serviettes proof that it had been a busy night. There were still a few patrons left outside, two chatting and laughing as they polished off dessert, two others settling their bill. All looked as though they hadn't a care in the world and Roxy envied them that. She longed suddenly for Max's favourite Sydney eatery, an Indian restaurant that used to drive her nuts. It was located about halfway between their two homes and was a decent cheap eats as far as cheap eats went, yet Roxy had grown bored by it and by Max's insistence on going there over and over again.

A creature of habit herself, Roxy had found it most annoying in others.

Now she longed for a creamy butter chicken, Max sitting across from her, teasing her about her fetish for death, her habit of cutting out crime stories and pasting them into scrapbooks. She longed for his enormous, clench-your-heart smile, and she wished he were around to smile upon her again.

"Sorry, ladies, our kitchen is-eh closed!" came the voice of the sleazy waiter she had spoken to earlier that night. He was leaning against a railing outside, dragging on a rolled cigarette, his eyes squinting lasciviously at Caroline. He had clearly moved on from Roxy and it didn't bother her one bit.

She pulled Caroline forward so he could get a better look and said, "Oh we're not after a meal. We're looking for someone, a man this time."

She produced Max's photo and he stared at it for a few moments then shrugged. Roxy was fast learning this was Italian for "I don't know and I don't care".

"Have you seen him?" Roxy asked.

"Not tonight, no."

"But you *have* seen him?" Caroline persisted and he nodded very slowly, a slight frown crinkling his forehead.

"He boyfriend of you?"

Caroline frowned back at him. "Certainly not. He's my brother." This cheered him up and he sucked on his rollie again. "Can you remember when you last saw him?"

The waiter blew out a long plume of smoke. "I no remember. You speak-eh to The Boss." He nudged his head inside.

"Oh?" Roxy said. "Ted, is it?"

He looked at her like she was thick. "No, no, no. Maria.

She know *everything.*"

There was a slight edge in his voice and when he nudged his head towards the bar at the back, his eyes rolled a little.

Roxy followed his nudge towards a tiny, dark-haired woman who was sitting at the bar at the back, deep in conversation with an equally small, fair-skinned man with a Fedora on his head.

"How long-eh you in town?" the waiter was asking Caroline and Roxy held a hand up to her.

"You stay here, see what else he knows. I'll just be a sec."

Caroline looked appalled by the suggestion but Roxy ignored this and made her way inside the café and towards the bar where the dark-haired woman was now patting the man's back as though soothing him. From the side, the woman looked Italian, her nose strong and protruding, but as Roxy got closer she realised they were conversing in English. The man had an Antipodean accent and was saying, "I have no idea how I got there, Maria, you have to believe me. No bloody idea."

"Shh!" she said suddenly, turning to look at Roxy whom she must have spotted in the mirror's reflection. She gave her one of those smiles that don't quite reach the eyes and when she spoke, her accent was slightly Australian, with Italian undertones. "The restaurant's now closed. Thanks very much. Please come back tomorrow."

Roxy glanced quickly at the man and then back again. He looked vaguely familiar, his pale skin blushing slightly, his eyes not meeting hers. She turned to the woman and said, "Yes, I know you're closed but your waiter suggested I talk to you." She waved to the front of the café. "You're Maria, right?"

"Yes."

"I just need to ask you a quick question. It's very important."

Maria looked annoyed for a moment before leaning towards the man, her tone softer now. "We'll talk tomorrow. Okay?"

He seemed appeased by this and repositioned his Fedora on his head, grappled for his sunglasses and keys, and left without even giving Roxy a glance.

Maria had no such hesitation and was now moving her eyes up the full length of Roxy's body as if trying to work out who this annoying creature was and what she could possibly want at this hour. Roxy took the opportunity to check her out, too. She was very short, slightly overweight, and had a cropped haircut that sat like a ragged black mop above thick, sculptured eyebrows and deep brown eyes. There was a smattering of freckles on her nose but her skin was tanned and she wore almost no makeup, just a smidgin of pink gloss on her lips.

"So, what is your question?" Maria asked, those eyebrows now raised high.

Roxy sat down on the vacant stool beside her and produced her phone, showing the woman Max's picture. She glanced at it and then up at Roxy expectantly.

"Have you seen this man? His name is Max Farrell. He's Australian and he's gone missing."

"No," Maria said, jumping off the stool and revealing she was even shorter than Roxy had expected. She made her way behind the bar where she pressed a button on the cash register, causing it to ping loudly before crashing open.

"Can you take another look?" Roxy pleaded. "He's been staying at Ola's Villas and Ola says he came here for breakfast last Friday morning."

The woman glanced at the picture again and then down at the till. She pulled out a wad of euros and began thumbing through it. "No, sorry." She glanced up, her expression more apologetic this time. "We get a lot of visitors here as you can imagine. I don't remember every one."

"Fair enough." Roxy closed the phone down again. "Were you working that morning?"

"Morning?"

"Last Friday. The morning he disappeared."

"Um ... no I would have been at the markets that

morning. I go every Friday." She stopped her silent counting and glanced up at Roxy sharply. "Wasn't that the day that ..." she hesitated, "... that the other Australian woman disappeared?" Roxy nodded and Maria stared at her silently for a few moments, her brown eyes boring into Roxy's. Eventually she said, "Maybe *they* were together?"

The look she gave Roxy then was almost accusatory and it sent her heart into a tailspin. She was speechless for a second as Maria produced another of those dead-eyed smiles.

"I'm sooo sorry. I *wish* I could help you but I just don't remember him." She looked down at the till and back again. "I really have to keep going with this or I'll never get out of here. Do you mind?"

Roxy mumbled her thanks and made her way back to the front of the restaurant where Caroline was now standing, tapping her toes, the waiter nowhere to be seen.

"I gave him the brush off," she told Roxy, shuddering dramatically as though he were a slimy insect she had literally just shaken off.

"But maybe he had something to share."

"Oh he wanted to share all right, but not what I was after. *As if.*" She shuddered again. "How'd you go inside?"

"Not sure. The boss, Maria, reckons she can't remember Max."

"But?"

"But for some reason I just don't believe her. She seemed, I don't know, dodgy or something. Fake. A little too saccharine for my taste."

"Maybe you just don't *want* to believe her," Caroline suggested and Roxy thought about this as she glanced inside again.

Maria was still behind the bar but was now talking into a mobile phone, gesticulating wildly as she spoke. She caught Roxy's eye through the restaurant window, dropped her hand and turned her back to her.

Oh no, thought Roxy. *There's definitely something dodgy about that one.*

CHAPTER 18

A harsh chopping sound woke Roxy from a deep sleep and she sat up with a start, unsure where she was and what she was doing there. It took another full minute before it all came flooding back and she dropped into the pillow, her heart heavy, then glanced towards the window. The shutters were still closed but bright light was streaming through the slats, and she could hear a helicopter hovering overhead.

She pulled herself out of bed, noting that Caroline was also up, clearly busy in the bathroom, the sound of water rushing through the pipes. Roxy flung the shutters open and looked out. It was a warm, sunny day and all around her, people were doing the same, some leaning out of windows, others looking up from street level towards that manic chopper.

"They've found something," came Caroline's voice, flat behind her, and Roxy looked around to find her friend wrapped in a crimson silk bathrobe, her hair in a white towel.

"How do you know?" Roxy asked and Caroline shrugged, pulling the towel off her hair to reveal wet, knotty locks.

"I just do." She began tugging her fingers through her

hair, flinching as she did so.

She didn't look too good today, and Roxy said, "Still jetlagged?"

"No, just stressed, actually. Another text came through to your phone from Gunter. I'm surprised it didn't wake you. Max still hasn't shown up for work."

"Did you really expect him to?"

Caroline glared at her like she'd never heard anything so shameful, then stalked across to her handbag, which had been dumped on the dining table and rummaged through for her cigarettes. Roxy didn't say a thing as she pulled one out and lit up. She then stepped across to another window, thrust open those shutters, and dragged on it deeply as she watched the helicopter disappear beyond the ridge.

"I'll have a quick shower," Roxy told her. "Then we can get some breakfast. I think it's time we both got a decent meal into us, okay?"

"Oh, well, if *you* say so," Caroline snapped.

Roxy stared at her. "Sorry?"

She held a hand up. "Never mind!" Then she turned her back to Roxy and continuing sucking on her cigarette.

Roxy watched her for a few seconds and was about to say something when she decided against it. Perhaps reality was finally sinking in for Caroline and she didn't like it one bit. She located her bathbag and headed for the shower.

Twenty minutes later the two women made their way back outdoors and towards the café they had used soon after they'd arrived. Caroline was keen to check the Internet again, and Roxy wanted to get hold of the "Big Breakfast" she had seen advertised on the chalkboard yesterday. For the first time in days, she was famished, and she knew it was time to refuel properly.

Caroline, however, barely ate a thing. After checking her e-mail, Twitter and Facebook accounts—"nothing, damn it!"—she nibbled a slice of *ciabatta* and jam despondently, and Roxy didn't blame her. It was now officially one week since Max had spoken to his mother and they felt no closer to finding him. As far as missing person cases go, Roxy knew that a week was nothing at all. Most law enforcement agencies around the world would sniff at that, laugh at her, tell her to go home and *chillax*, but Roxy knew better. She knew Max. He might have lost contact with her but he would never deliberately avoid his mother or his sister, or his job. It was not his style. He was loyal and he was loving, and he would never put them through such unnecessary worry. Nor would he leave his luggage behind in some strange hotel room, his bill unpaid.

Nope. Max was missing and something had happened. The hovering helicopter seemed to slam the point home. They may be searching for a missing Australian woman, but Roxy feared they might find themselves a missing Australian man at the same time.

"We need to speak to the local police," Roxy announced. "It's time to get them on board."

Before Caroline could reply, the large American woman from the day before came shuffling through the front door of the café, her husband a few steps behind, still sweating as though he'd just stepped out of a sauna. It surprised Roxy considering the weather was actually quite mild; it was autumn here, after all.

"Oh it's you two again," the American said loudly and Roxy nodded halfheartedly, not in the mood for small talk. "Vern, can you see, it's these lovely Aussies." She pronounced it O-sees.

"Have they found something?" Caroline indicated the sky above.

"Sounds like it, don't it? Poor old Donald is beside himself."

"Donald Marlow? Have you seen him this morning?" Roxy asked, interested suddenly.

"Oh, yes, darlin', he's havin' breakfast down at the pier."

"Which restaurant?"

"The one he's usually at, love. What's it called, Vern? Strange name, not Italian at all."

"You mean Ted's?" asked Roxy.

"That's the one, Ted's."

There was that restaurant again.

The woman wobbled her doughy chin and rolled her eyes. "Now, who ever heard of an Italian restaurant called Ted's?"

"It's short for something, my love," Vern said, speaking for the first time.

"Short on common sense, I'd say, and far too pricey for us! I says to Vern, I says, 'Why pay the equivalent of six bucks for a coffee just so you can stare at some stinky old boats?' I mean, we can get takeout and sit down by the pier and stare at the boats any time we like for free. O' course, the coffee's very good there, you gotta admit that, but I says to Vern, I says—"

"Is he still there?" Roxy interrupted her.

"Vern? No, darlin', he's right—"

"No." Roxy tried not to growl. "Donald Marlow."

"Oh, well, I can't see why he wouldn't be. I mean, he was just orderin' when we passed. Poor man's a bundle of nerves, what with all the helicopters passin' overhead and it has been quite a few days now since his wife disappeared, so ..."

Roxy jumped to her feet.

"Where are you going?" Caroline demanded.

Roxy glanced from the woman to Caroline and reached for her bag again. "I think it's time we checked out this expensive coffee for ourselves. If you'll excuse us?"

The woman stepped back looking surprised, while the two Australians paid their bill and then headed for the jetty.

"Can you slow down a bit!" called Caroline, puffing heavily as she tried to keep pace with Roxy.

Roxy turned and stared down at the strappy cork wedges Caroline had chosen to wear with her high-waisted linen shorts and bright yellow shirt. She scowled. "What were you thinking, Caroline?! Why didn't you just put some sneakers on like me, we're going to do a lot of running around today."

Caroline looked mortified. "I am *not* running around the Italian Riviera in a pair of sneakers! Puh-lease!"

Roxy rolled her eyes and resumed walking.

"Anyway," Caroline yelled out, "you're the one who's not thinking! We can't just waltz up to the poor man and demand to talk to him."

"I don't see why not," Roxy called back. "This guy is central to all of this, to Max, his disappearance. We *have* to talk to him, we've got no choice. Ahh, there's the restaurant now."

They'd just emerged from the underground tunnel and saw Ted's Trattoria across from the jetty. The sleazy waiter was not at his usual post but the place was bursting with patrons this time, every table occupied, both inside and out.

"How do we know what he looks like?"

Roxy glanced around. "I guess we just ask."

She spotted the café manager, Maria, handing menus to a Japanese couple inside and walked straight across.

"Hi, Maria."

Maria's eyes were lined today with thick, black kohl pencil and they widened when she recognised who it was. "Oh. You're back."

"'Fraid so."

Maria looked around her. "Sorry, no tables spare."

"That's okay. We're actually looking for someone."

"Again? I told you I have not seen—"

"Oh, no, different man this time. We're looking for Donald Marlow, you know, the man who lost his wife."

Maria's eyes narrowed considerably and she stepped back. "Oh. I don't think I've seen him."

"Yes, yes, Mr Marlow, he outside!" came a voice behind them and Roxy looked around to find the pretty young woman from last night, Sofia, standing there, a white apron around her shapely hips. She had swept her thick hair into a high ponytail and her claggy black eyes were now glancing out towards the patio.

Roxy followed her gaze and was about to enquire further when she spotted a man sitting under an umbrella who caused her to do a double take. It was the fair-skinned fellow she had seen talking with Maria at the back of the restaurant last night, but this time she recognised him.

"That's not Donald Marlow over there, is it?"

Before either woman could reply, she was making her way out to the patio and towards his table.

"Donald Marlow?"

The man looked up, startled. There was a laptop opened in front of him and, beside it, an empty champagne glass and the remains of something eggy on his plate. He was wearing a crumpled white shirt and the same Fedora as last night and, despite oversized black sunglasses—the kind you get from the Skin Cancer Council—he still couldn't manage to hide his splotchy red cheeks. Staring down at him now, Roxy realised why he'd looked so familiar last night. She had seen his face on the television news, albeit between his fingers as he struggled to block out the flashing cameras. It was definitely Candy's husband, and she wondered then, as she wondered now, what he was hiding from. She also wondered how someone as sporty looking as Candy could end up with this pale, limp-looking creature. He was more accountant-meets-computer geek than the outdoorsy type, but then perhaps that's why Candy had reached out to the likes of Max.

Roxy nudged the thought away and repeated herself. "You are Donald Marlow, right?"

His voice cracked a little as he said, "Yes?"

"I'm sorry, I know this is a really difficult time, but we were wondering if we could have a quick word with you."

He closed the laptop lid but not before Roxy spotted a website for the National Australia Bank. "Sorry, who are you?"

"I'm Roxy Parker and this"—she waved back to Caroline—"is Caroline Farrell, *Max Farrell's* sister." She waited for Donald to register the name, but when he continued staring at her blankly, she said, "Like your wife, Max has also gone missing. Here in Riomaggiore. We're very worried about him."

Was that anxiety that raced across Donald's face then? It was hard to tell in those enormous glasses but when he spoke his tone was more sympathetic than anything. "Oh God, I'm sorry about that, but I'm not quite sure what this has to do with me."

Maria appeared then, no trace of sympathy in her voice. "There is no room for you at this table, ladies. I have one inside if you'll—"

"Oh we'll manage," Roxy replied, pulling a vacant chair from another table and sitting down. Taking her lead, Caroline sat in the chair opposite Donald.

"Two lattés, thanks," Roxy said, flashing her a smug smile before refocusing on the Australian man.

An inscrutable look passed between Donald and Maria, then the latter pulled her lips into a tight smile, bowed her head and walked away. Roxy cleared her throat, wondering how to play it but the man was suddenly babbling away, his cheeks blushing even more crimson as he spoke.

"I'm sorry to hear about your mate. Bloody hell, those paths are treacherous, aren't they? What an amazing coincidence, two Aussies missing now, amazing. You *are* Australian, right?"

Roxy caught Caroline's eye. *Was the man playing games or just plain stupid?* "Yes, we are. We wondered whether Max might have been with your wife."

"My wife?" He looked at her like she was the stupid one. "Why would he have been with my—" He stopped short. "Oh right, yeah, I see." He was now twisting his serviette into a tight knot, his head bobbing up and down. "I see, I see. You think your friend might've been the one who escorted Candy that day ... the day she ... you know." His jaw tightened.

"Yes, we do." Roxy produced her iPhone. "This is Max." She held the phone in front of his glasses and watched closely as he stared at it for a few moments, his expression unchanged. "You don't recognise him?"

"No, no, I don't." He looked from Roxy to Caroline and back. "Should I?"

Roxy sighed. This was going to be harder than she'd thought. "Well, yes, actually. Max was up at Mt Pilatus with you guys."

He looked at the picture again. "He was?"

"Hm-mm."

"So?"

"So we think he first met your wife up there." She scrunched her eyes together. "They became *friendly*."

Again he said, "So?"

Her eyes widened. *What was this guy playing at?* "He was seen having breakfast with Candy last Tuesday morning at the Hotel Bellevue, then they went on a hike."

Donald sat back in his chair just as Maria returned with the lattés. Her smile was still stiff at her lips but it was clear she was worried and Roxy was sure she'd just given Donald an inquisitive look. He did not say a word as she handed the cups over and it wasn't until Maria was out of earshot that he spoke again. This time he sounded a little more sure of himself.

"I see what you're getting at. Listen, I've told the police already. My wife liked to take her walks with other people. She always did, it meant nothing. Your mate must have accompanied Candace on one of those walks in Switzerland, perhaps they compared itineraries and decided to take another hike together here in Italy. I'm still not sure how I can help. Perhaps you should be telling all this to the police. I can give you directions if you—"

"Oh for pity's sake," Caroline broke in suddenly, her own cheeks blushing with anger. "I haven't got time for this crap! We know all about the affair, Donald, so don't even try to give us the run around."

Roxy would have given Caroline a swift kick under the table were she not so startled by Donald's reaction. He had leapt out of his chair, his face drained of all colour, and he was clutching his twisted serviette in front of him.

"It's ... it's not true!" he stammered. "I love my wife, I would never do that. Never!"

Caroline looked at Roxy, confused, then back at Donald and Roxy realised he must have misunderstood what Caroline was saying. She was about to set him straight when a piercing wail caught everyone by surprise.

They all swung around to find a police patrol car with flashing lights and wailing siren attempting to make its way down the steep cobbled road towards the café, pedestrians and shop attendants scuttling in its wake. Roxy looked at Donald again and noticed that his colour had returned and his jaw was now clenched shut.

Maria was standing beside Sofia, at the doorway of the café, shouting something to a police officer who was leaning out of the car as it made its way towards them. She suddenly swung around to Donald and said, "Donnie, quick!"

"Oh, God," he said very softly beneath his breath then collected his laptop and wallet, and began to make his way out, past the other patrons, most of whom were now staring at him, wide eyed and open mouthed. The whole time he didn't give Roxy or Caroline so much as a second glance.

And why would he? thought Roxy. Judging from the grave expressions on the policemen's faces, he was about to get some very bad news.

CHAPTER 19

Back in the café, Roxy took a first sip of her latté. The American woman was right, it was good, so good in fact, she decided not to bother with the sugar. Yet for the life of her she couldn't enjoy it. The police must have found a body, why else would they come rushing down the street to see Donald?

But what if the body they'd found was not Donald's wife? What if it was ...?

She couldn't finish that thought, felt nausea well up inside again, yet as she tried to calm herself down, it was clear Caroline was on a totally different train of thought.

"What the hell was he on about?" she was saying. "He seemed to think I was suggesting that *he* had an affair. I was talking about his wife and Max. You got that, right?"

Roxy tried to drag her mind back to their earlier conversation. She sighed, picked up the sugar dispenser and unloaded several shots into her cup.

"But why would he think that?" Caroline persisted. "Unless ... maybe he's deflecting. Trying to get us off Max's trail." She was shaking her head. "What a hideous little man. He was *obviously* lying about Max, right? I mean, yeah, *sure* he's never seen him before. Like we're gonna believe *that!*"

"I don't know, Caro. He did seem genuinely surprised by the mention of Max. Confused, even."

She scoffed. "Nonsense! He was lying through his itty bitty little teeth. Did you see them? They were so tiny and sharklike. And what about that skin. Eeew. Do you think he suffers from rosacea, or maybe hives?" She mock shuddered. "Horrendous man."

Roxy hadn't even noticed the man's teeth, wasn't sure what his skin condition had to do with anything and suddenly felt like they were barrelling along the wrong track. "Caroline, that man has lost his wife. They might have just found her body, might be telling him right now."

"So?! Whose fault is that?"

"Well, we don't know ... yet."

Caroline shook her head at Roxy. "What's got into you?"

"I don't know. Now that I've met Donald Marlow, I'm just not convinced he even knew Max."

"Oh come *on*, Roxy! The guy is a weasel. He's up to no good. I can tell! Looks familiar, though. Was he here last night, as well?"

Roxy thought about this. "Yeah, he was talking to Maria at the bar. So why, then, would Maria act like she doesn't even know his wife?"

"She said that?"

"Not in so many words, but that's the impression I got."

Caroline eye-rolled her. "Maybe she was just consoling him, doesn't mean she knew his wife. Honestly, I can't understand you at all, Roxanne. You seem to have it in for her, yet act like the grubby hubby is all innocent and light!"

She went to defend herself and stopped. What was the point? Caroline was clearly in a bad mood today and she didn't have the energy to argue with her. Instead, she finished her coffee and looked up the road, noticing the large American couple talking to a police officer. He was holding a hand up as though trying to direct them away.

"Speaking of light," Roxy said, "let's see if we can shed a

bit more on what the police have found."

By the time they'd paid for their coffees—Maria not bothering to hide her sneer as she snatched their euros from them—the officer had disappeared and the American woman was waddling down the road towards them, her husband in his usual spot at her rear end.

"Oh, look, Vern, it's the O-sees again. Hey, gals, did you hear the news?!" They sidled up to her, shaking their heads. "They found a body! Washed up on a beach somewhere."

She sounded excited and Roxy couldn't believe the woman's insensitivity, like she was chatting about a plotline from an Agatha Christie novel. She glanced at Caroline who was suddenly looking stricken, her eyes wide, her arms folded tightly around her chest.

"Do they know who it is?" Roxy asked and the woman snorted.

"Well, who else is it gonna be, darlin'? Donald's being taken there now." She leaned in closer. "To identify the body." She snorted again. "But it has to be *her*! Of course it's her. I mean, who *else*?!" She gave them another of her "knowing" looks before waddling past them and away.

"I can think of at least one other person," Caroline said hoarsely and Roxy reached for her hand.

"It's not him, Caro. He's okay."

Caroline snatched her hand away with a huff. "Is that what helps you sleep? Blind optimism."

Roxy frowned. "Who says I've been getting any sleep?"

"Well you seem particularly relaxed today. Suddenly you're trying to say that guy is all innocent. Like Max just wandered off on his own and all is fine with the world. It's like you don't want to find him or something."

Roxy stared at her, confused. "What are you on about?"

"I want to know why you're so calm. Like none of this matters."

Roxy bristled. "Of course it matters. I'm here, aren't I?"

"Sure, but why? I mean, you didn't even want him

around, did you? You wouldn't move in with him."

"Sorry?"

"Back in Sydney! Maybe if you had, he might never have taken that stupid bloody job in Berlin—"

"Stupid? You were so excited for him."

Her mouth widened, her hands dropped to her hips. "Oh so now it's all *my* fault?!" Caroline's voice was rising and Roxy held both hands up to placate her. They were still standing on the street outside the restaurant and Sofia was now watching them keenly, a mobile phone at her ear, while several shop owners and tourists were staring towards them, one or two looking amused.

Roxy took a deep, settling breath and lowered her voice. "It's nobody's fault, Caroline. We don't even know what's happened yet, so we can't lose our heads. Not yet."

"No, you never lose your head, that's the problem." She turned away and began striding back towards the underpass en route to their apartment, and Roxy sighed and followed her.

She was feeling waves of anger now and was trying to deflect them as she raced to keep up with Caroline who was moving swiftly despite the ridiculous heels.

"Hang on a minute, Caroline," she called out, not caring suddenly who saw or heard what. "You're the one who's been acting like everything's hunky-dory!"

"I have not!" she screamed back. "He's my *brother*, Roxanne!"

"So you keep telling everyone."

"Well at least I'm happy to admit it. You can barely say his name without flinching."

"That is not true."

"You never call him your boyfriend."

"That's because he's *not* my boyfriend. We broke up months ago, remember?"

"No!" She stopped and swung around then, her eyes blazing, her hair flying about her face. "*You* broke up with *him*, you broke his heart and now he's ... he's ..."

Caroline looked as though she was about to burst into tears and Roxy tried to reach out to her again but she shook her off and continued storming up the road. Roxy followed silently, spotting their apartment owner, Hugo, standing at one side in front of a small convenience store, a mobile phone at his ear, a frown on his face.

"*Ciao, bella*!" came a voice to one side and Roxy glanced around to find Monty at his usual post, his smile wide. He clearly didn't realise the women were mid-fight.

Caroline ignored him completely and Roxy managed a small, weary wave as she followed her into their building and up the stairs to their apartment. When Caroline reached their door, she swung back to Roxy with a huff.

"I haven't got the key."

Roxy grappled through her handbag and felt a renewed surge of anger swell up inside. For days now, Caroline had been behaving like a narcissistic airhead, barely bothering to blink when Max's flatmate had showed up murdered in his apartment. Ever since they'd arrived she'd been more interested in looking good than finding her brother and now she had the hide to say Roxy was the blasé one. She was infuriated but she could also tell exactly what was going on and it helped douse the flames of her anger.

She looked up at her friend. "I know what you're doing, Caroline, and you can cut it out."

"Oh really Miss Smarty Pants, what am I doing?"

"You're hurting so you're lashing out." She took another calming breath while Caroline folded her arms defiantly and refused to meet her eyes. "But you're picking on the wrong person, and if you weren't so bloody terrified, you'd see that. If you want to find your brother, get a grip. I don't know if Donald Marlow has anything to do with this but I'm not going to point fingers until we get some more evidence. *Real evidence.* In the meantime, pull yourself together. Max's disappearance is not about you or me. And it certainly has nothing to do with whether or not he's my boyfriend!"

Still Caroline refused to look at her and Roxy's mood

turned dark again. "Listen, Caroline, we don't know why Max has disappeared but we need to find him and we're not going to do that by screaming at each other in the middle of Rio-bloody-maggiore! Got it?!"

Before she could reply, Roxy threw the keys at her and flung herself back down the staircase, two steps at a time, leaving Caroline blinking rapidly behind her.

By the time she got out to the street, Roxy was gasping for air and shaking with indignation. She tried to take some deep, gulping breaths to calm herself down. Like Caroline, she was hurting, too, and terrified to the core, but she couldn't lose her head, not now. She had to find Max. That was all that mattered. She whipped around and spotted Monty again but this time he was pretending to be deeply interested in an Adidas cap.

She strode across to him and without any pleasantries said, "You need to direct me to your local police station. Now."

CHAPTER 20

The *Comando Stazione Carabinieri*, Riomaggiore's Police Command Centre, was less than a ten-minute walk from the main drag, on the northwest end of the town, just below a crumbling church and across from a boutique hotel.

The front door was open when Roxy arrived and she stepped inside to find the room empty, a long, high desk cluttered with forms and brochures, some in Italian, most in a variety of other languages. There was a bell on the desk and she rang it just as a muscle-bound, uniformed officer stepped out from an internal room on one side.

"*Benvenuto*," he sang out then, checking her further, added, "Can I help you?"

Roxy produced Max's photo. "Yes, I'd like to report a missing person."

"Another one?" he said, and she nodded, holding the photo closer.

He looked at it carefully and then at Roxy. "His name?"

"Max Farrell."

"Ah. We have been expecting you. Please come with me."

Roxy felt that familiar wave of nausea again but managed

to nod and follow him as he opened a small trapdoor at one side and then led her into the room from which he'd just come. Inside, there was a table with several chairs, no window and a rickety fan leaning like an old drunk in one corner. Leaving the door open, he indicated for Roxy to take a seat across from him and watched as she did so, his dark brown eyes cool and steady. He looked like something out of central casting—chiselled jaw, bulging biceps, empathy enveloping his handsome face. His uniform was stylish and militaristic, a dark blue jacket with silver braiding around the cuffs and collar and edges trimmed in vivid red with silver epaulettes. His matching blue trousers had long scarlet stripes down both sides, and Roxy was grateful Caroline was not around. She'd be dribbling all over him by now.

"You can call me Officer Giuseppe," he said, offering her a plastic water bottle, which she took gladly. "Commander Rossi is currently occupied but you can talk to me." He pulled a pad of lined paper and a pencil from a drawer below the desk, sat down and opened it to a fresh page. "Okay, so, your boyfriend's name is Max Farrell—"

"Friend," she corrected then blushed. *Caroline was right on that score at least.*

"He was staying at Ola's Villas?" When she nodded, he asked, "What is your name?"

She told him. "I'm here with his sister, Caroline, on behalf of their parents who are back in Australia."

"And where is this sister?"

Drowning herself down at the jetty, I hope, thought Roxy. "She's back at our apartment. I can call her, if you like."

"That is not necessary at the moment. If you can answer some questions?"

"Yes. But, can I ask ...?" He stopped writing, looked at her expectantly. "I heard you'd found a body."

He gave a quick, dismissive shake of his head and continued writing. "It is a woman."

She felt the nausea dissipate and her shoulders relax

before a ping of guilt. "The missing Australian woman?"

"Identification is still under way." He looked up from his paper. "Do you know Mrs Marlow?"

"No, I don't." She hesitated. "But I think Max did."

Roxy took a long sip of her water and then tried to outline the facts as best she could. She told Officer Giuseppe about that strange call Max had made to his mother a week ago, how he had checked out of his Swiss hotel early and promptly disappeared, and how she and Caroline had caught the first plane to Europe to try to track him down. She explained how the Hotel Bellevue staff told them they had spotted Max and Candy together and how he must have followed Candy to Riomaggiore where he booked a room at Ola's Villas with another man. She went on to point out that Max's luggage was still in his room and he had not been seen or heard from since Friday morning when Ola believed he had breakfasted at Ted's Trattoria.

Glancing up from his pad where he'd been scribbling away, he said, "Really? Maria's place?"

"Yes." Giuseppe looked intrigued by this but waved her on. "Here's the most baffling bit. We think the man Max checked in with was his Berlin flatmate, Jake Conway. According to Ola, that man fit the description of Jake—a skinny American with lots of tattoos. Anyway he also disappeared on Friday morning, and his things are gone, so Ola assumed he left, but that Max is coming back. In any case, we don't know for sure if that was Jake who stayed with Max, but what we do know is, sometime between late Friday and early Saturday morning, Jake was murdered back in his apartment in Berlin, and Max hasn't been seen since."

She bit into her lower lip, knowing how bizarre it all sounded, and the look on the officer's face reflected it back to her. He had stopped writing and had a deep frown line between his eyes.

She didn't know if he was confused or simply thought she was insane, but eventually he pushed the notepad aside and said, "You must speak to Commander Rossi. Where are you staying?"

"Oh, I don't actually know the name of the street. Or the number." *Duh!* "It's an apartment above a hat shop that—"

"Hugo's place. Okay. Do you have a cell phone number?"

She gave it to him and he made a note of it, then stood up and walked her out. "Commander Rossi will call you at his first opportunity."

"And in the meantime?"

"In the meantime, you come back if you find your boyfriend."

Friend, she thought sadly. *Friend.*

As Roxy returned down the steep cobbled road towards town, she spotted Caroline rushing up towards her. The woman had tears streaming down her face and held her arms wide.

"I'm so sorry, Rox," she blubbed as she reached her, hesitant to embrace. "I'm an idiot, I know that."

Roxy shook her head and then pulled her into a fierce hug, holding her tight for several long minutes. Eventually, she said, "It's okay, Caro, you're just scared. So am I." She pushed her back, holding her at arm's length as she stared into her eyes. "But we're in this together, okay? We need each other. We can not turn on each other."

"I know, I know, I'm sorry ..."

Roxy hugged her again. "Shhh, it's fine. To be honest, I think I prefer you screaming at me than pretending everything's okay."

Caroline sniffed and wiped her eyes. "Miss Super Cool. Who was I kidding, right?"

"Well, you had me going for a minute there. I was starting to wonder whether you had ice running through your veins."

Caroline half smiled. "I just thought that if I didn't really accept he was missing, that it was all a bit of a lark, well, then it wouldn't really be real, you know?"

Roxy nodded, leading the way back down the hill towards their apartment.

Caroline stopped and Roxy turned back to her. "But it is real, isn't it, Roxy? He really is missing?"

"Doesn't mean he can't be found."

"But what if he's ..."

She couldn't bring herself to say it so Roxy said it for her. "Dead?"

Caroline choked back a sob and Roxy felt her own eyes welling up again. "That's something we might also have to face." She reached out and wrapped her arm through her elbow. "But we'll face it together, okay? No matter what, we will find him and we will bring him home."

Caroline nodded and sniffed loudly again. "I'm so grateful you're here, Roxy. I don't know what I'd do without you. Normally, Max is the one I call when I need help, you know that. My whole life, he's been looking out for me. I just have to ring and he jumps. Now ... well ..."

She flashed Roxy a look that wasn't quite apologetic, but it was close enough. And as they continued down the road together in silence, arm in arm, holding each other up, Roxy understood more clearly how terrified Caroline must be. She was Max's spoilt baby sister and he had been looking after her, her whole life. She had grown used to that, knowing she could simply click her elegantly manicured fingers and he'd appear to sort out whatever mess she'd landed herself in. Max was always on hand to pick Caroline up from a drunken night out, scare away an overly zealous admirer or fill up her bank account when she lost interest in yet another 'career' and ran out of money again.

Not this time.

Now it was Caroline's turn to sort out Max's mess, and she was failing miserably. They both were. Roxy, too, felt a lump of guilt. This journey with Caroline had shone a light on her own relationship with Max and she realised, now, why he had chosen her, pursued her so keenly over the past few years. Roxy was the antithesis of Caroline. She was Miss

Independent. Miss I Don't Need Anybody. She had never called Max, not once, to sort out her life. He had loved that about her, but it had irked him, too.

"You don't need anyone, do you?" he'd said to Roxy once and she had scoffed because she knew then as she knew now, that she did need someone in her life. She just didn't like admitting it.

Eventually Caroline said, "What do we do now?"

Roxy took out a small packet of tissues from her handbag and handed one to Caroline, then gave her own nose a good blow. "Well, I just spoke to a local police officer and reported Max officially missing. That's a good start."

"And the body they found?"

"Definitely a woman, probably Candy. I told them all we know about Max's friendship with her, and Officer Giuseppe is now arranging an official meeting with the commander in charge, a guy called Rossi. But he's busy right now."

"So in the meantime?"

"In the meantime, we go back to Ted's and see what Maria's got to say for herself."

Maria was nowhere to be found when the women returned to her restaurant but the creepy waiter was back and watching Caroline warily, as though she might bite. Roxy didn't know what Caroline had said to him last night, but she felt for the guy. She'd just experienced Caroline's bite herself, and it wasn't pleasant.

She was about to speak to the man when Caroline grabbed her elbow and held her back.

"I've got this one," she whispered, stepping forward and swishing her long hair so it swirled in front of her shoulders. "Hi again," she all but purred and the waiter's wariness started to drop away. "Have you got a minute you can spare for me? Pleeeease."

He glanced around then raised one shoulder lazily. He was still pouting a little but he couldn't help himself. He had a thing for blondes. "Maybe."

Caroline smiled. "We're still looking for my brother, Max. Remember, we showed you a photo last night?"

Roxy produced the image and he glanced at it shrewdly again.

"He no you boyfriend?"

She shook her head firmly. "We're so worried. We heard he likes to come here."

He shrugged. "Yes-eh. But not-eh today, no?"

"No, but he *was* here last Friday, right? The day the Australian lady disappeared?"

He considered this. "Oh yes, and the day before. He talk-eh to Candy."

Both women had to contain their surprise. "Really?" Caroline said. "Candy Marlow."

"Of course. I tell-eh the police. He talk to Miss Candy up-eh the back."

They glanced inside. "Near the bar?" Roxy asked and he looked across at her and shrugged.

"Was Donald there, too?"

He thought about this. "He outside."

"So Max didn't talk to him?" He shrugged again. "Did you hear what Candy and Max were talking about?"

"No." He sniggered suddenly. "But he no happy, no? I t'ink he try his luck and she tell him to piss off." He sniggered again but there was a dark look in his eyes. He had obviously tried his own luck with Mrs Marlow in the past. "Candy *bellissimo* but she also big-eh tease. How you say, a prick—"

"Valentino!"

They all turned around to find Maria staring at them from the back of the cafe. She had a menu in her hand and was waving it in the air, indicating for him to get on with it.

He glanced at Maria then back at the women, looking completely unfazed. "Okay, I go now. *Scusi.*"

As he turned towards the patio, a loud "toot" caught the women's attention out on the street and they turned to watch a small van attempting to squeeze its way through the thick pedestrian traffic. Apart from emergency vehicles, cars were generally prohibited from the narrow cobbled roads but this one was obviously delivering supplies, most of the tourists ignoring it as it tried to weave its way down.

"Should we have a word with Maria?" Caroline said but Roxy was staring at the vehicle like she'd seen a ghost. "What is it?"

"The car!" Roxy said. "Whatever happened to Max's Mercedes-Benz?"

CHAPTER 21

The young parking attendant had a face full of acne and badly dyed white hair cropped short with what looked like a black soccer ball etched into one side. He was leaning out of the toll booth as the women arrived, handing a docket over to a small family in a 4WD the size of a tank, and Roxy wondered as she watched, how the enormous vehicle ever managed to navigate the notoriously narrow roads of the Italian Rivera. She didn't even like its chances of squeezing into the tiny spaces in the cramped parking lot. It seemed like a pretty silly car to bring to this part of the world and as it proceeded slowly down the road and into the station, the parking attendant watched it go with a snicker that suggested he was thinking the exact same thing.

After realising they had forgotten all about Max's loaned Mercedes—where was it? Did it hold any clues to his disappearance?—the two women decided to check out the parking station for themselves, just in case it was still in there, gathering dust.

Along the way, Caroline insisted they stop at their apartment and, while she dashed upstairs, Roxy waved to Monty but he didn't see her; he was busy for once, grappling to release a sombrero from a high perch while an eager-looking man with a painfully red face watched on. The sun was now making its way back down again, but he was obviously not going to make the same mistake tomorrow.

"Ta-dah!" came Caroline beside her and Roxy swung around to find her friend holding one long, tanned leg out for her to admire.

"You changed your shoes," Roxy said, noticing she was now wearing bright orange and white trainers.

"Well, we can't be glamorous all of the time. Besides, they're Nike Air Max Lunar 90s."

Whatever the hell that meant. Roxy just smiled and said, "Come on then."

They continued up the street, faster this time, and as they walked Roxy began berating herself aloud. "I can't believe I forgot all about Max's car!"

"You think it really matters?"

"Absolutely. If we find the car we find more clues that lead to Max."

"Okay, I can see that. But how do you know it'll be at the parking station? He could've parked it on any of the side streets up the top."

"No way. It's the only parking station in town and I doubt he'd leave a loaned luxury vehicle out on the street overnight."

"But what makes you think it's still there?" Caroline persisted. "We didn't see keys for it in his room. Or a parking docket."

No, Roxy thought, we did not. She thought then of Max's elusive travel companion. Had he taken off in Max's Mercedes? If it had been Jake, it would certainly explain how he got back to Berlin so quickly. Yet it seemed strange that Max would let him take the car, in effect leaving him without a way home. A slight shiver ran through Roxy's spine. What if Jake had pinched the car without Max knowing? What if someone else had?

She shook the thought away and told Caroline, "Let's

look for the car and worry about the rest later."

The young parking attendant had finished snickering at the 4WD and was now flicking through what looked like a sports magazine on a bench top in front of him. Roxy stepped closer and said, "*Ciao.*"

He looked up with surprise. "*Ciao!* You want your car?"

"Actually, we're looking for a friend's car." She pulled out her iPhone picture again. "An Australian tourist called Max Farrell has gone missing." She thrust the picture under his nose. "We think he parked his car here and we're wondering if it's still around."

"Bad week for tourist, yeah?" He stared at the picture. "I no see this man."

"He was driving a Mercedes."

"What type?"

"That's a really good question," she said, thinking, 'I am such an idiot! Why didn't I ask Gunter?'

He placed his magazine aside and began flipping through what looked like a large, tattered log book. Eventually he said, "I have three Mercedes today. You got docket?"

"Sorry no." She was about to explain that Caroline was Max's sister, that she had a right to look for his car, but he was already opening the small door to the booth and stepping out.

"You want come look?"

"Sure," said Roxy, giving Caroline a quick, victory smile.

The attendant peered up the road as if checking for cars and, satisfied his services were not in demand, waved a hand for them to follow him down the road towards the parking lot where the young family were still attempting to park. The wife seemed to be berating the husband, her mouth flapping fast, while the two children in the backseat stared resolutely out the windows, earphones in place.

The attendant chuckled as he passed them and continued towards an internal stairwell. He led them up a flight and past a stream of parked cars before stopping at a rusty gold-coloured Mercedes sedan. It had to be at least twenty years old and Roxy shook her head.

"I don't think this is his," she said and then leant in to peer through the windows. There was a large straw hat sitting on the backseat with a floral scarf wrapped around it. On one window, a sticker had something written in French with a tiny French poodle beside it. It also had French numberplates.

"This must belong to someone from France," Caroline said and Roxy stared at her.

"D'ya think?" She turned to the attendant. "Definitely not his."

"Okay, you follow." He then led them to a silver Mercedes SUV, slightly dusty with several discarded coffee cups inside and a copy of *Elle* on the backseat.

"Oh that's where I left it!" Caroline exclaimed. "You don't happen to have the keys on you, do you?"

Roxy glared at Caroline so she held her palms out as if to say, "Okay, sorry, it was worth a try."

"This one's ours," Roxy told the attendant and he looked it over, impressed.

"Okay, one more."

They returned to the stairwell and went up a final flight, bursting out into the sunlight. They were now on the rooftop and there was no shade at all which explained why there were far fewer cars parked up here. The attendant looked around and then pointed towards a small, red convertible that was sitting alone on the very far side of the roof. This one looked newer but Roxy doubted Max would have agreed to park it outdoors, let alone leave the top down. In any case, they walked across and checked it out. It did have a German number plate but it also had several stickers along the bumper bar, one for FC Barcelona, another for Real Madrid.

"You think he's been to Spain lately?" Caroline asked and Roxy shook her head.

"I think this car belongs to a soccer fanatic, which you

and I both know is not Max Farrell."

"True, but it was a loan, so maybe someone else put those there."

There were no obvious items inside the car, probably because it was open to the elements, and eventually both women agreed this, too, was unlikely to be Max's.

"Any other Mercs?" Roxy asked, hopefully.

"No more."

So where is his car, then? Roxy pulled out her phone and began tapping away through the contact list. "I should have done this earlier." She clicked on a number and held a finger up to stall Caroline's impending question. Two seconds later it answered.

"Hello, Gunter? Hi, it's Roxy Parker. No, no we haven't. You?" She paused to listen for a few minutes, adding a few "oh, rights" and "yep, yeps", before saying, "Listen, I was wondering if you could tell me what kind of Mercedes Max was driving. It obviously hasn't shown up back there yet? ... No, didn't think so ... Yep, oh, okay. Do you have a number plate or anything? Right ... No, that's fine, can you just text it to me when you get it? Thanks, Gunter. ... No, we're trying to locate it now ... Okay, sure, I'll let you know. Thanks again."

She hung up and turned back to Caroline. "Okay, so Max's Merc hasn't been returned, as we thought. Gunter says it was a brand-new compact SUV, exactly like the one we have but a slightly newer model, and it's a deep maroon colour. He doesn't have the numberplate on hand but will text me when he gets it."

"Ma-rhone?" the man said.

"Yes, like a deep reddish brown colour."

The attendant held an open palm out. "Oh, I forget this one! Come, come!"

Metaphorically holding their breaths, the two women followed the attendant who was already striding quickly towards the staircase again. He led them all the way back to the ground level where, at one end, the family had managed to park, the parents now squabbling over something in the boot. Their children were leaning against the car, earphones still in place, looking mortified, and Roxy felt for them. Family holidays were not always what they were cracked up to be. She didn't get to experience many before her own father passed away but those she remembered were marred by her mother's constant nagging and her father's brooding silence, while Roxy sat in the backseat wishing it was already over. She gave the kids an empathetic smile before following the attendant right to the back of the parking lot where several cars had been parked in by others. These cars were going nowhere fast. He was pointing towards a yellow Peugeot and she looked at it and then behind it to where a dusty maroon coloured vehicle had been wedged in.

He beamed at her. "You friend's car?"

Roxy spotted the familiar three-pointed Mercedes star symbol and then the Berlin numberplates and felt a small swoop of victory.

"That has to be it!" Caroline was saying, rushing past the Peugeot and throwing herself at a door, hoping to get in. Of course it was locked. All three then stood around the car, hands cupping their eyes, peering inside the windows. The first thing Roxy saw was a camera tripod resting against the backseat and what might have been a light meter beside it.

"Yep, it's Max's car all right." She turned to the attendant. "I don't suppose you have the keys?" He shook his head. "How long did he book in for?"

He shrugged. He would have to check his files.

"Can you give us a minute?" she asked, wanting to inspect the car further.

The attendant agreed, making his way back outside while Roxy and Caroline continued staring through the windows. There was an empty bottle of Coke lying on the floor on the passenger side and the cup holders contained two Styrofoam coffee cups. On the windscreen, Roxy noticed a Swiss motorway sticker that was dated eleven days ago. They were also supposed to get one when they crossed the border, a compulsory tax for using Swiss roads, but were in such a hurry, they decided to risk it. Max had not been so delinquent. She also spotted several discarded receipts on the dashboard and Roxy thought she could make out the word Milan on what looked like a parking docket. Had he stopped there on his way to Riomaggiore? And if so, why?

If only she could get in.

Caroline turned to Roxy. "I think we should check for the keys again in Max's room. See if we can open it."

"Okay, but let's see what the attendant has to say first."

They made their way back to the toll booth out front where a black BMW was just pulling in. As they waited for the attendant to process the order, Roxy filled Caroline in on her earlier conversation with Gunter.

"He told me the Berlin police have been in to see him twice now, looking for Max."

"Oh puh-lease! They don't honestly *still* think he killed his flatmate, surely?"

"No, nothing to do with Jake. Mercedes have officially filed a missing person's report. They've also spoken to the Australian Embassy, apparently. But it's not good news."

"What do you mean?"

"Both the police and the Consulate-General in Berlin have told Gunter that it's not their jurisdiction because Max disappeared while in Switzerland. Italy, actually, but that's not the point. Technically the German mob are off the hook."

"So they're washing their hands of him?!"

"Sounds like it. They asked Gunter to call if Max turned up, but that's all they said. Oh, that's my phone again."

She could hear a quick beeping sound coming from her handbag and pulled out her phone to find a text waiting from Gunter. She read it aloud: "*Mercedes M-class SUV, Berlin plates.*" Then she rattled off the number and Caroline nodded.

"Yep, that's the same as the maroon one."

Roxy was glad Caroline had remembered to take note of

the plate; it hadn't even occurred to her. Finally they were working as a team and she felt lighter for it.

"Oh, he's ready for us now," Caroline said.

The attendant was ushering them over as the BMW drove away and he had the book in his hands again. He began flicking through it, towards the front, and stopped at a page, smacking one palm down on it.

"Okay, yes, you car come 7:25 p.m. last Wednesday and book for three day."

"But it's been about six!" said Caroline. He stared at her like he had no idea what the problem was and she frowned. "Didn't you wonder where he was?"

He shrugged. "More money for us, yes?"

Couldn't argue with that, thought Roxy. "Did you check him in?"

He thought about this and then shook his head. "I work day shift, Henri work night."

"I think I met Henri last night. Is he around? Can we talk to him now?"

"No, he sleep now. You come back tonight. After five o'clock. You talk then."

"But we want to talk now," Caroline persisted and again he looked at her unfazed.

"Thanks, anyway," Roxy said. "What was your name?"

"Me, Aris."

"Okay, thanks Aris. I'm Roxy, this is Caroline. If you see Henri, can you explain that we'll be back to have a chat?" He looked at her confused, so she quickly said, "Just tell him we'll be back."

"Okay then. *Ciao!*"

Roxy took Caroline by the arm. "Come on, let's see if we can find the key."

"And if we can't?"

"Then we report this to Officer Giuseppe. Maybe he can break in for us and see if there are any more clues in the car."

This seemed to satisfy her and they headed back into

town and down the hill, past the fishing boats and up the path to Ola's Villas. Roxy still had the room key so didn't bother ringing the front door bell, simply let them both in and led the way up the stairs to Max's room. They were a few steps short of the landing when Sofia appeared at the top, a look of surprise on her face.

"Hello," Roxy said, noticing she had a clump of keys in her hands.

"Why you here?!" Sofia demanded, her sticky black eyelashes scrunched together tightly.

Roxy held up Max's room key and was about to ask her the same question when she flicked her blonde ponytail behind her and swished past them down the stairs.

"She gets around," Caroline said and Roxy squinted after her, thinking, "Yes she does."

"Well come on then, woman. Let's get in."

Shrugging, Roxy opened the door, then sighed sadly as they stepped inside. The room was even gloomier in the harsh light of day.

"So we're paying for this dump now as well?" Caroline said and Roxy nodded.

"I don't think we should give it up yet. Not until the police take a proper search. Maybe they need to fingerprint the place."

"Oh God, that sounds so serious." She held up a hand. "I know, I know. It *is* serious. Okay, I'll go back through his bag with a fine-tooth comb, check all pockets, inside and out. You check the rest of the place."

Roxy noted that "the rest of the place", albeit small, was still fifty times bigger than the duffle bag, but didn't bother to point this out as she began to search. She was just happy Caroline was finally being useful.

Over the next ten minutes, Roxy inspected every corner of the room again, looking under the beds, behind the lamps, and through every drawer. She spotted a small wicker basket of knickknacks she hadn't taken much notice of before, which included a luggage padlock, TV remote control and some tobacco papers, but no keys.

Meanwhile, Caroline was pulling all the clothes back out of Max's bag, going through each item methodically in case the keys had got caught up between the shirts or inside the leg pants.

"Nothing," she called out, slipping a hand into a side pocket where she uncovered a dirty pair of boxers Max must have hidden away and squealed. "My brother is soooo gross!"

A minute later she was squealing again but her tone was very different. Roxy looked up to find her holding a cap high in the air. It was actually a sun visor, a small, bubble-gum pink one, with the word "Billabong" in white cursive writing across the brim.

"This has to be Candy's," she said, staring at it triumphantly before a flicker of confusion crossed her face. "What the hell's it doing here?"

CHAPTER 22

The two women stared from the pink visor to Caroline's iPad which was now open on Max's Facebook page.

"It's a match," Caroline said, tapping one long fingernail at the picture of Candy at the top of Mt Pilatus, smiling widely as she stood in front of that stunning view, arms spread wide, candy pink visor on her head.

Roxy squished her lips to one side and studied the picture. It seemed like a lifetime ago that she had first seen the image up at the Hotel Bellevue and the same feelings of jealousy and hurt gushed through her veins, but this time they were quickly quashed by a deep sense of sadness. Whatever ill feelings she had felt for this perky-looking blonde now subsided. This was probably one of the last happy moments of Candy Marlow's relatively short life.

She shook herself a little and tried to focus. Why was Candy's cap in Max's hotel room? And how had they not spotted it earlier?

"Where exactly did you find it, Caroline?"

She put the iPad down and showed Roxy, plunging her hand into a small pocket on one side of Max's duffle bag. "I am sure I checked this yesterday," she said, sounding defensive. "Someone must have slipped it in overnight."

"Whoa, let's not get ahead of ourselves. Maybe you forgot to check this pocket. It's only small, easy to overlook."

"No way, I checked it, Roxy. I am not a moron."

"I didn't say you were. But, you know, it does have his stinky boxers in it. You might not have checked it thoroughly."

Caroline had to concede the point but was still adamant that someone might have slipped it in afterwards.

"Okay, I'll play along," said Roxy. "Assuming, then, that it got put in after our search, why would someone want to plant the cap here?"

"To make it look like Max had something to do with Candy's disappearance, of course."

"But who could've done it? I mean, apart from Ola, we're the only ones with a key, surely?"

"Oh, I doubt that. There's probably a cleaner or two, maybe someone who's stayed here in the past." She began clicking her fingers furiously. "What about that woman we just passed on the stairs, the one with the embarrassing dye job?! Isn't she the waitress from Ted's? What was *she* doing here, that's what I want to know?"

Roxy considered this. "Yeah, I wondered that myself. Of course she could be a cleaner. It's not unheard of to have two jobs, you know. Plus she obviously knows Ola; she helped me out last night when I first came here. Or, rather, didn't help, but you know what I mean."

Caroline looked like she had no idea what she meant but said, "Doesn't mean she didn't plant the visor."

True, thought Roxy, pulling her phone from her bag. "We have to call Officer Giuseppe. Tell him what's going on."

Just as she said it, her phone began to ring. She lifted her eyebrows, surprised, and spotted Gunter's number. He was keen to hear the latest on the car and Roxy explained that it was still at the parking station, assuring him it was safe although he didn't seem to care about that.

"The problem is, we just can't open the car. Can't find a key."

"It is not a normal key, no?" he replied down the crackly line. "It is one of those new smart keys."

"Smart key?" She'd never heard of such a thing. Her own car, an old VW Golf, was almost at vintage stage. There was nothing smart about it.

"Yes, it has a keyless entry remote. You can activate the ignition without needing to insert a key. It's only small, it looks like a—"

"Remote control!" Roxy yelped, jumping to her feet and reaching across to the side table where the wicker basket sat with its motley collection. She rifled through until she found the black and silver remote. She studied it properly this time and saw the tiny Mercedes logo in one corner. She also looked around and realised there was no television set in the room. She eye-rolled herself this time.

"I have it!" she told him.

"Good work. You are a super sleuth, yes?"

"Oh I'm no super sleuth, Gunter. If it wasn't for you I'd still be looking for the TV."

"What did you say?"

"Never mind. Thanks again and I'll call if we find anything."

Roxy was about to explain the smart key to Caroline but the younger woman's confused expression stalled her.

"What is it?" she asked.

Caroline was still holding the sun visor but now had a black and white Converse sneaker in her other hand and was staring at it like she'd never seen anything so strange.

"What?" Roxy persisted, and Caroline glanced up at her.

"Where's the other one?" she asked.

"The other shoe?"

"Yes."

"Was it here last night?"

She looked uncertain. "I'm not sure, to be honest. Maybe. Do you remember?"

"I remember the shoe, but can't remember if there was one or two. Have you checked everywhere? Under the bed? Near the front door?"

She nodded but they both did a second search and failed to turn up the matching Converse.

"It might never have made it to Riomaggiore, of course. Max probably just packed in a hurry and left it behind in Berlin."

Caroline began nodding vigorously. "Or he could have left it at Mt Pilatus. Leon did say Max took off in a major hurry."

"Or maybe," Roxy said, holding the smart key in the air, "it dropped out of his bag and is currently sitting in the boot of his Mercedes just waiting to be discovered. Come on, let's go check it out."

On the way back to the parking lot, the two women grabbed another slice of pizza to keep them going, mushroom this time with thick shavings of parmesan, and then made a detour to the police station to report the cap and see if a police officer could accompany them to Max's car. If there were any items of interest in his Mercedes, they wanted an expert on hand to bag it. Caroline had already smudged her paw prints all over Candy's cap and Roxy didn't want to compromise any more potential evidence. Yet when they reached the station, the front door was securely locked and no one answered their knock.

"Probably out on smoko," Caroline suggested but Roxy was already reading a sign on the outside wall.

She hadn't noticed it before because the station had been open, but it gave a full list of operating times and an out-of-hours number to call in the case of emergencies.

"According to this sign," Roxy said, "the station is closed Monday to Friday. It's only opened on weekends outside of summer. Mustn't be enough business to warrant it."

"But didn't you say you spoke to someone here earlier today? It's Wednesday, isn't it?"

"Yes, I guess with all the commotion over Candy's disappearance, they're manning the station more regularly. Oh well, let's check out the car anyway. I'm not waiting around for them to show."

Back at the parking station, Roxy showed Aris the key and he happily waved them in where they made their way straight to the Mercedes that had been parked in by the yellow Peugeot. Roxy gave the smart key a gentle air kiss and then clicked it into place just as Gunter had instructed, and *kabam*! The entire car unlocked with a very soft, subtle "click".

"Smooooth," Caroline said, reaching for the door handle.

"Hang on a second!" Roxy produced a tissue from her handbag. "Use this so we don't leave our prints all over it this time."

"Oooh, look who's been watching *CSI*."

"It's called common sense, Caroline, you should try it some time."

Roxy wrapped her own hand in a second tissue and then went to the boot of the car and was about to open it when she had a sudden, horrifying thought. She hesitated.

He wouldn't be in there. *Would he?!*

She braced herself then leaned down towards the boot slowly, forcing herself to inhale as every nerve in her body stood on high alert. All she could smell was a smoky petrol scent. She gave herself a shake—*you're being ridiculous, of course he's not in there!*—then, using the tissue, clicked the boot open. It sprang out and up with one swift move, and she jumped back, not daring to look.

"You all right?" It was Caroline beside her.

"Yes, I'm fine!" Still, she took a sideways glance into the boot and was rewarded with a gloriously empty interior. Upon closer inspection, she did discover the usual paraphernalia hidden away under the floor matting: a spare tyre, a first aid kit, and emergency stopping gear including a bright orange reflective vest.

"No shoe?" asked Caroline and Roxy looked at her confused for a second. Her nerves were still jangling about.

"Oh, no, not here. Anything inside the car?"

"Nothing very interesting. But see here," she dragged Roxy back to the front seat where she leaned in and tapped a pen at the passenger-side Styrofoam cup. "No lipstick marks. Whoever his passenger was, it had to belong to a man." She grinned. "See, I can be a super sleuth, too."

"Of course, not all women wear lippie all of the time," Roxy pointed out, but when Caroline looked at her like she was speaking nonsense, she quickly added, "Still, I reckon you're right. I'd bet any money that cup is dripping with Jake's DNA."

Caroline grimaced and backed away from the cup. "So you definitely think Jake was the guy Max showed up with that first night?"

"Yep, and, if you'll excuse me for a second, I have a hunch these might prove it." She indicated for Caroline to step back out and then she leaned in and, using her tissue again, reached across the dashboard for the toll receipts.

She then laid them out on the car's bonnet in chronological order. There were several familiar ones, for the autobahn between Germany and Switzerland, for the Alpnachstad parking station, and for the road down to Riomaggiore. They, too, had coughed up for those tolls and they were not cheap. Yet it was the Milan receipt that had her interested. It was dated early Wednesday afternoon and was for a parking station at a Milan Bus Depot.

"Didn't the freeway bypass the city?" Caroline said. "We didn't stop there."

"No. So why, if Max was in such a hurry, did he stop and park in Milan?"

"Bite to eat?"

"At the bus depot?" Caroline shrugged. "Nope, I've got a theory that's where Max met up with Jake. I bet Jake caught a bus from Berlin to Milan and then hitched a ride with Max for the final leg here. We know Jake wasn't at Mt Pilatus, so they must have met up somewhere."

"But why would Max even *want* to meet up with Jake? That's the bit that seems totally bizarre to me. I mean, if my brother was planning a romantic rendezvous with Candy on the Italian Riviera, he'd hardly drag his freeloading flatmate along, would he?"

"Maybe Max called Jake from Switzerland to let him know he was heading to Italy and Jake begged a ride off him. Maybe he had some business here; who knows? He was a muso, probably a pretty spontaneous guy, might have thought it'd be fun to tag along."

She set the receipts aside and did her own internal check of the car, searching through the various nooks and crannies, the glove box, the ashtray, the seat pockets at the back, and produced nothing more of interest, just the photography equipment and Coke bottle they'd spotted earlier, a half empty packet of gum and an old iPad charger—yet more evidence that Max's devices were not short on battery power.

"Oooh, I know!" Caroline reached in towards the car's CD player. She frowned. "You want to start the car up so we can see what's inside?"

Roxy doubted it mattered but placed the key, as instructed, on the round keypad below the steering wheel, impressed as it all came to life, the control panel illuminated with vivid neon colour. At the same time a blast of sound came rushing out of the speakers. It was heavy and it was rock, and it had Caroline recoiling again.

"Ewww! That has to be Jake's. No way Max would listen to that crap!"

Roxy located the volume and turned it right down, then clicked the CD off and watched as Metallica's self-titled album popped out. Roxy had to agree that, unless Max's musical tastes had changed dramatically in the three months he'd been in Germany, this was indeed more likely to belong to an American rocker with bad tatts.

Roxy's phone rang again and she pressed the answer

button to find Officer Giuseppe on the other end. She began to tell him all about Max's car, begging him to get a team together to do an official search, but he soon cut her short.

"Do not worry about this for now," he said, sounding breathless. "Commander Rossi has returned and he wants to speak to you immediately. He has heard from your boyfriend Max."

Friend, Roxy would have corrected him, if her jaw hadn't just hit the ground.

CHAPTER 23

Commander Rossi and his petite sidekick Detective Constantini—"please, just call me Carmela"—bounced off each other like an old married couple, finishing each other's sentences, squabbling over minor details and slapping each other playfully about the shoulders from time to time, and as Roxy watched them in action she couldn't help thinking of that old English puppet show Punch and Judy. Except, after they dropped their bombshell, it was Caroline who looked ready to pull on the boxing gloves.

After bolting as fast as they could to the police station, neither woman daring to think anything lest they be disappointed all over again, Giuseppe had met them at the front door and taken them through to the interview room to meet Rossi and Carmela. Roxy noticed that Caroline barely blinked twice at the hunky officer, a sure sign she was not herself today.

The interview room was the same one where Roxy had sat earlier. This time the old fan was whirring in the corner but she couldn't feel any benefit and was sweating now beneath her light cotton shirt. She noticed the door had been shut and wished they'd open it a crack.

It was clear Giuseppe had already filled his superiors in on most of what Roxy had told him yet some of his information was incorrect and, while they spoke surprisingly good English, Roxy still spent the first fifteen minutes clarifying details and setting the record straight. When she had finished, she took a deep breath and said, "Look, I'm sorry to be impatient, but Officer Giuseppe said you had heard from Max and ... well ...?"

Both women looked at him, eyes as wide as saucers, and Rossi cleared his throat, knowing he was about to disappoint. "We are not a hundred percent sure it is Mr Farrell, you understand, which is why we have called you here." He leaned across the table to a small recorder on one side and pulled it towards himself. "Can I play for you?"

"We would like you to identify the voice," added Carmela. "It is very mumbled, you must listen, carefully, yes?"

Caroline glanced worriedly across to Roxy and she gave her a reassuring nod.

Rossi attempted to press play several times but the machine was not cooperating. He hissed something in Italian under his breath and kept stabbing at the Play button. Eventually, Carmela smacked him across the shoulder, pulled the recorder from his hands and got it working. After an agonising few seconds, a loud crackling sound could be heard, followed by an Italian voice saying, *'Polizia, qual è la vostra emergenza?'*

There was another crackling sound then a man's voice appeared speaking softly. *"I ... ah... I need to speak with the police, please."*

Caroline's eyes widened. "That's Max!"

Roxy nodded, holding a finger to her lips as the operator said, *'This is the police. What is your emergency?'*

There was another pause before Max's voice returned, even softer than before. It was as though he were whispering. *'I just need to speak to someone, is there someone there I can speak with?'*

"What is this regarding, please?"

Another pause. When he started speaking again Max sounded almost embarrassed, certainly unsure of himself. *"I don't know, um, you see, I think ... I mean, I'm pretty sure there's going to be a ... crime."*

"Crime? What kind of crime?"

"Um, well, I'm just worried, that's all. I mean, I could be wrong. Oh, shit—"

The line suddenly went dead and all that remained was the recorder's eerie whistling sound. Rossi turned it off and looked up at them. Both women were still staring at the machine, Caroline tearful, Roxy with a hand to her mouth.

"Can you tell me, please, Miss Farrell, is that the voice of your missing brother, Max Farrell?"

Caroline sniffed and then nodded.

"For verification purposes, Miss Farrell, I need you to indicate verbally please."

At first Caroline didn't seem to understand him and Roxy reached out and grasped her hand. "Say yes, Caro," she said and Caroline blinked back a tear.

"Yes."

"When did he leave this message?" Roxy asked, trying to control her own tears which were threatening to spill.

"It came through to our emergency call service at 8:08 p.m. last Thursday."

Roxy began doing the maths, her brain clicking into gear as her heart plummeted. "That's *before* he disappeared. Before Candy—"

"Hang on," said Caroline, her voice trembling a little now. "Are you saying you got this message last Thursday and you ignored it?"

"No, no, we did not ignore it," Rossi said and then Carmela explained.

"This station is closed weekdays outside of peak season, so any calls from Riomaggiore come directly through to our head office in La Spezia. If it is an emergency, a team is despatched."

"And that didn't seem like an emergency to you?" Caroline said, her voice now quivering with contained rage.

Rossi held his palms up. "You have to understand, please, Miss Farrell. Your brother said no more than that. He did not give his name or explain what this, er, 'crime' was. Then, as you can see, he hung up."

"He might have been referring to a shoplifter for all we knew," added Carmela.

Sensing a fresh wave of anger, Rossi quickly added, "In any case, we did send two officers out the next day, around midday, and everything seemed to be okay."

"Okay? Two people were missing!" said Caroline.

"No, no, not then you see," said Carmela. "Our men patrolled the main town for hours. They spoke to shop owners and locals but could not find any problems to report. Nobody tell us these people are missing. It was only later that evening that Mr Marlow approached the officers and reported his wife missing. The officers began a search that evening and we brought in the helicopters and coast guard for a full-scale search the following morning. We later learned that your brother, too, disappeared that Friday morning."

"*Before* your officers got here," Caroline said, barely able to conceal the contempt in her voice.

Rossi coughed to clear his throat. "We still have no evidence that a crime has been committed."

"What?! Surely Max's message ...?"

"Again," interjected Carmela, "it is not specific enough. We need more evidence."

"Which brings us to the camera," Rossi said. He reached below the table and produced what looked like a clear evidence bag. Through the bag they could see an iPhone encased in hot pink plastic.

"That has to be Candy's," Roxy said and Rossi looked at her inquisitively so she added, "I know she has a thing for pink, that's all."

It was located with the body, he explained. "Which has

now been formally identified as Candace Eloise Marlow."

Roxy and Caroline shared a glance then, and Roxy thought how horrendous it was that someone else's death could fill them with such relief.

"Anyway, lucky for us, she had it inside her waterproof jacket, so we got it working," Carmela was saying as she snatched the bag from Rossi and began clicking the phone to life through the plastic. She continued clicking until she got to the page she wanted. She held it out for them to see and Caroline's shoulders dropped.

"Oh, Maxy." Her voice was brimming with deep despair. She showed it to Roxy who was also overwhelmed with a sense of melancholy.

It was a photo showing Max standing in front of a stunning alpine view with one arm slung around Candy's shoulder, the other by his side, the same slightly worried look in his eyes. It was almost a mirror image of the one on his Facebook page and Roxy realised they must have given both their devices to a third party to take the photos.

"That is a picture of your brother, Max Farrell, yes?"

Again this was directed at Caroline, again she struggled to answer until Roxy prompted her. "Yes, that's Max."

"We thought so," Carmela was saying. "There are six pictures with Mr Farrell."

"They were all taken last Tuesday at the same place," added Rossi. "But we do not know this place. Can you identify?"

Caroline slowly clicked through all six images and both women agreed it had to be Mt Pilatus. They spotted the familiar caves, the circular-shaped hotel, a bright red train sitting at an impossible angle in another.

"Did you find any pictures with Max here in Riomaggiore?" asked Roxy. "Or maybe on that walk between here and Manorola?"

Both detectives shook their heads.

It was the best news Roxy had heard all day and her heart lightened a little. "So you have no evidence that Max accompanied Candy on her walk last Friday, the day she disappeared?"

"No, but …" began Rossi.

"It does not mean he was not with her," finished Carmela.

Yes it does, Roxy wanted to exclaim. The last time they went on a walk, up at Mt Pilatus, they took a stack of photos together. Why would this walk be any different? Instead she asked, "Did you find any pictures of anyone else with Candy?"

Carmela glanced at Rossi as if getting permission to answer and when he nodded she said, "Not on the day in question, no. But there were several shots from that day, taken around the time we believe she fell off the pathway." She paused, glancing at Rossi again. "They are of the deceased. Alone."

"But someone must have been with her, to take the shots," said Roxy.

"Could've been selfies," said Caroline.

"Selfies?" asked Rossi and Carmela hissed at him.

"You know selfies!" She slapped him across the shoulder, lighter this time. "All the youngsters they take the selfies all the time." She held the phone up in front of her and turned her wrist around as though about to take a photo of herself. "She could have done this."

"Can I see?" asked Caroline and Carmela handed the evidence bag over.

Caroline flicked through with her forefinger, passing across a range of images as she did so. At one stage she glanced up at Roxy, a surreptitious look in her eyes, before continuing through the shots until she found the ones Carmela was referring to on the hills around Riomaggiore. They sent a small chill through her body. Each one was slightly different but they all showed Candy standing on the edge of a cliff with a bright yellow cap on, squinting slightly into the sun. In one she was holding her arms wide as if presenting the view, in another she was pointing down towards the stunning blue sea, the same sea that would soon claim her life. Caroline noticed she wasn't smiling as widely in these pictures as she was in the ones with Max at Mt Pilatus. If she was with someone, she wasn't nearly as happy.

"I don't think these are selfies," Caroline said. "There's too much distance between Candy and the lens, and see this one, with her arms out, she's not holding the camera in that one at all. Of course, she could have set the camera up on a rock face somewhere, but it's not so easy to do with an iPhone. I bet somebody else took them for her."

"Which means somebody was definitely with Mrs Marlow on the track," Rossi said.

"Or she could have asked a passing tourist to take them," said Carmela, scrunching up her nose, "but six shots? I doubt that. No, no, I agree, someone was with Mrs Marlow on her walk and they were very careful not to be photographed."

Roxy stared at her for a minute. "You think that person was Max, don't you?"

"We do not know. We have no evidence at this stage. He did not send you any messages telling you where he was going? Telling you about Mrs Marlow?"

Both women shook their heads and Caroline said, "The last time Max spoke to my mother he was in a hurry and didn't say much. Mum misheard where he was going but she says he never mentioned anybody else. We're as surprised as everyone to learn that he started up an affair with Candy Marlow."

"And nothing about Donald Marlow?"

"No. We never even heard the name Marlow until we got to Mt Pilatus. Why?"

The detectives shared a glance but did not answer the question.

Now Rossi asked, "Has your brother ever come to Riomaggiore before?"

"Not that I know of. I don't think so." Caroline glanced at Roxy who nodded agreement.

Rossi reached out for the phone and said, "Officer Giuseppe has told me that you have located Mr Farrell's car. If you will hand over the keys, we will make an inspection."

Roxy did so, explaining how the smart key worked. He looked confused and Carmela snatched it off him.

"He's useless with technology. I will do the opening!"

Now it was Rossi's turn to give his partner a light whack across the arm. "I am not so bad, you know!" He turned back to Roxy. "Okay, Ola's room key, too, please. I think this one is easy to work, hey?"

"Just a boring old door key," Roxy told him, handing it over. They had already relinquished the pink cap and Rossi had given it to Giuseppe to take into evidence. Roxy had explained their concerns that it had been planted, and asked about Sofia, yet neither detective knew whether she worked for Ola. Giuseppe had been ordered to look into it.

"And you have received no more word from your brother?" he asked of Caroline. She shook her head. "No more pictures on the Twitter?"

"Well, he only posted messages on Twitter. The pictures were on Facebook."

Carmela hissed again but said nothing as Rossi pushed away from the desk and stood up. "That will do for now. You are staying in town in case we have more questions?"

"We're staying in town until we find Max," Roxy corrected him.

"Okay. Maybe we can help you with this. We will check out your friend's hotel room and his car. Maybe you lucky and he just go away for a few days and he be back, all will be happy days, no?" He didn't sound convincing and they weren't buying it. "You can go now, ladies, but first, please see Officer Giuseppe. We need to get your fingerprints."

"Ours?" they said unison.

"Not to worry," said Carmela with a smile. "You have put your prints all over everything, we need to discount them from the evidence."

Before they left, Roxy asked, "Do you have any idea what

happened to Candy? Whether she fell accidentally or was pushed?"

The two detectives shared another look and then Rossi said, "That is the sixty-four-dollar question."

"Sixty-four-*thousand*, you silly man!" interjected Carmela, giving him a final smack across the arm for good measure.

CHAPTER 24

Half an hour later the two women were wedged tightly together in their apartment bathroom, swiping at their fingertips with tissues soaked in heavy duty eye-makeup remover.

"See, it pays to bring plenty of crap along," Caroline said.

She was having a dig at Roxy but her heart was not really in it. Hearing Max's voice again and seeing his face on Candy's iPhone had sent her emotions into freefall right alongside Roxy's. "Why do you think Max left that emergency phone message? Did he suspect that Candy was going to be killed? Is that what he meant by a crime?"

Roxy thought about this as she squirted more remover onto a second tissue. "Obviously he suspected something was going to happen. Maybe he got some bad vibes off Donald, or maybe Candy told him she was worried and maybe that's why he followed her down here in the first place." She sighed, exasperated. "If only he'd given more details before he got cut off."

"And *why* did he get cut off, that's what I want to know? Do you think maybe he was overheard? Maybe Donald followed my brother to the police station and spotted him

182

using the phone, so he ... so he ..."

The two women stared at each other in the reflection of the mirror. It was too unbearable to even contemplate. Roxy lobbed her used tissues into the toilet and returned to the lounge room where she slipped off her shoes and dropped onto the sofa with a loud sigh. Caroline went directly from the bathroom to her handbag where she located her cigarettes and lit one up.

Stepping across to the open shutters, she said, "You won't believe who else I saw photographed on Candy's iPhone." Roxy looked up. "Go on, guess!"

Roxy dropped her head to one side. "I don't know. Sophia Loren?"

Caroline looked at her, confused, then took an interminably long time to exhale before saying, "Maria, from Ted's."

Roxy sat up with a start. "What? Really?!"

She nodded. "After that police woman gave me the camera, I was flicking through the images and there were a stack of Candy and Donald, obviously taken here in town."

"As you'd expect. They were here for a few days before Candy disappeared."

"Right, well, several of the shots were clearly taken at Ted's Café, I recognised the patio out back."

"So you saw Maria in the back of some shots, then?"

"Not the back, no. She was sitting *between* Candy and Donald looking all chummy, chummy, smiling like nobody's business. They were holding cocktails up as though about to do a toast or something."

"Like friends?"

"Like *best* friends."

Roxy couldn't believe it. "So why did I get such a strong impression that Maria didn't even know Candy before she disappeared?"

"Dunno, but she obviously did."

Roxy tried to recall her first conversation with Maria, at the back of Ted's. She realised she had only *assumed* Maria didn't know Candy because she'd spoken of her in terms of "another Australian woman". She had never used her actual name.

But why?

Had she done that to deceive Roxy or was it because she didn't want to go into it with a total stranger. She frowned and said, "Still doesn't explain much. I mean, why would Maria want to kill Candy? And how? She's pretty bloody small. I doubt she could throw a Chihuahua over a cliff, let alone a grown woman. We're also forgetting that Candy went on a walk with a *man*, not a woman."

"Yeah, but what if Maria was sleeping with Donald, huh?"

Roxy sat up further. "Go on."

"Think about it, he *was* very defensive about his marriage when we spoke to him, acting like we'd accused him of an affair. I don't know about Candy and Max, but maybe Donald and Maria have also been seeing each other and Donald bumped off Candy so they could hook up. The woman's obviously got appalling taste in men, but that doesn't mean it didn't happen. So, if you think about it, we could both be right. It could be Donald and Maria acting together." She paused. "Plus, she's clearly got a bug up her arse. Did you see the way she spoke to Valentino? She's a vicious one, that one."

Roxy's head was spinning now as she tried to lock the various pieces into place. It still didn't explain Jake's murder, nor could she see either one of them pulling it off. When it came to brute strength, Donald wasn't much bigger than Maria.

Caroline finished the last of her cigarette and said, "Oh well, I thought it was exciting." She glanced at her watch. "Dinner time soon and I need a shower. Desperately. Mind if I go first?"

It was the first time Caroline had bothered to ask and Roxy tried to hide her surprise. "Sure, go for it." Then she dropped back onto the sofa.

That night, despite long showers and a fresh change of clothes, the women felt too flat to move much beyond their apartment and decided on the café across the road for dinner. The Marina was more basic than Ted's but the food was tasty and they settled on eggplant ravioli and seafood pasta.

"And a bottle of Peroni," Roxy told the waiter, knowing only too well how abysmal their wine selection was. Caroline held two fingers in the air, following suit.

When their beers arrived, the women sipped them quietly for a while just watching the buzz of happy tourists around them, feeling sadder than ever. Eventually Caroline said, "I hope that fat American doesn't come in. I've had enough of her and her sweaty husband."

"That's a bit mean, Caro. She's harmless."

"Yeah, as harmless as a brown snake. And I hope to God we don't run into that Valentino guy, either. Did you notice he's wearing a wedding band? What a slimeball. I pity his poor wife."

Roxy scoffed. "Bloody hell, Caroline, you're sick of everyone."

"Not true! I haven't reached my limit with you yet."

"So that tiff we had earlier today?'

She waved a hand in the air. "That was nothing. You'll know when I'm really over you."

"Oooh I'm shaking in my boots."

"Your cute, creamy leather boots?" Caroline stared down at Roxy's feet. "Managed to squeeze those into your itty bitty little bag, I noticed." Her eyes swept up to the front door suddenly and she groaned. "You have got to be kidding me."

Roxy glanced around to find the aforementioned American waddling in, a bright floral dress clinging to her enormous curves.

"Hi, gals," she said, catching their eye, but this time she didn't stop at their table, instead brushing her way past them to a table at the back of the restaurant where another couple had been quietly sharing a bottle of wine.

All that was about to change, Roxy thought, watching as the American burst into loud chatter and sat down to join them.

"Thank God she's found some new friends," Caroline said.

Roxy wasn't so grateful. She wondered what other gossip the nosey American had managed to glean during the day. "Did we ever show her the picture of Max?"

Caroline looked alarmed. "Does it matter?"

"It might. She goes on about Monty, but I reckon she's the font of all knowledge around here. I think I'll ask her if she ever saw him."

"Well, do it after dinner, when I'm safely back in the apartment, so I don't have to deal with her calling me an O-cee again!"

"Fine. I wonder where her husband is."

"Again, does it *matter*?"

"Probably not. So, how's the ravioli?"

She licked her lips. "Not bad. Yours?"

They continued swapping small talk for the rest of the meal, both too weary or worried to broach the subject of Max again. Yet it was clearly at the back of their minds. Another full day had passed since anyone had heard from him and it was becoming harder and harder to remain positive. Each passing day chipped away at their optimism and Roxy wondered if they would ever find Max, let alone bring him home alive.

She thought of her Crime Catalogues back at home, the scrapbooks that Oliver collectively dubbed her "Book of Death", and of the various news stories she had cut out and pasted in there over the years. No one seemed to understand why Roxy kept those articles, why she persisted in cataloguing such misery and mayhem, and the truth was Roxy couldn't really explain it herself. If pressed, she would say it was for research, and in some cases this was true. At least twice in the past two years, the scrapbooks had revealed information that had helped solve real-life crimes. Mostly, though, it was more sentimental than that. Roxy suspected her scrapbooks were there to bear witness, to show that someone cared: a life might be taken, but it lived forever in the scrapbooks in her sunroom.

The missing people cases, though, were a whole different kettle of fish. Thinking of them now, she realised those stories were the most haunting of all. Amongst the many tales of the dead and mutilated were occasional articles about a missing person, a loved one lost forever in time. Sons and daughters, children and adults, dozens of souls who'd simply vanished without a trace.

There one minute, gone the next.

Were their families still searching, she wondered now, still clinging to futile hope? Or had they finally given up and pretended to get on with their lives knowing full well that nothing would ever be the same again?

Could she and Caroline—the entire Farrell clan for that matter—ever find the courage to do that?

A loud burst of noise cut through Roxy's thoughts and she looked up to see the table at the back rollicking with laughter. Caroline, too, was looking around, perplexed, and Roxy wondered if she'd been thinking the same thing, also struggling to hold onto hope.

"I'm heading back to the apartment," Caroline said then, her eyes welling with tears.

"Are you okay?"

"Yeah, yeah!" She swiped at her eyes with a chuckle. "I just need to pep myself up a bit, that's all! Might pop on a face mask, oil the locks a bit." She swept a hand through her hair. "I must look a horror! Best tidy myself up before we see that gorgeous copper again."

Roxy smiled. She was no longer irritated by Caroline's self-absorption. You did what you had to do to get by.

"I'm gonna hang around and see if Mrs America has more info." Caroline nodded and went to produce her purse when Roxy held a hand up. "I've got this one."

"Goodo, I'll see you back up there?"

"Of course you will."

As Caroline left, Roxy ordered another beer then leaned back in her seat, feigning boredom. It took less than a minute for the American woman to holler across the café.

"On your own there, darlin'? Why don't you come join us?"

Roxy turned to face her with a smile, thinking, "Hook, line and sinker."

The American woman's name, as it turned out, was Lily-Anne Wavers—"I cannot *believe* I never introduced myself, I'm losing my style!" Her husband, Vern, she explained, was back at the hotel, suffering from heat stress. "Poor darlin', he just don't cope well here in the tropics."

The fact that they weren't actually in the tropics was neither here nor there to Lily-Anne whose adopted state of Michigan was "cold as a welldigger's ass". The other couple, she quickly explained, were from an equally chilly part of the world, Ireland. "But they're used to the warmth, come here every year, been comin' forever!"

"John and Beryl McDonald," the man announced, rising to shake Roxy's hand and see her into the spare chair. He was well into his fifties with a mop of orange hair, and his wife was not dissimilar, although her hair was lighter, with silvery streaks through it. They were both well dressed without being ostentatious, he in a long-sleeved blue shirt, a gold Rolex on his wrist, she in a flowing white dress with matching pearl earrings and necklace. "We come every autumn, to be sure," John was explaining, his Irish accent lilting and melodic. "That way it's not too hot and we miss the dreaded crowds, ye see."

"Oh yes," said Lily-Anne. "I can't stand all these tourists! So loud, so obnoxious."

Roxy stared at her, not sure whether she realised the irony of what she'd just said.

"Anyway, enough about that, I've got a bone to pick with

you, young lady!" Lily-Anne began waggling a fat finger in the air. "Why did you gals never tell me you were also searching for someone?! I just heard that your boyfriend Matt is missing. I am soooo sorry!"

"Max, actually," she corrected her. "And he's not really my boyfriend, he's Caroline's brother." She reached for her phone and showed them Max's mugshot. "You never saw him around here, did you?"

"Now I can't say I have, but you best show that to Vern when you see him tomorr'a, he's got a better eye for faces than I do. What about you, guys?"

Roxy presented the picture to the other couple but they, too, shook their heads.

"Are you saying your friend also went missing? From Riomaggiore?" Beryl asked, trying to keep up and Lily-Anne nodded her wobbly chin.

"It *is* confusin', all these O-cees disappearing off the face of God's earth. Now listen, what do you think's happened to your darling friend Matt?"

"Max," Roxy corrected again. "We honestly don't know. But he was mates with Candy so we're worried he might have ..."

She didn't need to finish that sentence, Lily-Anne's hand was already at her face, a look of horror in her eyes. "No!"

"What is it?!" gushed Beryl.

"She thinks the poor man may have gone over the cliff with your friend Candy. Ain't that right, sweet pea?"

Roxy nodded, there was no point pretending otherwise any more. *But hang on a minute.* She looked across at Beryl. "You knew Candy Marlow?"

The Irish woman half smiled, looking almost apologetic. "Ai, but we weren't the best of friends. Just enough to say hello to, that kinda thing. We often saw each other on our trips here, occasionally we got talking." She put her wine glass down and explained: "Candy owns a place here, ye see. And, like us, she prefers to visit in the quieter seasons when she gets the cliff walks all to her—" Beryl stopped, realising what she had said and her husband put an arm around her shoulder while Lily-Anne tutt-tutted beside her.

"Terrible, terrible tragedy," the American said, her eyes squinting as she turned them upon Roxy. "Now tell me, have the police found any signs of your dear friend yet? Any signs at all?"

Roxy shook her head. "He's been missing now since Friday, but his stuff is still in his hotel room and his car's still in the parking station so ..."

"Oh dear," said John. "It does not look good for your young fellow."

"Oooh now, hush!" said Lily-Anne. "Enough of all the negative talk. What can we do to help, my darlin'? There must be somethin' we can do."

"Well actually there is," Roxy replied, turning her eyes upon Beryl again. "You can tell me everything you know about the Marlows."

CHAPTER 25

Candace and Donald Marlow had been married just four years when Candy disappeared, she on her first husband, he his second wife. They had no children between them but a stack of cash thanks to a large inheritance left to Candy by her wealthy elderly parents. Donald wasn't exactly a pauper, though, and made good money, or so he told everyone, on his real estate investments back home in Western Australia. Despite this, it was Candy's real estate—the sweeping seaside apartment in Riomaggiore—that brought them to the region each year.

"Candy must have bought the place some years before she met Donald," Beryl explained. "She told me she'd been coming to this part of the world since she was a wee lass. Always loved it, had fond memories of the place, so didn't hesitate when an opportunity to buy an apartment came up."

"Good on her," said Roxy. "And didn't I read that she co-owns it with someone?"

"That's right," John said. "I don't know what the story is now, but back then, foreigners couldn't own property outright in Italy, ye see? They had to be sponsored by an Italian national. She didn't care, she'd do anything to own a little slice of Riomaggiore."

"Still," chimed in Beryl, "it's sad that the place she loved so much became the place that killed her."

And they all reflected on that for a moment before Roxy's brain began ticking over. "So now she's gone, do you think Donald will sell his share of the apartment, or keep coming back?"

John shrugged. "I'm not sure it's his to sell, dear. Candy co-owned it with an Italian local, so it's up to her, I'd say."

"Her?" Roxy's eyes widened. "Who are you talking about? Who did Candy own property with?"

"Why, Maria, of course," said Beryl.

"Maria? From Ted's?"

Beryl blinked a few times. "Aye, dear, she and Candy were the best of mates. Knew each other back in Australia, I believe, although Maria was born here. She moved to your country when she was a young lass and only came back about a decade ago to take over the restaurant when her father passed. Renamed it, of course, tried to make it sound more Western, I don't know why. Anyway, she had a little money to spare so went halves in the apartment with Candy. Now you have to remember, this was quite a few years back and I believe they got a very good deal. This town has gone through the roof since then, apartment must be worth a pot of gold now." She sighed. "Poor Maria, she really is most distraught."

I bet she is, thought Roxy. The plot had just thickened up.

****

"Hang on, I am so confused," said Caroline, who was sitting up in bed when Roxy returned, gooey green gunk covering her face, thick white cream in her hair and the latest copy of *Grazia* by her side. Despite the gunk, or perhaps because of it, she looked much improved, her eyes brighter, the tears now gone. "Are you saying Maria and Candy *owned* a place together? Here in town?"

"Yep, they were more than best friends, they were business partners. This opens the whole thing wide up."

"How do you mean?"

"Think about it. We've been suspecting Donald Marlow all along, but what if he had nothing to do with it? What if it was about money, not sex? I mean, it works to Maria's advantage to bump off Candy because then she gets to have the apartment all to herself. It sounds pretty swanky. It's huge, which is unusual for this tiny, cramped village, and it's right on the sea, has a fantastic view, or at least that's what Beryl says."

Caroline was making her way to the bathroom to wash the mask off. She stopped at the door and said, "Except surely Candy's half reverts to her husband now she's dead?" She raised her creamy eyebrows a few times and sang, "Yet more reason to suspect Dooooooonald."

As she disappeared into the bathroom, Roxy dropped down into the sofa and gave it some more thought.

"They have to be in it together!" called out Caroline.

"What?!" Roxy called back.

"Donald and Maria! Obviously in cahoots."

Two minutes later she was back, patting softly at her face with a fresh towel. The goo had all been removed and her skin was glowing. She looked like a new woman and Roxy was impressed. Apart from a regular soaking in the tub, Roxy didn't spend a lot of time pampering herself, yet it obviously worked wonders on Caroline, who was now reaching for some moisturiser and applying thick globs to her arms and décolletage.

"So we're back to square one," Roxy said. "Donald did it, with help from Maria, so they could continue seeing each other *and* get the inheritance."

"Double motive," Caroline added.

"Yeah, it is starting to stack up."

Roxy recalled the first time she had seen Donald, two nights ago when he sat with Maria at the back of her café, talking in strained, almost intimate tones while Maria had patted him gently on the back. Now what had he said before she'd hushed him up? Something about having no idea how he'd got there. Or something like that.

If only she could remember.

A shrill ringing sound shook Roxy back to the present and she sprang on her handbag to retrieve her phone. "It's Holly!"

"Who?"

Roxy frowned at Caroline as she took the call. "Hi Holly. How's things in *Berlin*?" She gave her friend a pointed look.

"Yeah, not bad," Holly replied down the line. "Pigs have still got the tape around Max's door, which is sooo creepy, I just wish they'd solve this thing and leave us all in peace, you know? I don't s'pose you've found him yet?"

"Sadly, no, and we're getting more and more worried. Do the police have any idea what happened to Jake? Do they still think Max had something to do with it?"

"Well, actually, the crazy loons seem to think the opposite now."

"Sorry?"

"Look, it's the reason I'm calling so late. I thought you might want to hear this."

"What?"

"It's a load of bollocks, of course, but they now seem to think Jake had something to do with Max's disappearance."

"Why would they think that?" Roxy dropped back into the sofa again as Caroline watched her, her eyes wide as if to say, 'What?!'

"Well, Reggie—that's the bass player from the Angry Euros, right—he told the coppers that Jake rang him just before he bussed it down to Italy to meet Max."

"So he *did* get the bus to Milan! I knew it." There was no doubting it now. Jake was the man who had shown up with Max at Ola's Villas on Wednesday.

"Yeah, well, according to Reggie, Jake said he'd be back for Saturd'y's gig, right, but that he was going to Italy to clear his debts with Max once and for all." She hesitated. "Reggie reckons Jake said, 'Once I get this out of the way, I won't have to worry about Max ever again.'"

Roxy felt a shiver run through her body. That sounded ominous. "What do the police say?"

"I haven't spoken to them, right? I just ran into Reggie, you see, and he's been telling me all this."

"Okay, so what does Reggie say?"

She hesitated. "You might not want to hear this."

"It's fine, Holly. Just say it."

She hesitated again. "Reggie reckons the cops think Jake must have owed Max quite a few quid and so he met up with him in Italy and, well, got rid of 'im, so to speak." She couldn't quite bring herself to say the word "kill" and Roxy was glad. She didn't really want to hear it now. Once again there was a kind of logical sense to this, at least from a time line perspective.

"Still doesn't explain who then killed Jake."

"That's what I said but Reggie reckons they're working on some double-crossing theory."

"Huh?"

"Cops insinuated, right, that Jake might have been in it with some Italian geezer, that the two of them robbed Max at the same time. Reckon they might've pinched his good cameras and cleared out his bank account, that kinda stuff, and then they either got into a fight when they got back to Berlin or this Italian bloke double-crossed Jake, killed him and took off with everything. Reggie says they're checking Max's bank accounts to see if he's had large amounts of cash removed, that kind of thing."

Roxy was shaking her head at the phone now. No way, she thought. Max didn't have that much worth stealing, plus it was all too complicated, it just didn't add up. Why not just kill him at home in Berlin? Unless, of course, they thought the anonymity of Riomaggiore was preferable. The shiver intensified.

"Look, sorry but I gotta go, this is costing me a friggin' fortune. I really just wanted to see how you guys are holdin' up. You oright?"

"We're okay, thanks, Holly, we appreciate your call. And please call if you hear any more. Or send me a text and I'll call you back."

She promised to do that and hung up, then Roxy looked across to Caroline, unsure how much to reveal.

"No secrets, remember?" Caroline said as if reading her mind, and so Roxy repeated what Max's neighbour had said. "That's the most ridiculous thing I've ever heard," she spat. "It's just plain ludicrous."

Roxy thought about it some more. Eventually she said, "It might not be as ludicrous as we think, you know." Before Caroline could protest again, she added, "I mean, we've worked out why Max came to Riomaggiore: he obviously fell for this Candy woman"—funny the way she struggled to use her name, it reminded Roxy of the way her mother referred to Max—"but that doesn't explain why Jake came along." She sighed. "It brings me back to an earlier theory of mine."

"Oh really, which theory was that? I'm having trouble keeping up."

Roxy ignored her sarcasm. "The theory that Max rang his flatmate to say, 'I'm heading to Italy' and Jake begged a lift. Only he didn't do it for the fun of it, he did it because he saw his opportunity to get rid of Max and clear his debts once and for all."

Caroline looked incredulous. "So what about Donald and Maria? Where does that leave them?"

Roxy shrugged. "Maybe they have nothing to do with any of this."

"Then—duh!—why is Candy dead?"

Roxy groaned. "I don't know! Maybe that's a whole separate crime. Maybe that's our problem, we keep linking the two deaths together, but maybe they're not connected. Maybe when Max called the police, he was worried about Jake, not Donald. Maybe that was the 'crime' he was talking about—he suspected his flatmate was up to something."

Caroline was shaking her head. "I just don't buy it. Not

one bit. They *have* to be connected, they just have to."

Roxy sat forward suddenly. "Maybe we're looking at this the wrong way around! Maybe Candy was the one who got in the way when Jake was trying to kill Max. Maybe she stumbled upon them having a fight on the cliff top and that's how she ended up over the edge."

"What, like collateral damage?"

"Exactly. *She* was the one who was in the wrong place at the wrong time."

The words hung like heavy drapes across their hearts and the two women didn't speak then, not for a long, long time. All the benefits of Caroline's makeover had dissipated and her face looked strained again. Roxy, too, was chewing at her lower lip, trying to connect so many seemingly unconnected dots.

It all seemed so senseless yet there was a kind of evil logic at the same time.

****

A firm tap sounded at the apartment door and at first Roxy thought she'd imagined it.

Tap, tap, tap.

There it was again. She struggled to sit up, her limbs entwined in the sheets, and tried to find the switch for the lamp. It was still dark outside, only a slight glimmer of light coming through the shutters from the street below. She peered at her watch. It was 5:03 a.m.

Tap, tap, tap! Louder this time.

"Coming!" Roxy croaked.

"Wha—" said Caroline, her head lifting sightly from her pillow, completely covered in a mess of blonde hair.

"Someone's at the door."

"Wha—"

Roxy groaned and got up, found Caroline's silk bathrobe on the edge of a chair and wrapped it around herself, then padded across to the front door and said, "Who is it?"

Thinking, "At this hour, it'd better be bloody good."

"Officer Giuseppe!"

Oh God, she thought, *anyone but him.*

She stepped back, her heart in her stomach again. She looked across at Caroline who was now sitting up in bed, hair all over her face, the sheet pulled up to her chest. She had the same terrified look in her eyes but gave Roxy a nod.

They would face this together, come what may.

Roxy unlatched the lock and swung the door open to find Officer Giuseppe standing down one step. He was not in his usual uniform, had a thick blue sweater and blue trousers on, and a stern look on his chiselled face.

"Do not be alarmed," he said, clearly reading the panic in her eyes, "but I need you to come with me, now. We have found something."

CHAPTER 26

The Converse sneaker was looking soggy and unloved. The shoelace was missing and the front was fraying just slightly, but other than that it was a dead ringer for the one in Max's hotel room.

The two women stared at it forlornly for a few minutes before Caroline burst into tears.

"Oh my God," she spluttered. "He's gone!"

Roxy leaned across and wrapped an arm across her back. She felt oddly cold, strangely unmoved. "It's just a shoe, Caroline. Loads of people misplace shoes on their walks—"

"It's *his* shoe! It has to be!" She buckled over, sobbing again.

Rossi coughed. "Are you saying, Miss Farrell, that you believe this shoe belongs to your brother, Max Farrell?"

Caroline sniffed and then blew her nose into a tissue that Carmela had handed her across the table. They were back at the police station, in the small interrogation room, and both detectives were wearing dark tracksuits, their eyes droopy, coffee mugs close by. Rossi's hair was wisping up on one side as though he, too, had just been dragged from his pillow.

"There was a matching one in Max's hotel room," Roxy explained. "Just the one."

"Yes, we saw that one, too," Carmela said. "Giuseppe has gone to retrieve it now. We will check for the size, but ..."

"We're pretty certain this belonged to your brother," Rossi said to Caroline.

"Where did you find it?"

"It washed up just near the jetty. One of the local boys found it very early this morning, caught in some fishing line."

Roxy thought about this. "But didn't you say Candy was located miles away?"

"Yes," said Carmela. "But the tides have been all over the place this past week. It would have been easy for things to scatter."

Roxy stared at the shoe again. It was in better condition than you'd expect after a week floating about in the tides. "Did you find anything else?"

"Just the shoe."

Caroline sobbed again at the mere mention of it and Roxy patted her back gently.

"We are organising the helicopters to do another search today," Rossi informed her. "We will find his body."

That set her off even harder but Roxy's thoughts were heading in a different direction. She began to shake her head. "You know, if you think about it, it doesn't make much sense."

"Yes, madam, murder, it is senseless," Rossi began but she shook her head again.

"No, no, I mean, he couldn't have been wearing his Converse sneakers when he went walking because—"

"Because they're useless for hiking!" Caroline chimed in now, sniffing again into her tissue. "Plus they're not cheap. Why ruin a perfectly good—"

"No, no, it's not that. One of them was still in his hotel room. So he couldn't have been wearing them when he disappeared. Don't you see? It makes no sense. Maybe he lost one the day before, or something, but he must have returned to his room to place the other one back in his bag."

"Unless someone else placed it there," said Carmela, her eyebrows arched skyward and Roxy blinked a few times.

"But why? Why would someone do that?"

"To make it look like he returned, to deflect the blame for Candy's death onto him."

"Oh, yes," said Caroline, warming to this idea. "They probably planted the pink visor at the same time!"

As they continued talking this over in circles, Roxy's head felt more and more muddled. It just wasn't clicking into place for her. She had plenty of experience solving mysteries and they usually, eventually, made sense. This one was all over the place again.

One minute they were suspecting Donald, the next they were pointing the finger at Maria, then both of them. Just last night, Jake was suddenly the main culprit. And now? God knows who was under the spotlight now. She was losing track.

Commander Rossi had no such doubts. He cleared his throat and said, "I wanted to inform you that we have issued an arrest warrant for Donald Marlow. My men are in the process of picking him up now."

Both women stared at him. Caroline's eye lit up, her tears draining away. "I knew he was dodgy! I knew it!"

Despite herself, Roxy couldn't help feeling surprised. "On what evidence?" she said.

Carmela and Rossi shared another of those glances before Rossi said, "We can not tell you that, I am sorry."

"Motive then?"

A small cough and Rossi said, "There is a very substantial inheritance."

"I knew it!" Caroline said again and Roxy wanted to smack her.

Yes, yes, she thought, *we've already been there, thought that.* "What about Max?"

"I am sorry to say but we believe Mr Farrell got in the

way," Carmela said. "We know he accompanied Mrs Marlow on her walk at Mt Pilatus, we have confirmed this with the staff there. So it makes sense that he also accompanied her the day she died." She glanced down at the Converse sneaker as if that was all the proof they needed. "We believe that Mr Marlow followed them and pushed them both over the edge. We believe he only intended to kill his wife, but that Mr Farrell was just in the wrong place at—"

"The wrong time, yeah, yeah," Roxy interjected. "I'm sorry to sound cynical, but are you really saying that Donald Marlow managed to overpower both Candy and Max, all on his own? I know you haven't met Max, but he's really tall, broad shouldered, strong. There's no way that wimpy little man could overpower him. No way."

Perhaps it was just wishful thinking.

"Ahh, but anyone can be pushed when their back is turned," Carmela said and Caroline made a kind of strangled sound. "Plus, he may have had an accomplice."

"Maria!" Caroline exclaimed, and now it was Carmela's turn to look surprised.

Roxy said, "We already suspect she and Donald were sleeping together, but it still doesn't add up. Unless she's lying, Maria told us she was at the markets that Friday morning. She might have an alibi. Have you checked that?"

Carmela glanced at Rossi and he sighed wearily then gave a small nod. She said, "We have looked into it, yes, and at the moment we have no proof of this. The markets are in Monterosso, you see."

"Monterosso? One of the other five towns?"

"The farthest town from here, in fact. The parking attendant remembers her leaving Riomaggiore at 9:05 a.m. that morning, but she did not return until just after midday. No one recalls seeing her in Monterosso, she has no alibi."

"So she could have parked somewhere along the road and walked down to meet Candy on the Blue Trail?"

"Yes."

"And Donald? Also no alibi?"

"He was last seen at Ted's Trattoria, having breakfast, around 10:30 a.m. He did not appear again until around 3:00 p.m. He can not properly account for his time."

"He can't tell you where he was between 10:30 a.m. and 3:00 p.m. that Friday?"

Carmella hesitated, glanced quickly at Rossi and did not answer.

"Can you at least tell me when Candy was killed, do you know?" Roxy asked.

"The coroner can not tell us precisely, you understand?" said Rossi. "The deceased's body was too decomposed by the time we found her, and while there were numerous fractures and some serious contusions around the head area, we do know she died from drowning. That is a fact. Judging from witness statements, we believe Mrs Marlow fell from the edge of the trail sometime between 11:00 a.m. when she set off on the walk, and about 1:00 p.m. that Friday."

Roxy went to say something but knew she had to tread carefully. She couldn't believe the detectives were being so forthcoming and she didn't want to scare them off. "Okay, so both Donald and Maria have plenty of motive and no clear alibi. But surely you need more than that? I mean, do you have any actual evidence that they were at the cliff at that time, that Candy was even pushed over the edge?" She paused. "I'm not saying that Donald and Maria *weren't* having an affair, but is there any evidence to actually pin this on them? I'm playing Devil's Advocate here, but maybe Candy found out about the affair and threw herself over, out of despair."

"Really?" said Caroline, her eyebrows high. She hadn't thought of that.

"We do not believe so," said Rossi. "There is evidence that Donald Marlow had made threats against his wife."

"What kind of threats?" Roxy said.

"At this stage I cannot tell you more than that."

"And Max?" she asked, frowning down at the shoe. "Any other evidence that he was anywhere near the trail at that time? Did anyone actually *see* him, do you know?"

"Mr Farrell was last seen that morning, also at Ted's Trattoria, also around 10:30 a.m." Carmela said. "Then he just vanished. No one remembers where he went or in which direction. He was never seen again."

Caroline, who had been watching this exchange with a fascinated expression, dropped her head into her hands and began sobbing again, and Roxy felt like joining her but tried to remain strong, swallowing her own tears back down. She had just one more question and everything rested on it.

"What about Jake Conway?" The two detectives looked at her, blank expressions in their eyes. "Max's flatmate. How does he fit into all of this?"

Carmela shrugged her shoulders slightly. "We have been speaking to the Berlin police but we are not sure he has anything to do with this."

"They are getting back to us with more information tonight," added Rossi, "but I am sorry, Miss Parker, his death, at this stage, appears to be unconnected."

Roxy nodded. She knew they'd say that.

Rossi was sighing now and pushing himself away from the table and up to his feet. He looked drained, even a little defeated, and Roxy wondered whether he'd ever had a case so baffling or if he just needed his sleep.

"We will continue the search for your brother, Miss Farrell," he was saying to Caroline, reaching down to give her shoulder a few quick taps. "We will find him, you not to worry." Then he looked at Roxy and said, "You are okay?"

Not really, she thought but just nodded again.

By the time the two women had left the station and begun walking back to their room, Roxy's head was spinning again. She realised she should be jubilant. The police were making an arrest, the bad guy was going to be locked up. So why did it all feel so wrong? And why were there so many questions still unanswered?

Like: How did a scrawny guy like Donald Marlow

overpower two sporty people on a cliff face? Even with the help of his shrimp-sized lover?

How did Max's sneaker end up in the water while the other one remained in his hotel room? And if it had been there for almost a week, why was it not in worse shape?

But, most importantly, how the hell did Jake fit into all of this?

Roxy thought about that some more. To her Jake was the key to everything, the piece of the puzzle that was refusing to fit. The German police seemed to think he killed Max. The Italians didn't seem too interested in him at all. And yet she felt that he was at the centre of it all. He just had to be.

Roxy chewed her lower lip, tried to juggle her brain into gear. *Think, Roxy, think!*

She must have groaned aloud then because Caroline was looking at her with a worried crinkle in her brow. "You okay?"

They were now standing out the front of Monty's hat shop and while his door was slightly ajar, the shopkeeper was nowhere to be seen.

Roxy shook her head, no. "But I will be, Caroline. First I need to take a good, long walk."

"Really? After stomping up and down these streets for *days*. You have the energy for that?"

"I need to see this Blue Trail for myself. I need to see where Candy fell, where Max might have ..." She let that dangle. "I need to go there."

She was referring to the cliff path, of course, and Caroline's look of worry turned to one of horror. "You're not really going up there? Tell me you're not!"

"I have to, Caro. I need to see for myself. And I need to clear my head. Everything is so mixed up."

While beauty treatments might be the perfect elixir for Caroline, it was vigorous walks that did the trick for Roxy. They never failed to clear out the cobwebs and reboot the brain, but not if Caroline could help it.

"It's too dangerous, Roxy, you can't go!"

"Everything okay-eh?" Monty had come out of his shop and had a stack of wide-brimmed straw hats in his hands.

Caroline stepped towards him and grabbed his arm. "No, Monty. Roxy's being a bloody idiot. Tell her that cliff walk is too dangerous! Tell her she can't go."

He looked with sympathy at Caroline then turned to Roxy and said, "You want, I come with you, no?"

"Thanks, Monty," she replied. "You're very sweet but this is something I have to do alone."

"But ... but ..." stammered Caroline.

Roxy pulled her into a tight embrace. "I'll be okay. I promise. What could possibly go wrong?"

CHAPTER 27

The first leg of the nine-kilometre *Sentiero Azzurro*, or Blue Trail, between all five towns of the Cinque Terre was relatively easy, just a twenty-five-minute walk that linked Riomaggiore to the south, with its closest neighbour, the village of Manarola, to the northwest. Or at least that's what the sign said.

Roxy had made her way through the underpass and up past Ted's Trattoria where Sofia was standing out the front, apron in place, chatting with Hugo. Both locals turned to wave at Roxy and she waved back but kept right on walking, past the small alleyway that led to the back of Ted's and up the steep, stone steps to the start of the trail. As she read the sign, a small lump had lodged in Roxy's throat. According to the inscription, this part of the coastline was known as the *Via dell'Amore*, or The Way of Love.

The lump in Roxy's throat hardened and tears began welling in her eyes. Had Max and Candy decided to rendezvous on the Way of Love? Was this where it all went terribly wrong?

Dabbing at a tear that had spilled down her cheek, Roxy gave herself a quick pep talk then securely fastened her handbag across her body, pushed her Gucci sunglasses into a better position on her nose, and set off.

The path was not as wide as she'd hoped, but it was relatively flat and paved in most places with slate tiles. While there were none of the usual warning signs she had come to expect from cliff walks around her home country—clearly litigation lawyers had not caught up with the council here— there was a metal fence along most of the cliff side and sheer rock face along the other. The fence was a little rickety in parts and just waist high, offering very little protection should someone want to throw you over, she thought darkly as she walked.

Along the way she noticed hundreds and hundreds of "love locks", small padlocks that had been secured to the fence by lovers past. She stopped and read some of the inscriptions—JB 4 RS, S+V—and felt herself choke up again. She wondered if Max and Candy had placed one somewhere, then shook her head. He was a natural romantic, but even that seemed a little twee for Max Farrell.

She sighed. *Oh Max. Where are you?*

Stepping closer to the railing now, she held on and leaned out, looking down at the rippled blue sea below. There were splashes of frothy white where it crashed into the coastline, and while she couldn't picture Max down there—or perhaps she wouldn't let herself—she kept having flashes of Candy's muscular body being smashed against those rocks. She shuddered and stepped back.

Then she pushed her sunglasses into place and kept walking. As she did so, Roxy's brain returned to the American flatmate Jake.

What was he doing in Riomaggiore?

Why was he killed?

How was his murder connected to Max?

Perhaps Jake had witnessed Donald and/or Maria killing Candy and Max and that's why he was murdered. Perhaps one of them drove Jake back to Berlin where they bludgeoned him with his own guitar.

She shook her head. *No, no, that didn't work.* Unless they owned a Learjet there was no way either of them could do it. The drive between Riomaggiore and Berlin was at least twelve hours long and she knew for a fact that Jake had been killed some time very late on Friday night. Yet according to Riomaggiore police, Maria had only been out of town between 9:00 a.m. and midday that Friday. Donald had been missing longer—between 10:30 a.m. and 3:00 p.m.—yet still not long enough to drive to Berlin, kill Jake and return again.

She stopped in her tracks. Perhaps there was a third party? That would help explain it. But who?

She groaned again and kept walking, this time trying hard not to think, just letting her mind rest. God knows it needed a reprieve. Eventually, after another ten minutes or so, Roxy stopped again and leaned out against the railing, watching as a fisherman ploughed his vessel through the waters far below. Then she flinched when she realised that was no fishing boat. It had a blue stripe along one side and what looked like large spotlights attached to the roof.

It had to be the coast guard.

For several minutes she watched it bobbing in and out of the white caps as it made its way around the bay, hugging the shore the whole way. She knew what it was looking for and she felt deep sadness again.

Come on, Roxy, she told herself. *Keep going.*

Another hundred metres along, just after she'd taken a steep turn, the path came to an abrupt halt. A section had been cordoned off by blue police tape, some of which was flapping freely in the breeze where it had freed itself from its wiring, and there was a small sign on one side, with the words "Danger! No Pass!"

There was no way through.

Roxy stood then for many minutes just staring at the spot where Candy must have fallen. Why else would the police rope this bit off? She tried to find evidence of a landslip, loose rocks or broken branches where she must have grabbed for her life, but she could see nothing out of the ordinary. It looked just like the rocky terrain she had passed, peaceful and untouched. The fence was still in place and there was a smattering of plant life clinging to the rock below, including some agaves and cacti. Roxy glanced around. It hadn't occurred to her before, but that explained why no one else had passed her on the walk. It was out of bounds now. Candy's death, in effect, had put a stop to the Way of Love. At least for now.

A loud screaming sound caught Roxy off guard and she swung around, heart thumping in her chest as she clung tighter to the metal fence which was vibrating a little. She couldn't see the source of the noise but there was also a slight shaking of the earth below her feet and she wondered what was going on. Was it an earthquake?

"It's just the train," came a deep, unexpected voice, and Roxy looked back to find a figure standing in the middle of the pathway on the Riomaggiore side.

She could not make out who it was. He had his back to the sun and was just a silhouette in the harsh morning light. Her heart now pounding like a jackhammer, she tried to take some calming breaths as she stepped away from the fence and wedged herself deeper into the rock face on the other side.

"There's a tunnel, you see, dug through the rock," the man was saying, his voice slightly familiar. "Must have been quite a feat of engineering to get those tunnels in place."

"What ... what do you want?" Roxy managed to say, her throat dry, her heart so loud she wondered how he could hear her voice over it.

The man stepped forward and that's when she saw his face clearly for the first time. She felt her mouth drain dry as he gave her a small, flickering smile.

"I've come to find you," Donald Marlow said.

Then he took another step towards her.

CHAPTER 28

Caroline was right. Donald Marlow was not an attractive man, but now, wanted for two murders with a life sentence hanging over his head, he looked almost grotesque. Without his Fedora and enormous sunglasses, his splotchy skin was glowing red and his pale, semi-balding head made him look like a hairy egg as wisps of hair fluttered about in the breeze.

"You scared the crap out of me!" Roxy hissed, patting her hammering heart.

"Sorry. Didn't mean to." He stepped back and leaned against the fence, just a metre away. "It's beautiful here, don't you think?"

She breathed deeply again but didn't have the energy to answer him.

"Candace loved this part of the walk best. They call it the *Via dell'Amore*, you know?" The Way of Love.

"Yes," Roxy managed. "I read that."

He looked down at the sea. "All she wanted was for me to accompany her on this walk. So many times she asked, so many times I said no." He turned to face her. "It was her thing, you see, I wasn't really into hiking ..." He emitted a small groan and she wondered if he was crying. "If only I'd walked with her ... instead ...”

“What do you want, Donald?” Roxy interrupted, her confidence returning.

He turned to face her full on then and his eyes were red and wet. “I didn’t kill my wife, or your friend. I didn’t do it, you have to believe me.”

Roxy glanced around him, hoping to see someone, anyone, come along the path. There was not a soul about. “So why do the police think you did?”

His shoulders drooped. After several minutes he said, “They think I’ve been having an affair.”

“With Maria, yes, I know.”

“But it’s not true! It’s just not!”

“So why would they say it?”

He sniffed loudly and his eyes filled with something akin to embarrassment. “Because ... while my poor wife was here, walking with some other man, I ... I was in Maria’s bed.”

“What?”

Donald leaned his back against the fence and dropped his head into his hands, his voice muffled now as he spoke. “I’m so confused. I ... I drink and I black out. I woke up in her bed that day ... In Maria’s bed. We must have ...”

He didn’t say any more, his face still hidden by his hands and Roxy knew she had to act. She needed to get away from this precarious part of the cliff walk. She glanced around and spotted a grassy ledge a few metres back towards town. It was flat and it was safer than the rock face she was now wedged against.

She took another deep breath and said, “Do you mind?” He looked up and she pointed towards the grass. “I just need to sit down, over there. My back is killing me.”

Her back was fine, but he didn’t need to know that. Donald looked around and then nodded, so she slowly edged her way past him, trying hard not to touch him as she stepped along the path to the grassy patch. She dropped down onto it with a flood of relief, and after a moment he joined her, sitting within spitting distance of where she was now perched.

He was squatting and there were tears in his eyes. "You have to help me. The police ..." He glanced back down the pathway nervously. "They're gonna come, they're gonna arrest me, but I didn't do this. You have to believe me!"

Roxy held a hand up to calm him down. "I do believe you, Donald."

He stared hard at her. "Really?" He did not look convinced.

"Yes, but you need to back up a little. Let's start at the beginning, that Friday your wife disappeared. Can you tell me what happened?"

He swallowed hard. "We had breakfast together."

"At Ted's?"

"Yes! We always have breaky there. Maria and my wife are business partners. We eat there to support her. We always do. Did."

"Okay, so you had breakfast at Ted's. What time was this?"

"I don't know, 9:30ish."

"Okay, did you see my friend Max there? We know he was also eating there that morning."

"No! I swear to God I did not see him." He looked at her, his eyes fluttering wildly. "I know you don't believe me, but I never met your mate. Candy mentioned him but I never met him, not here, not at Mt Pilatus. I promise!"

"Okay, forget him for now. So what happened, after breakfast?"

"I ... I don't remember."

"Think!"

"Okay, um, Candy told me she was going on a walk. I told her to be careful." He looked around. "You can see the path. It's not as safe as people make out." She nodded, urging him on. "She just laughed at me, said she'd be safer here than with me." He looked stung now, could barely meet Roxy's eyes. "I didn't know what she meant. She'd been saying crazy things like that for days. Anyway, that's when she told me she had an escort so she'd be perfectly fine. She always used that word, escort. She rarely named these blokes, but she was a bloody flirt, my Candy. She always found one willing guy or another." He met Roxy's eyes then. "You have to understand, she was perfectly harmless, she just flirted with whoever she needed to flirt with to get them to accompany her on her walks. It never went anywhere, I can assure you."

That did assure Roxy, but she wondered if Max knew; if he had been led up the garden path by Candy, both literally and figuratively. Still, it wasn't really the point now.

"Did your wife say who was escorting her on the walk that day? The day she disappeared?"

"No! I assumed later that it must have been your friend, the one that also went missing."

"Max."

"Yeah, well, that makes sense, right? You said he had walked with my wife at Mt Pilatus and then came here, so I assumed that must be the man. I told the police this but they won't believe me."

"But why didn't Candy tell you his name?"

"I don't know! I wish she had, God I wish she had. She just said she was heading off and then she laughed and said, 'If I'm not back by four, send out the search party.'" His eyes filled with tears. "I thought she was joking."

Roxy shivered a little at the woman's prophetic words but she knew she didn't have much time so she had to hurry him along. He was right, the police were no doubt searching the town for him now and she needed to find out everything she could before he was locked away and out of her reach. "So what happened then? Candy left the café to go for a walk. When was that? Exactly?"

"I told Rossi, Candy left Ted's to get ready for her hike some time before ten, at least that's what I remember. I stayed around to finish breakfast and it's all a blur after that." He offered a remorseful smile. "I'd been drinking mimosas at brunch, Candy didn't, she wanted to keep a clear head for her hike, but I was relaxed, you know, I was chilling out. I was on holiday." He sighed. "Anyway, I must have drunk more than I realised because the next few hours are ... well, they're a wipeout."

"That's a lot of champagne."

He nodded his head sadly. "I woke up around three-ish."

"That Friday afternoon?"

"Yes. Oh God, this is the bit I don't understand ... I woke up in Maria's bed, I was shocked."

"How did you end up in her bed?"

"I don't know! That's the crazy bit. I just don't know. I'd never been there before, I swear to you! I have never slept with her before. Ever, in my life. We've been coming to Rio' for years now and I never so much as looked twice at Maria. Why ... now?"

"Was Maria there? In bed beside you?"

"Of course not!"

"So how did you know it was her bed?"

He looked confused for a second, said impatiently, "Because her things were in there, of course, and because it was upstairs, in the back of her café. I know she has a room back there. She stays there, sometimes, when she's fighting with the hubby. Which is, like, always."

"Maria's married?" That was the first anyone had mentioned that.

"Yes," he said and went to say something else when an Asian man suddenly appeared from around the bend in the path, followed quickly by a petite woman and a young boy. They were clearly tourists and the man was holding a large iPad out, snapping away furiously.

"The path is closed!" Roxy called out to them, eager to get them out of the way. She didn't believe Donald was a threat, but she didn't want to risk it either. "You have to go!"

They looked at her, uncertain for a few minutes then said something to each other, bowed their heads and turned back the way they had come. When they disappeared behind the bend again, Roxy exhaled then glanced at Donald who didn't seem to have even noticed them.

She was running out of time. "Okay, so when you woke up around three on Friday, you were still at Ted's, in Maria's room? Is that what you're saying?"

"Yes! I stepped out of the room and down the stairs and found myself in the corridor, just outside the kitchen. I had a throbbing headache and I just needed to get out of there. I used the back exit and took off."

"Why the back exit?"

He held his head to one side. "I'm not an idiot. I knew how it'd look. Doesn't matter, anyway, I got busted."

"Someone saw you? Who? Valentino?"

"No, thank God! Jesus, he would've punched me out. Nah, it was Sofia. She was just knocking off for the day." He groaned. "Oh the look in her eyes! It was mortifying."

"Sofia saw you? The waitress?" He nodded. "Okay, then what happened?"

"Then I took off! I went back to our apartment and had a shower and a lie down. I was confused, I didn't understand what had happened. I woke up quite a bit later and Candy still hadn't returned from her walk. I waited another hour and then, remembering what she'd said, I went out to look for her. I went back to Ted's and spoke to Maria but she hadn't seen her either, so I searched her favourite haunts. Nothing. That's when I saw the two officers, walking down the main road. You rarely see police in Riomaggiore, at least not at this time of year. So I reported Candy missing."

He took a small step towards Roxy then settled back into his squat. "I might have woken up in Maria's bed, but I did *not* sleep with her, I know I didn't. I haven't been having an affair, I never have."

"So how did you end up in her bed?"

"I don't know! As I said, I must have had too much to drink and I must have stumbled back there to sleep it off. I didn't go there with Maria, I promise!"

"Okay, okay, calm down." His skin was glowing crimson again. "So what does Maria say about all of this? Surely they can just check with her and she can set the record straight.”

“She denies it, of course! But the police don’t believe her, that’s the problem. Someone seems to have given them the impression that we’d been having it off for ages. Someone ...” he swallowed hard, “someone has been telling them lies, telling them that I threatened my wife. That I wanted her dead.”

“So you could be with Maria?”

“Yes, but it’s not true! None of it. I loved my wife, I would never hurt her, I would never betray her, never!”

Roxy sighed with exasperation. “But who would do this to you, Donald? *Why?*”

He looked up, defeated, and whispered, “I wish to God I knew.”

Roxy didn’t know whether Donald Marlow was spinning her a lie or whether he really was speaking the truth, but her instincts told her the latter. He seemed too distraught and strung out, but perhaps he was just a very good actor.

Then it occurred to her. “That’s your alibi.”

He blinked rapidly. “What?”

“Whether you were sleeping with Maria or not, you woke up in Maria’s bed so you couldn’t have killed Candy. Don’t you see? You have an alibi.”

He was shaking his head again. “You don’t get it. I woke up *alone.*”

“Yes, but Sofia saw you come out around 3:00 p.m. She can vouch for you.”

“No, no, the police are saying I snuck in the back door of the restaurant after killing my wife and *pretended* I’d been in Maria’s room all that day. I most certainly do not have an alibi.” He began shaking his head like a crazy man again. “Don’t you see! Someone’s doing this to me! Someone’s lying about me, they’re trying to pin this on me!”

“But why would they do that, Donald? Why?” When he didn’t answer, she said, “Could it be Maria?”

“Noooo,” he said, shaking his head. “She wouldn’t do that to me.”

"Are you sure? Did Candy leave Maria anything in her will? Her share of the apartment they co-owned?"

"No, that comes to me ..." His head stopped shaking. "Unless of course something happens to me, then it reverts to her. Oh bloody hell! Do you think ... But no, she wouldn't. Would she?"

His eyes were fluttering madly again and the splotches on his skin had formed a giant red blush.

"How much is this apartment worth?"

"A seaside apartment on the Italian Riviera? A shitload!" He was coming back to life now as the realisation dawned on him. "Candy never let Maria rent it out to tourists, always wanted it available should she drop in without notice. She also didn't like the idea of strangers sleeping in her bed. But Maria tried to change her mind a few times. Candy always refused. I thought ... I thought Maria was happy, I thought she was fine with the arrangement."

"So she and Maria never used it as a holiday rental?"

"No, well occasionally when Maria made a real fuss, but most of the time, no. Which is crazy, really. They could rent it out for a bomb."

"So how did they make their money back?"

"They didn't. Candy had more than enough, she just didn't care about that."

Ah yes, thought Roxy. *But perhaps Maria did.*

Before Roxy could say another word, a loud voice came out of nowhere, making them both jump.

"Police! Stay where you are!"

Roxy looked up to find Officer Giuseppe standing at the very edge of the path where it dipped around and disappeared back towards town. She snuck a glance at Donald but it was as though he hadn't heard him, his head back in his hands again.

How would he react? she wondered, not daring to look to her left where the cliff edge dropped away. Sure, there was a fence there, but she still didn't like her chances.

She looked back at Giuseppe who was motioning for her

to come towards him with one hand as the other held a gun, pointed straight towards Donald. A second officer appeared behind him.

Roxy took a deep breath and edged her way on her bum, a few paces away from Donald, towards the police.

"I should just end it now," Donald said then, so softly Roxy could barely hear him.

She stopped moving. "What?"

He rested his chin on his hands and stared out at the view. "Maybe it's time I joined my wife."

Roxy held a hand up to Giuseppe who had been creeping forward, hoping to stall him. She said to Donald, "But you didn't kill her, right?"

He shifted his eyes to look at her. There was hurt there now, and something else. Was it relief? "You really believe me?"

"And they will, too." She indicated the police. "But not if you throw yourself over. Then whoever's doing this to you will get away with it, and you'll go down in history as a murderer."

She shuffled her bum back towards him. "It's time to stop this, Donald. You need to hand yourself in."

"I didn't do it," he said softly again. "I didn't kill my wife and I didn't hurt your friend either."

He dropped his head back down and began to cry then, loud, gut-wrenching sobs, and Roxy stayed exactly where she was as the officers closed in. Giuseppe grabbed her right arm and dragged her out of the way as the second officer pounced on Donald, pushing him to the ground and pulling both his hands behind his back, cuffing them into place.

"Are you okay?" Giuseppe asked and Roxy nodded.

"He hasn't hurt me. I'm fine."

She stepped aside as he took Donald into custody, reading him his rights in Italian, whatever good that would do.

"I'm innocent," were the last words Donald said, his eyes beseeching hers as he was led back down the path.

CHAPTER 29

Back on the main read, just next to Ted's, Roxy, Caroline and Sofia were watching the police load Donald in the back of their patrol car, his head bowed low, his skin oddly pasty now.

Giuseppe said something to the officer and then stepped across to Roxy. "Can you come up to the station later, for a statement?"

She nodded. "Of course. But please, you need to understand, he never harmed me. He just needed to talk."

"Terrifying place to have a conversation!" Caroline spat, still convinced the man was a lunatic.

"Be sure to be there by midday," Giuseppe added, "because we will be closing up the police station this afternoon. Commanders Rossi and Constantini will be returning full time to La Spezia now."

"And you?"

"I will be back tomorrow afternoon." He turned to look at Caroline. "We will resume searching for your brother then. I am sorry we can not do it any sooner. We have a major emergency back in La Spezia, we just do not have the manpower."

Caroline looked outraged but before she could object, Roxy quickly asked, "How did you find me?"

"You can thank Sofia for that," Caroline snapped. "She alerted the police who had no idea where Donald had disappeared to." She glowered at Giuseppe. "You guys had been chasing your tails for the past hour. If it wasn't for Sofia, well ..." She mock shuddered, not daring to think.

Sofia smiled sheepishly. "I see Mr Marlow take-eh the path, just like you. I worry for you."

"And thank God you did!" gushed Caroline.

But Roxy was not so worried. She turned to Giuseppe. "So what will happen to Donald now?"

"I will take him back to La Spezia where he will be detained until his bail hearing."

"Oh God, he won't get bail, will he?" said Caroline.

Giuseppe ignored this and said, "You will be safe now, Miss Parker. I can assure you."

Roxy thought about this. She had never felt unsafe in Donald's presence. At no point had he threatened her and she couldn't see him threatening his wife or Max, for that matter. She couldn't imagine that small, fearful man overcoming either of them and throwing them to their deaths. None of it made sense.

She considered Maria's part in all of this. If Donald was telling the truth, was Maria the guilty party? She had no alibi, after all, and she had a lot to gain from the removal of the Marlows. She shook her head. If Donald couldn't throw two adults over the cliff, there was even less chance that Maria could.

Oh no, she thought, if she's guilty of this, she must be working with someone. That was the only solution. There had to be someone else involved. She kept coming back to that.

But who could it be?

Giuseppe bid them farewell then and returned to the police wagon. They watched as it blasted short, quick sirens into the air, clearing tourists in all directions, before it began to wind its way back up the narrow cobbled road, Donald barely visible in the back, his head bowed low.

Sofia turned towards Roxy. "I 'ave to get back to work now. You okay?"

She nodded. "Thanks so much for all your help."

She shrugged elaborately, her ample bosom lifting and dropping, then made her way inside the restaurant as Caroline grabbed Roxy's elbow.

"I don't know about you, but I need a strong coffee, badly."

Roxy was happy to be dragged along, this time to a small café on a narrow side street where they had never ventured before. It was little more than a hole in the wall and they settled into a tiny table at the back, glad of the privacy. It was well away from the madding crowd.

"Lily-Anne won't find us here either," Caroline said and then frowned. "Although I wouldn't put it past her! She's already found me once today and it's not yet," she glanced at her watch, "ten."

"Oh?"

"Yes. While you were taking your *walk*," the way she said the word was full of recriminations, "I was having a coffee at the Marina, and who else would wander in but that dreadful woman."

"She's not so bad."

Caroline snorted. "Your standards are dropping, sweetie. The woman's a horror. Anyway, she seems to think you're fabulous, too, because she asked me to tell you she's meeting some Irish people for Happy Hour at Ted's tonight if you want to join her."

"That was nice of her. Not sure I've got the energy though." She wasn't sure if she was ready to face Maria, either.

"Of course you haven't," Caroline was saying. "Anyway, it's not until 4:00 p.m., so if you change your mind, your new BFF will be waiting there for you with her sweaty husband, no doubt." She quivered a little. "Now, Missy, you had better fill me in on what that crazy lunatic had to say for himself. What happened? Did he hurt you?"

Roxy shook her head firmly. "He just wanted me to listen. He was pleading for his life."

As they ordered and then ate a breakfast of coffee and toasted *ciabatta*, Roxy proceeded to fill Caroline in on the conversation she and Donald had shared on the *Via dell'Amore*. When she'd finished, she said, "Donald reckons someone's trying to frame him, and I wonder whether it could be Maria."

"What? So she can own an apartment she already owns?"

"Only half owns."

"Oh for goodness sake. The woman's obviously got her hands full as it is, more than she could want. She owns one of the top restaurants in town, Roxy, why on earth would she risk jail for half an apartment? Why would Donald think that? Oh, I know," she began clicking her fingers together, "maybe the little weasel is *lying*! Ever thought of that?! He's trying to throw the blame back onto Maria which makes me think he's guiltier than ever." She scoffed. "He really sucked you in, Roxy. You fell for his sob story."

This made Roxy bristle. She usually had great instincts, but they were all over the place with Donald. Why couldn't she just accept that he killed his wife for the inheritance? Was it because she then had to accept he must also have done away with Max at the same time?

"I just feel like we're overlooking something," Roxy said. "Or *someone*. I don't know whether Donald did this thing, or whether or not Maria was involved. But I do know there had to be a third party. There's no way it could all be pulled off without one."

"So who, then? Could it be Sofia? I mean, I know she 'rescued' you and all today, but still, she does have access to Max's room. She could be working with Donald. Maybe those two were having an affair and plotted this together."

Roxy thought about that. "So why would Sofia call the

police this morning, tell them where Donald was? She wouldn't dob him in if she was working with him, surely? Besides, she's also got an alibi on the day Candy died. Donald said she was at Ted's that afternoon when he woke up in Maria's bed. That was 3:00 p.m. There was no way she could have driven to Berlin and back by then."

Caroline's eyebrows raised. "Ah yes, but that's what *Donald* tells you. Maybe he was just giving her an alibi."

Roxy frowned. "Maybe. But surely the police have already looked into that. Ahhh! It's all so frustrating. You know, it could be someone we haven't even thought about." She chewed on her coffee cup for a few seconds then dropped it back down with a clunk. "What about Maria's husband!"

"Husband? I didn't even know she had one."

"That makes two of us, but apparently she does. Maybe this elusive husband helped her out. It would certainly explain a few things. Maybe, while Maria was throwing Candy to her death, the hubby was driving Jake back to Berlin where he killed him."

"Except that Donald told you and everyone who'd listen that Candy was going on her hike with a man that fateful day. A *man*. Sorry, sweetie, but last time I looked, Maria was a fully grown chick. Well, not fully grown. The woman's almost a midget."

"Candy could have lied."

"Why would she? I mean, you usually lie about spending time with someone of the opposite sex, not the same sex, not your business partner. If she really did go for a walk with Maria, why wouldn't she tell this to Donald? What's to hide? Nope, I say she never said that to her husband at all because he was the one that accompanied her. I say, they both left Ted's after breakfast together and went on that hike. He took a few photos, making sure to stay out of all of them, and, once they got to a secluded spot, he threw her over the edge. He'd probably already pinched one of Max's shoes and chucked it over, too, so it'd look like Max had something to do with it."

"So how did Donald get hold of Max's shoe? He says he didn't even know him."

"How could he not!? There were pictures of Max all over Candy's smartphone, for God's sake. He must have seen them and become *livid*. That's why he threw her over. Then, he returned to town and pretended to everyone that he'd woken up in Ted's." She began clicking her fingers again. "The cops are right, it would have been easy for him to slip through the back door and pretend to wake up in Maria's bed. Problem was, Maria wasn't buying it. She wasn't playing ball so he could have an alibi." She clicked her fingers again. "Maybe they really had slept together in the past and he thought Maria would defend him, but she's obviously more honourable than *you* give her credit for!"

Roxy scratched her head and then tried to massage her neck. She could feel a headache coming on. "Okay, okay, if that's true, once more, I have to ask, where does all this leave Jake? Who killed him? And why?"

Caroline's cockiness did a nosedive then, her smile deflated, the fieriness in her eyes extinguished. She picked up her coffee cup and drank the rest of it in silence.

****

The man looked across the room with a snide smile. "See, I tell you they go away! Now they have Donald in custody we can get rid of this one at last."

His partner was not so sure. "They still have the helicopters, they will still look for him."

He scoffed, waved a hand in the air. "No, it is not so much of a panic anymore. Now they find the shoe they are not so anxious. They will close the police office this afternoon and go back to La Spezia."

"But they will come back tomorrow again!"

He grinned. "Which is why we get rid of him tonight."

CHAPTER 30

Living with the constant fear that a loved one will show up dead does not erase the everyday monotonies of life, nor does the threat of being thrown over a cliff face. Sure, you lose your appetite for a while, you care less about appearance (unless, of course, you're Caroline) but eventually life goes on and hunger returns and you have to try to keep going. In turn, your clothes get dirty and need washing.

So it was, at the end of such a stressful day, the two friends found themselves sitting side by side in a sweaty Laundromat watching an industrial sized washing machine go through the spin cycle.

Earlier that day, after finishing breakfast with Caroline, Roxy had returned to the police station as requested. Giuseppe had gone back to La Spezia and there was a young policewoman at the front desk, waiting to take her statement before closing up shop. Once that was out of the way, Roxy made her way back to her bed, catching up on some much needed rest while Caroline sipped a bottle of *Limonata* on the sofa, flicking through yet another fashion magazine. *Harper's BAZAAR* this time. Where she got them all from, Roxy never bothered to ask. At some stage Caroline must have gone outside to fetch some lunch—a baguette, some feta cheese and the reddest tomato she had ever seen—but she found it difficult to eat, still feeling shaken up by the morning's events.

It was only later that afternoon, as they attempted to freshen up and head out for an early dinner, that both women looked at each other and knew it was time to get practical. Thrusting their dirty clothes in plastic bags, they gathered their loose change and headed back outdoors. At the convenience store, they invested in a small packet of laundry powder and then found their way to the local Laundromat, which happened to be across the road from their apartment in a basement room below street level. Roxy marvelled that they hadn't noticed it before, and wondered what real treasures this beautiful town possessed that had been lost to them in their single-minded quest to find Max.

It was hot inside the Laundromat and every machine was on overdrive so they had to wait a few minutes for one to free up. They dropped their bags to the floor and sat to the side, Roxy attempting to clear her mind while Caroline took the opportunity to catch up on her social media.

She illegally tapped into the nearby Marina Café's Wi-Fi then logged into her Facebook site, yelping as the page came up. It was clear the word was now out about Max's disappearance and she had been deluged with mixed messages of encouragement and despair.

"There's 262 messages on Facebook alone," she told Roxy. "I'm too scared to look at Twitter."

"All about Max?"

"Every single one. Oh, no, here's one from Oliver, for you."

Roxy glanced up at her. "Oh?"

"God, that's a terrible picture. Does your agent never shave? And how many chins has he got now?"

"Caro."

"Sorry, but really, it's shocking. Okay, so he says he's been madly calling your mobile and wants me to ask why you haven't phoned."

"Because my old number's useless over here, I'm using a different SIM card, of course." Roxy tried not to think of all the messages her poor mother must have left on her old number as well.

Caroline began tapping away. "I'll tell him to stop being a stress head, that you're perfectly fine and will be in touch when we find Max." She stopped typing, sighed sadly then resumed typing again.

As Caroline continued making her way through the messages, Roxy glanced out of the tiny barred window right at the top of the wall, which offered a small, dusty view of the street above. It was just starting to get dark outside and the crowds were thinning out as they did most evenings, the day-trippers heading back to their hotels or homes or wherever it was they all came from.

She longed for her own home, then, for the apartment she once thought was tiny but now realised was spacious by Riomaggiore standards. She longed, too, for her sun-dappled office looking out over Australian gums and lush ferns. She yearned for her old laptop, her comfy lounge and her tiny TV set. But most of all she longed to speak to her mother and her agent, to tell them both that everything was okay.

If only she could tell them that.

Something on the road above caught Roxy's attention and she squinted to get a better look as she watched someone walk past. That's when it occurred to her: Someone else had disappeared unexpectedly last Friday, the same Friday Candy and Max had vanished.

She'd forgotten all about that.

Before she could give it more thought, Caroline was jumping up. "Free at last!" she said, striding towards a washing machine that had just finished its cycle, its roaring motor winding down as the door emitted a clicking sound. Caroline swung it open and began hauling the wet clothes out.

Roxy was appalled. "You don't want to wait for the

owner of those?"

"God no! We haven't got time for that. Besides, it's their own damn fault for deserting their laundry at the end of a busy day." She placed the wet clothes on top of the machine then pushed her own gear inside. "Where's your stuff?"

Roxy stood up and emptied her laundry bag into the machine, then sprinkled some washing powder over the top. They counted their coins and placed six into the requisite slot, jamming it in and out quickly so the machine could start.

After watching for a few seconds, Caroline said, "Cool, let's get outta here."

"What, and desert our own laundry? At the end of a busy day?"

Caroline ignored this and made her way back up the stairs and onto the street level again, Roxy fast behind. They looked around.

"So what now?" Caroline asked.

"I hate to say it, but I need to find Lily-Anne." Caroline looked at her as if she were nuts. "I have two really important questions I need to ask her. Do you think she'll still be at Ted's?"

She shrugged. "Don't know, don't care. I'm thinking I might just get takeaway and head back to the room. Not really in the mood for a lively restaurant tonight." She blinked. "God, I never thought I'd hear myself say that!"

Roxy smiled. Perhaps Caroline was finally growing up. "Do you think you can get enough takeaway for me, too? I won't be long."

"Of course. I might even get some gelato as well. You know, we've been in Italy for days and haven't even treated ourselves yet."

"Good idea. But first, can I ask you a huge favour?"

Caroline shrugged. "If it'll help find Max."

"I think it just might." Roxy glanced at her watch, it was a few minutes before five. "While I talk to Lily-Anne, can you go back to the parking station as fast as you can? You need to talk to Aris again before he finishes work. If he's already left, try and find him. He can't be far."

Caroline stared at her, perplexed. "Okaaaaay," she said. "What's going on? Why do I need to speak to the parking attendant?"

"Because we've all forgotten to ask the most obvious question."

"Which is?"

"How did Jake get back to Berlin last Friday? Or, more importantly, with *whom*?" Caroline looked confused so she explained: "We know for a fact that Jake didn't use Max's car. It's still there, right? So who took him?"

"He could've used the train."

"Nope, he never would have got back so quickly on public transport. He had to go by car. Who was the driver? It couldn't have been Donald or Maria, so who was it?" She shook Caroline by the shoulders. "This is really important. You need to ask Aris for a list of all the cars that left town some time last Friday morning and then returned after midday on Saturday."

"That's a lot of cars, Roxy."

She held up a finger. "Here's how you can narrow it down. We only want to know about the cars that left with two people on Friday, and returned with just one on Saturday."

"You think that was the person who killed Jake?"

"Bingo!"

As Caroline made her way to the parking station, glimmers of confusion still on her face, Roxy wound her way back down to the pier and towards Ted's Trattoria & Music Bar. It was now early evening and the place was beginning to come to life again. The cocktail crowd were gathering in their flowing dresses and linen shirts, sipping creamy, bright concoctions, their only care: what to order for dinner that night. Roxy could not see any of the usual staff—Maria, Valentino, Sofia—but she did spot a black man wielding a cocktail shaker behind the bar and two female waitresses, both looking a lot like German backpackers with broad shoulders and no-nonsense expressions.

"Oh, Roxy, my darlin'!" came an American accent from the patio and she glanced around to find Lily-Anne, champagne glass in hand, sitting with Vern and the Irish couple.

Roxy made her way over as John found her a chair.

"I'm soooo glad you could join us, you must be desperate for a drink after your ordeal," Lily-Anne was saying.

"So you heard about that then."

"Of course we heard! How *dreadful!* You poor, poor pumpkin! Held hostage! And by a crazed murderer!"

"Well, I'm not sure—"

"Now, now, don't you beat yourself up about it, my dear! That Donald Marlow had us all fooled, didn't he, Vern? I never would've believed it of him, never in my life! I says to Vern, I says, 'He seemed like a perfectly normal gentleman. A little funny looking, that has to be said, but perfectly normal.'"

Beryl was nodding keenly. "Aye, he took us all by surprise, me dear. We've known him much longer, to be sure, and he always seemed so polite, and so *devoted* to Candace!" She glanced around furtively then lowered her voice. "I never would have suspected that he and *Maria* ..." She said the name with a hush and they all nodded fervently again.

Roxy sighed. So that gossip had reached them, too.

"I mean, I know Maria wasn't exactly happy with Valentino, but still."

Roxy's ears pricked up. "Valentino?"

"Aye, her husband."

Roxy sat back in her chair with a small smile. That was her first question answered. Then she frowned as the reality of it sank in. "I thought he was just the hired help."

Lily-Anne burst into a fit of giggles and wobbled her chin at Roxy. "Oh that's *hilarious!* Don't let Valentino hear you say that! He'd be mortified! Of course, we all know who wears the pants in *that* relationship." She raised her eyebrows a few times, mischievously. "She's very bossy, that woman, and I can tell he just don't like it. A man don't like to be bossed about now, does he, Vern?"

Vern stayed quiet beside her.

"But ... but ..." Roxy was struggling to understand. "He was always so flirtatious, so sleazy ..."

"Oh, he's just *Italian* is all. They can't help themselves. It's their nature."

"So Maria is married to Valentino." Roxy still couldn't picture it and Lily-Anne was laughing again.

"Ooh yes, my dear, Mr and Mrs Valentino Tedesco." She glanced around. "Not that I've seen either of them tonight. You seen them, Vern?"

Vern grunted something this time and dabbed at his forehead with a handkerchief but Roxy's head was now spinning in a whole new direction.

"Did you say Valentino *Tedesco*?"

"Hm-mm. Why, dear?"

Roxy glanced around. The penny had finally dropped. "So *that's* why this place is called Ted's? Short for Tedesco, Valentino's surname?"

Now where had she heard that name before?

"Aye, Maria felt it sounded more Western-like, would be more appealing to the tourists," John was saying but Roxy was no longer listening.

She stood abruptly and turned to go when she remembered her second question. She turned back. "Lily-Anne, you said you got badly sunburnt one day last week. Can you remember what day that was?"

Lily-Anne blinked at her, confused by the change of tack but, sensing her mood, she tried to think. "Oh dear, I really can't remember." She glanced at her husband. "Vern, you're good with detail now, ain't ya? You must remember, when was that?"

Vern, who had uttered very little throughout this

exchange, turned his watery blue eyes upon Roxy and said very simply, very matter-of-factly, "It was last Friday."

The look he then gave Roxy suggested he knew exactly where she was going with that and wondered what had taken her so long.

CHAPTER 31

"What's taking so long?" demanded Caroline, crouching in the dark beside Roxy. "My legs are going numb."

"Shh," said Roxy. "Not long now."

It was just after midnight and the fishing village was almost still. The shops, eateries and bars had all closed, their twinkly lights out for the night, and no one was on the streets except a few stray cats and a sleepy dog. That is, until they had crept out of the train tunnel and up the stairs towards the jetty and spotted the small group of youngsters sitting on the stone wall, dragging on cigarettes and sharing a bottle of something they were no doubt too young to be sharing.

"Bored bloody teenagers," Roxy said. "Doesn't one of them have an Xbox at home?"

"Why can't we just wait until morning and get the police then?" hissed Caroline, equally as bored, and Roxy shook her head.

"Because it could be too late by then."

"Too late for what?"

Roxy didn't dare to say. "Shhh!" she said instead, wishing the teenagers away.

They watched from the shadows of the stairwell for some time, one eye on the kids, the other on Ted's Trattoria directly across the road. Finally, after what seemed like a lifetime, but was probably more like ten minutes, one of the teens threw the empty bottle into the water and they all jumped up and made their way past Ted's and along the thin dark street that Roxy knew led away from the main road and towards Ola's Villas.

She watched them disappear from sight then took another good look at the restaurant, checking for movement of any kind. There was a small light on outside the front door but the rest of the place was shrouded in darkness. Eventually, after what seemed another lifetime, Roxy said, "Let's go."

At the same time, she thought, "I just hope we're not too late."

"But why Ted's?" Caroline persisted, following close behind.

"We need to get inside and look around, we need to see for ourselves."

Caroline grabbed Roxy's hand. "Oh my God! You think Max is in there!"

Roxy shook her head firmly. "No, Caro, I just hope he is."

A few hours earlier, Caroline and Roxy had met back in the apartment where, over takeaway calamari and mouthwatering strawberry gelato, Caroline had told Roxy everything the parking attendant had said. They now knew exactly who had come and gone between Friday morning and Saturday afternoon, and it was starting to make sense. Finally, after a week of frustration, the oddly shaped pieces of this puzzle were clicking into place.

There was just one final piece outstanding and she had a strong hunch it was waiting for them somewhere inside Ted's.

Clinging to the sides of the buildings where the

moonlight was darkest, they edged their way slowly along the cobbled road and then past Ted's front door and into the side alley that led to the back. It was pitch-black there and they waited a moment to let their eyes adjust before Roxy crept up to the back door and tried the handle.

She softly groaned. It was locked.

"She's hardly going to leave it open with a welcome sign on the mat, is she?" Caroline whispered beside her, but Roxy was already looking around for a key. She wiped her hands above the door frame, searched a nearby pot. No luck.

"We need to break in," she whispered back. "We—"

A sudden noise made Roxy stop. It sounded like a footstep, then another, then two more. They were coming from inside the restaurant and getting louder.

"Shit!" Caroline hissed and they glanced, terrified, at each other before racing back down the alley to the main road.

"Over here!" Roxy had spotted a large dumpster near the takeaway pizza shop. They ducked behind it just as a dark figure emerged from the alley.

At first they could not work out who it was and Roxy tried to lean out farther to get a better look.

"Be careful!" Caroline whispered.

Roxy took a deep breath and was rewarded with the putrid smell of rotting garbage and fresh urine. She grimaced and tried not to breathe through her nose as she edged forward, crouching now at the side of the dumpster in the shadow of a smaller recycling bin. She squinted, trying to get a better look, and that's when she recognised who it was. She was not at all surprised.

"Is it the sleazebag?" Caroline hissed and Roxy glanced around and nodded.

"Yep, Valentino."

Aris had already told Caroline how Valentino had taken his car from the locals' section of the parking station at around 11:30 a.m. that fateful Friday, an unfamiliar man in the passenger seat beside him. Valentino had told Aris, in hushed tones, that he was heading to Rome to see a cousin, but Aris had wondered about that because the strange man had looked up then, surprised. When Valentino returned, the following day, the passenger was nowhere to be seen but Aris did notice, resting on the dashboard, a toll sticker for the A15 motorway, which Valentino had quickly pocketed.

"That's the road north of here, not south to Roma," he had told Caroline. "I tell the police all of this, but they no care."

Well, thought Roxy. *They'll care now.* She looked around again but Valentino had disappeared and she began to panic, glancing frantically up and down the street, when he suddenly reemerged from the alley, his back to her now as he hauled something out. It looked like a large, black sack.

Roxy felt her heart stop.

"What's he got?" Caroline whispered.

"Shh. There's someone else coming!"

A second figure had appeared, holding on to the other end of the sack, and Roxy stared hard for a few moments trying to work out who it was. Then she gasped aloud. She could not believe her eyes.

"What the hell ...?!"

"Who is it?" hissed Caroline but Roxy was now speechless. She dropped back behind the dumpster and shook her head over and over, trying to reconnect the pieces. She thought she'd had this thing solved, she thought the puzzle had been perfect, but now ...

"Oh for pity's sake!" Caroline climbed over Roxy and towards the side where she stuck her neck out to see for herself. A second later she was flat on the ground beside Roxy, also stunned into silence.

Eventually, she found the words. "That's Monty."

Roxy had no choice but to nod. Yes it was.

There in the dim light of the street lamps was their guardian angel, the Santa Claus look-alike with the mop of white hair and the thick white moustache, the same man who was always ready with an eager wave and a helping hand. Yet here he was helping Valentino lift the large sack, clearly struggling beneath its weight.

"But ... but how?" Caroline was saying. "*Why?!*"

Roxy shook herself out, there was no time to think now, she had to get back out and see what they were up to. Scrambling past Caroline, she edged her way to the shadows of the recycling bin and looked out to find that the two men now had a better grip on the sack and were carrying it slowly down the ramp, towards the water. Caroline, too, had given up hiding and was crouched just behind Roxy, her eyes wide.

"What have they got?" she hissed. "Is that ...?"

She couldn't say the name and neither could Roxy. They just watched, numb, for a few minutes as the kidnappers hauled the sack along the jetty and then dumped it with an ugly thud into a small runabout.

"They're heading out to sea," Roxy said and was about to say something else when Caroline stood up from the dumpster and began running down towards them.

"Oh shit!" Roxy cried. *What if they had a gun?*

It didn't matter to Caroline. She knew what was in that sack and she couldn't let them escape.

"Stop!" she screamed, her voice piercing the silence and echoing across the rocks on either side of the jetty. "Give me my brother back!"

CHAPTER 32

Monty and Valentino stared back towards Caroline, stunned and motionless for a few seconds before Monty shouted something to Valentino and he dashed across to the rear of the boat and began frantically tugging at something. It was the boat's motor.

Both women were now racing down the jetty ramp towards the boat but by the time they got close he had sparked the engine to life, released the rope from its buoy and the runabout was spurting away, heading out to sea, out into the murky darkness. Within seconds it had disappeared from sight.

"Noooooooooo!" screamed Caroline, dropping to her knees, one hand across her mouth, sobbing hysterically. "No, no, no, please, I just want Max!"

Roxy had reached Caroline and was pulling her up. "Come on, we need to follow them!"

Caroline looked like she was in a daze now, so Roxy rushed past her and jumped into the first vessel she found. Damn it! It had no motor. She jumped back out, nearly toppling into the water as she did so, then corrected herself and ran down the jetty a little farther until she spotted a small dinghy with an outboard motor. She threw herself into it and stared at it. How the hell did you start the thing?

"Get out of the way!" screamed Caroline who had caught up with her and had already released the connecting rope. She reached across the stern and pulled at some kind of lever, ensuring it was straight. Next she pulled out the choke, turned the hand grip on the throttle and yanked at the starter rope. It spluttered for a few seconds then died.

"Bugger it!" she said then took a deep breath and tried again, slower this time, and the engine suddenly roared to life. "That's more like it." When she spotted Roxy's look of wide-eyed surprise, she added, "That's how I spent *my* teenage years, in case you were wondering. Had a thing for yachties."

Within minutes she had manoeuvred them away from the other fishing vessels and was ploughing out through the bay, following in Monty's frothy wake.

"What do we do if we catch up to them?" Caroline yelled across the roar of the engine and the rushing of the wind, and Roxy shook her head, clinging for dear life to the side of the vessel.

She had no idea. She just knew they had to stick close, they had to follow Max, wherever that took them. Come what may.

"There they are!" Caroline yelled again, clutching onto the tiller as she steered the boat with one hand, her other hand pointing towards a rush of white water in the distance. It had to be Monty's boat, still flying, full throttle across the bay. Within minutes it would be through the inlet and out into the open sea.

"It's too far away!" Roxy screamed back and then gasped when a sudden ball of white light appeared from nowhere, just to the north of the kidnapper's runabout, followed fast by another ball of light from the west.

"What's going on?" screamed Caroline and at first Roxy had no idea.

Then she realised and felt a flood of relief. "It must be

the coast guard!"

Caroline took the motor down a notch and they watched from a distance as the larger vessels closed in on the smaller one, a flurry of Italian bursting out from a loudspeaker somewhere. They could just make out three or four dark figures running up and down the starboard side of one patrol vessel and what looked like guns pointing in the direction of Monty's runabout.

By now the runabout had stalled and there was a burst of noise again before several dark-clad figures jumped onto its bow, pushing the kidnappers out of sight, probably onto the floor of the boat to be handcuffed.

That's when Caroline buckled over, one hand still on the tiller, the other holding her mouth in wrenching sobs, and Roxy joined her at the stern, holding her tight as they both cried with joy and relief.

It was over at last.

"But what about Max?!" Caroline suddenly gasped, pushing away, a look of panic in her eyes. "Oh my God, what if he's ...?"

Roxy swiped her tears away then reached over and, using the technique Caroline had used earlier, revved the engine back to life. "Let's find out, shall we?"

Caroline grabbed her hand to stall her. "I'm not sure I can."

Roxy placed her other hand on Caroline's and gave her a reassuring smile. "Come on, Caro. We've come this far. We can go the final leg. We can do this. For Max."

Max's heart was still beating, but only just. As they puttered their way to the runabout, they watched with horror as two officers were leaning over Max's limp body, one performing CPR, the other monitoring his watch. The kidnappers had been hauled off and onto the second patrol boat, but Roxy couldn't even look their way. She never wanted to set eyes on Monty and Valentino again.

A familiar face appeared then, leaning out from the first

patrol boat. It was Officer Giuseppe with a life jacket on and a rope in his hands, which he was now flinging towards them. Caroline grabbed it and secured it to the bow then watched as Giuseppe and another officer pulled them close enough to tie the two vessels together. Within minutes the women had clambered off and were sitting to one side of the patrol boat, blankets wrapped around their shaking bodies, watching mutely as the officers continued working on Max.

After what seemed like forever, one of the officers yelled something in Italian to Giuseppe who yelled something back then turned to look at Caroline.

"We need to get him to a hospital, fast!"

Before she could respond, one officer was releasing the small motorboat Roxy and Caroline had used and was reversing it out of the way while two other officers were hauling Max's lifeless body onto their patrol boat, a third continuing with the CPR. As Max's body was set down carefully at the stern, both women gasped.

He looked like a total stranger. Max's gaunt face was unshaven and smudged with dirt, his usually floppy hair oily and clinging to his head, the clothes on his body filthy and torn. His eyes were not open and his limbs were not moving, but the vessel now was, at rapidly increasing speed, heading in a southerly direction, away from Riomaggiore.

Caroline, too, was flying across the boat, trying to get to her brother, but Roxy held her back. "I need to be with him!" she screamed. "I need to hold him!"

"Let them do their job, Caro. They don't need us getting in their way."

"But he's my brother!" she wailed and Roxy screamed back at her.

"And he's my *boyfriend*!" There she'd said it. "But it's not about us. We need to let them bring him back."

Caroline nodded wearily and dropped her head into her hands again as Giuseppe wrapped the blanket around her tighter.

The vessel was now flying across the bay and Roxy stole

a glimpse back towards the second patrol boat, which was following close behind. At the forward bow she spotted two men sitting cross-legged, their hands behind their backs, their heads hung low, several officers standing on either side. Suddenly one of the men looked up and straight towards her. Roxy couldn't see his face clearly, but it had to be Monty, she could just make out a mop of white hair, something white near his mouth.

A fierce wave of anger and betrayal rippled through her then and she wanted to raise her fists and scream at him, but she did none of that. She simply shook her head and looked away.

"Tea!"

Giuseppe was holding a flask out towards her and Roxy accepted it with a grateful nod. After a few refreshing gulps, she handed it back and asked, "How did you know?"

He looked over her shoulder to the second boat. "We have suspected Valentino for some time, but we were not sure about his accomplice," he called back, his voice difficult to hear above the drone of the boat's large engines. "I am sorry it had to get this far, but we needed to catch him in the act."

"Monty?"

"Yes, Monty Tedesco."

And then, in a whoosh, it came to her. It all made sense now and she was shocked that she had not realised it earlier. "They're related, right?"

"Monty is Valentino's uncle."

No wonder Valentino's surname had sounded so familiar earlier that evening. Suddenly, Lily-Anne Waver's words began ringing in Roxy's ears, the words she had used that first night they had arrived in Riomaggiore and Monty had helped them find lodgings: *"So Monty Tedesco strikes again,"* Lily-Anne had said. *"He's always at his bat perch, helping everyone."*

Too helpful, Roxy thought now, realising with a tremble how badly she and Caroline had been played. They had trusted this man and he had manipulated them, right from the start.

She recalled Monty's words, too, from that first evening, how he'd envied Hugo's five holiday rentals and sniggered: *"Life is too easy for him. He just rents the rooms then sleeps all day. I wish!"*

In fact, he'd wished for it so badly, he was prepared to kill anyone who got in his way.

Roxy didn't know if it was Monty's idea or Valentino's, but they must have conspired to get rid of Candy and frame Donald for the crime. That way they, too, could live the easy life. All they had to do was convince Valentino's busy wife Maria to let them start renting out that enormous seaside apartment, then they could just sit back and watch the money pour in.

And if Maria refused? Well, there was always the cliff top on a quiet and lonely day.

Roxy trembled again and turned back to Officer Giuseppe. "So why did you arrest Donald this morning? What was that about?"

"We needed to get him out of Riomaggiore," he yelled. "We needed an excuse to close down the station. I told you about this, knowing the word would get out. Sofia must have mentioned it to Valentino when she returned to the restaurant, and Valentino must have told Monty. This is what we were counting on. We needed them to think it was over and force their hand."

"You mean force them to get rid of Max?" She glanced across to her dear friend who was still being monitored by the patrol officers but had a little more colour in his cheeks now. Caroline had crept to his side and was clutching one hand, a look of shock on her face.

Roxy turned back to Giuseppe, her emerald eyes flashing with fury. "You risked his life!"

Giuseppe had the decency to look ashamed and said, "I am sorry about this." He edged closer to where she was sitting. "You have to believe me, Miss Parker, we had no choice. They had already killed two people, we needed to catch them, how you say, *red-handed*. We needed them to think the coast was clear and force them to act."

Well, they'd certainly done that.

The motor suddenly dropped down a few revs and Roxy looked up to find they were turning towards an unfamiliar coastline glistening with thousands of tiny lights.

"La Spezia," Giuseppe called out. "The hospital is not far away. Your friend, Max, will soon be okay."

Boyfriend, she wanted to correct him, but only nodded, hoping he was right.

EPILOGUE

Max did survive his seven-day ordeal, but he would be a changed man for life, and it saddened Roxy deeply as she watched him lying in his hospital bed, sleeping now, but probably not as peacefully as he once had. He'd probably never sleep quite so peacefully again.

It had been three days since his ordeal had ended, and while his health was now improving, it would be many weeks before his weight returned. Yet it was his spirit Roxy was most worried about.

As Max recuperated at La Spezia's Sant'Andrea Hospital, a drip in one arm, bandages on his forehead and around both wrists and ankles, Roxy thought of what he had endured at the hands of Monty and Valentino Tedesco. She felt bitterly angry but relieved, too, because he had not been killed as Jake had. They had spared him that. Not intentionally, of course, for it was only a matter of time.

From what Roxy had pieced together with Commander Rossi and Carmela, they had every intention of killing Max, but the police had arrived in Riomaggiore and so they had to put it off until the coast was clear, when they could quietly dump him out to sea.

Roxy shivered a little at the thought and watched Max sleep, most of her questions now answered, the whole, complicated puzzle now complete. What she hadn't worked out for herself, Max had filled in between groggy sleeps and doctor's visits. The police had managed to explain the rest.

The whole sorry saga had started for Max 500 kilometres away, in a whole different country at a whole different altitude. It was his first Monday night at Mt Pilatus and a perky blonde Australian with a silly name and a flirtatious nature had approached him at the bar below the stairs of the Hotel Bellevue. He was enjoying the complementary Swiss cheese between sips of good Belgian beer, happy in his own company, when Candy waltzed up, her husband back in his room with a headache. They were chatting within seconds, Candy waxing lyrical about her boring husband who often got headaches and always hated to hike.

"I'm hiking around the trail tomorrow if you want to come along," Max had said, fatefully as it turned out, and she had gleefully accepted. She had a knack for encouraging male escorts.

And so they had met for breakfast that Tuesday, Max in hiking boots, Candy with her bubble pink visor on and trekking poles by her side, all ready for a day around the mountain. The walk had been a lot of fun until Candy started to tell Max about a few "silly messages" she had recently received from her business partner in Riomaggiore.

"What sort of messages?" he had asked.

"Oh she seems to have it in her head that my husband can't be trusted." She laughed then, not believing it for a second, but at Max's insistence, told him how Maria's husband, Valentino, suspected that Donald was planning to "bump her off".

"It's ludicrous!" she'd said, but it must have played on Max's mind because, knowing the couple were heading for Cinque Terre the following day, he began to worry. Unable to convince Candy to take the threat seriously, he phoned his flatmate, Jake, offering to waive his overdue rent if he could get himself to Milan with Max's good camcorder and telephoto lens by lunchtime the next day.

"If this guy really is going to try to kill his wife, I'm going to film it all and make sure he doesn't get away with it!"

Next he called his mother in Australia and, not wanting to worry her, simply told her he was heading to a place called Riomaggiore. Any more and she'd panic. He should have realised that she would start panicking the minute she heard the tension in his voice.

And so Max had checked out of Mt Pilatus early and followed the Marlows down to Italy, stopping briefly in Milan to collect his camera gear from Jake. Being a spontaneous fellow, Jake had begged to come along and after some hesitation Max had agreed. He could do with the company.

That was his first major mistake.

Late that Wednesday night, the flatmates arrived in Riomaggiore and found a room at Ola's Villas. The next afternoon, Max caught up with Candy who was stunned to learn he had followed her all this way.

"You have to report your husband to the local police," he'd said and she had laughed him off. He was overreacting, she was sure it was all just a silly misunderstanding. "Well, I'm not letting Donald out of my sight," Max had told her then. "If he so much as tries anything with you, I'll not only have it on camera, I'll be there to stop him."

That conversation was Max's second mistake.

"Valentino overheard the whole thing," Commander Rossi had told Roxy and Caroline when they met again, just the day before.

They had all gathered in a small waiting room at the La Spezia hospital. The police had already interrogated the Tedescos and while Monty had not so much as opened his mouth, Valentino's lips were flapping.

"He is a big baby," Carmela had scoffed. "He is crying and trying to say it was all his uncle's idea. But we know that *he* is the one who killed Jake."

"Ah yes, but he tells us he did not mean to," said Rossi. "He only meant to drive him back to Berlin and leave him there."

"So what on earth happened?" demanded Caroline, but Roxy was already holding her hand up.

"Sorry, can we just back up a bit first? You said that Valentino overheard Max talking to Candy; that was at the back of Ted's, right, on the Thursday night? Valentino told us Max was trying to hit on Candy, but obviously he was lying. Max was trying to protect the poor woman."

"Yes," said Carmela. "That's when Valentino panicked. How could they possibly plant Candy's murder on Donald if Max was watching him the whole time? He quickly reported the conversation to Monty who was furious. His plan was about to go belly up!"

Little did any of them know, Monty's plan had been many years in the making, his envy of Candy and frustration with Maria, brewing to boiling point. Despite his outwardly friendly nature, Monty was a bundle of bitterness and regret, and he was fed up to his hind teeth with running the hat shop. It was a full-time, thankless job, and one that was so dull he spent his days loitering on the road watching as other people got to enjoy their leisurely lives. He had always longed for a holiday rental, an easy life like Hugo, but he didn't have the money and time was running out. Would he spend his final good years serving sunburnt tourists while Candace and Donald Marlow got to relax?

Not if he could help it.

Monty wanted to ditch his job and take over managing that enormous, seaside apartment that his nephew's wife was squandering away. He wanted to rent it out all day every day to rich tourists while he put his feet up. Yet Maria was having none of it. Candy didn't want to rent it to strangers and Maria didn't really have the time, her restaurant being a full-time occupation. She was happy with the status-quo, Monty not so much.

Eventually, as Valentino's marriage deteriorated—how

could it not, the man had eyes for everyone but his wife—Monty convinced his nephew to act, explaining that once Candy was gone, they would both be rich and happy. He knew that Candy's apartment alone could net more than Hugo's five crummy rentals. "You need never work in that dingy trattoria again, slave to your nagging fish wife!"

"The plan was supposed to be a simple one," said Rossi. "First they would plant the idea that Donald could not be trusted into Candy's head then, when the Marlows arrived for their annual holiday, Monty would take Candy on a secret walk along the cliff top to discuss his concerns in private."

"He needed to do it that first Friday morning," Giuseppe spoke up now, "when he knew I would not be in town. I only man the office on weekends when it is busiest, you see."

"That is right," said Carmela. "Monty planned to meet Candy in secret at the most secluded part of the Blue Trail, just near the end of the *Via dell'Amore*. He would take a few photos and then, while she was leaning out to look at the view, he would push her over."

"And while Monty did that, Valentino was going to stitch Donald up," said Roxy.

"That is correct," Rossi agreed. "He would drug Donald's champagne and juice—a drink he had every morning over breakfast at Ted's when he was in town—then, before Donald passed out, Valentino would get him into Maria's bedroom above the restaurant, where he would be out of the way and without an alibi. Valentino knew Maria would be at the Monterosso markets, where she was every Friday. If we did not believe Donald killed his wife for the inheritance, a suspected affair would seal his fate."

"Of course they knew Maria would deny it, but they were counting on a sceptical police force," said Carmela. "And if they could stick it to Valentino's nagging wife at the same time, then, great."

"But what if Maria had refused?" said Caroline now. "What if she had inherited the whole apartment and didn't want to let Monty take it over and rent it out?"

Rossi's eyes drooped sadly. "Then there is always the rocky cliffs of the *Via dell'Amore*."

Roxy thought about this and shivered. She hadn't exactly warmed to Maria, but she was glad she had been spared that. The plan was certainly foolproof, she thought, the perfect murder. Candy would be gone, Donald in jail, and the apartment would be theirs to do with as they liked.

But they weren't counting on Candy's White Knight, Max Farrell, and his sidekick Jake Conway.

"They must have been very frustrated," said Carmela, half smiling. "How could they pin this on Donald if Max and Jake were watching him the whole time? That's when they reworked their plan. Now they would have to get rid of those men, too. And quickly, before the weekend came and Giuseppe returned."

So it was, that Friday morning, as Maria headed off to the markets and Candy headed off for her hike, Valentino had to put Plan B into place. Instead of just drugging Donald, he also had to drug Max who was seated nearby.

"We believe he drugged Mr Farrell first," said Rossi.

"What kind of drug?" asked Caroline.

"We suspect Rohypnol, we have found several suspicious vials amongst Mr Tedesco's belongings so we will know more soon, when the forensics report comes back."

"Are you talking about Roofies, the date rape drug?"

"That is the one."

How typical of that sleazebag, Caroline thought, wondering why he even had the drug in the first place. She shuddered at the thought.

"We suspect he laced two glasses of the champagne and juice drink, er, what do you call it?"

"Mimosa," Caroline promptly answered.

"Yes, that is it. Mr Farrell tells us that Valentino offered him a complimentary mimosa with his breakfast, it's about the last thing he remembers, and we suspect it was laced with the strong sedative. When he became groggy, Valentino pretended to help him to the restrooms at the back but really he dragged him down to the wine cellar deep below the restaurant before he passed out."

"The cellar is not used anymore," explained Carmela. "Plus it has thick stone walls. A very good place to hide someone."

"But hang on," said Roxy. "What about that text message Max sent me: SOS. Was Max in the cellar then?"

Giuseppe nodded. "His memory is very vague, of course, but we believe he must have sent that message before he was properly tied up. Valentino must have left your friend for a few minutes while he drugged Mr Marlow and got him into Maria's bed. Mr Farrell must have come to at some point and sent that text before he fell unconscious again."

"And Sofia, the waitress?" demanded Caroline. "She was on duty that day, how on earth did she not notice all these men disappearing out the back, looking stoned to their eyeballs?"

Rossi shook his head. "There is no evidence that Sofia is involved and we do know that Valentino kept her busy with the tables out on the patio, so it is likely that she did not see any of this, but we are still checking. We have also confirmed that Ola does employ Sofia to clean her hotel rooms, so it is not suspicious that you saw her outside Max's room that day. Still, we are keeping an open mind."

Roxy said, "Okay, so Valentino drugs both men and gets them out of the way, but where is Jake in all of this?"

"Ah yes, the third man," said Carmela. "The one who has been confusing us all."

Understatement of the week, thought Roxy but she just listened as Carmela continued.

"Valentino had quite a lot of luck on his side. He did not have enough of the drug for all three men, but he was guessing from the previous morning that Jake would not come to Ted's for breakfast, he would be sleeping in."

"So," interjected Rossi, "according to Sofia, just before 11:00 a.m., Valentino suddenly put her in charge of the restaurant claiming his cousin had called with an emergency in Roma. He said to tell Maria he would be away overnight."

"But really he was heading straight to Ola's Villas to offer Jake a lift back to Berlin, right?" said Roxy and they all nodded. "He probably woke him up and told him they had to leave immediately." They nodded again.

While Valentino must have loathed the idea of a gruelling, twelve-hour drive, he knew he had little choice; he had to get Jake out of the way, pronto. The plan, however, was not to kill him, or at least that's what he told the police. He was simply going to get him to his apartment, freshen up quickly, then get back in the car and head home. The problem was, Jake started listening to his answering machine and there were dozens of increasingly frantic messages left by the Farrell family, desperately looking for Max.

That's when Valentino panicked.

As Jake left his first message for Caroline, Valentino grabbed the nearest object he could find and smashed his head in. Then he wiped all the other messages and headed back to Italy as fast he could drive, thinking he had got away with it and congratulating himself the whole time. Little did he know, the young woman in apartment 3A had heard some words of Italian being spoken in the corridor that night, and a young parking attendant back in Riomaggiore had a thorough knowledge of road tolls.

"Okay," said Roxy. "So while Valentino was doing all the heavy lifting, Monty was doing a little push and shove? Throwing Candy over the cliff?"

The detectives nodded again. "He was clever, our Monty," said Rossi. "The old-timer knew the path well. He knew there were bends where you could walk unseen, where you could push your victim off the edge and no one would notice a thing."

What Monty didn't know, thought Roxy, was that he would be noticed in absentia—when a loud American woman would get so badly sunburnt she would come calling for a hat. As she sat in the Laundromat that day, watching the spin cycle, Roxy realised that Monty, too, had no alibi at the time of Candy's death, yet she quickly dismissed this. After all, why would Monty want to kill Candy? He was just a helpful local. The husband was the one with the motive.

As if reading her mind, Carmela said, "When Donald woke up from his drug-induced sleep late Friday afternoon, still in Maria's bed, he had no idea what had just happened and absolutely no alibi."

"And what he didn't know," added Rossi, "was that it wasn't just Sofia who saw him coming out the back of Ted's. Maria had also spotted him."

Carmela laughed suddenly. "Poor Maria! She was so confused! She could not work out why he was in her room. She says she never looked twice at her friend's husband."

"And why would she?" chimed in Caroline, recalling his pale splotchy skin, his sharklike teeth.

"So what happens now?" asked Roxy. "Will Donald keep Candy's share of the apartment, do you know?"

Rossi shrugged. "I don't think he has given it much thought. He is still in La Spezia, organising to have his wife's remains returned to Australia. I believe Maria will accompany him for the funeral."

"They're going to bury her at home?"

"Cremate," said Carmela. "He said something about taking her ashes on one final hike, to her favourite lookout, somewhere in the Blue Mountains, is it?"

"Oh that's a beautiful spot," said Roxy. "So, he's going to escort his wife this time." She sighed. "If only he'd done that earlier, all of this might never have happened."

They contemplated that silently for several minutes before Carmela coughed discreetly and nudged her head sideways at Rossi. When he looked at her like she was crazy, she gave him a quick thwack across one shoulder and said, "The award, you idiot!"

"Oh, yes, *scusi*!" Rossi then told them the exciting news. His superiors had decided to honour Caroline and Roxy with one of Italy's highest commendations, the Civilian Valour

Medal for Bravery. "The ceremony will be later in the year, but the Force will be happy to fly you back for it."

"Oh my God!" squealed Caroline. "That's *amazing!* When do we get it? What does it look like?"

As she rattled away, Roxy smiled but couldn't help thinking she had all the reward she needed and he was lying under crisp white sheets in the Sant'Andrea Hospital.

Max stirred then, breaking Roxy from her reverie, and she watched as he struggled to open his eyes before he drifted back to sleep.

Oh Max, she thought, reaching for his hand and giving it a gentle squeeze. *You're the one who deserves the medal. If only you hadn't been so gallant.*

All those years he'd spent chiding *her* for suspecting the worst, for seeing crimes wherever she looked, he'd done the exact same thing. And it had almost cost him his life.

Indeed, underestimating Max Farrell had been Monty and Valentino's biggest mistake. They never would have guessed that Max would follow Candy to town, nor that he would take her words so seriously and contact the police. The problem was, as he left his message on the emergency phone line, he began to second-guess himself. It all sounded a little absurd. *No wonder Candy wasn't taking it seriously!* There was no substantial evidence and Donald Marlow looked harmless enough. And so Max had hung up without giving any more details, and that was his third major mistake.

It was also the thing that saved his life.

Not sure what to make of the confusing call, Commander Rossi had decided to despatch two officers to Riomaggiore the next day to investigate, but not until midday—too late for Candy as it turned out, but in time to stop Monty from disposing of Max, as planned, that night.

So Monty bided his time, waiting until Candy's body was found and the police had finally vacated the town, Donald in cuffs, a guilty shadow hanging over Maria. Once the police were gone, Monty and Valentino would dump Max out to sea, knowing he would be so weak he would easily drown and it would look like he had been there all along. Their plan would finally be complete.

Enter Roxy and Caroline.

When the two Aussies arrived a few days after Candy had vanished, enquiring about their missing friend, Monty began to panic. He knew he had to keep them close and so he had done everything to help them out, in effect to learn what they knew and to gain access to Max's hotel room. There, while Roxy called Caroline, he planted Candy's pink visor and retrieved the Converse sneaker. He later planted it in the fishing lines, hoping it would make them believe their friend was already dead.

Little did he know it would only encourage Roxy's insatiable curiosity because, as she pointed out to the local police, who would go hiking with just one shoe?

"Hey, Parker."

Roxy looked up from her thoughts again to find Max watching her this time, his eyelids heavy, his cheeks pale. She edged closer and gave his hand another squeeze. "Hey, Max. How are you feeling?"

He tried to smile, only managed a grimace. "Like I've been run over by a truck. Fifty times. Sorry, must have dozed off."

"Don't be sorry. Your body's still recovering. Those bastards fed you, but only just. Doc says it'll be a few more days yet before you're strong enough to get up."

"Caroline?" He tried to look around.

"She's downstairs, trying to get her mitts on some magazines, I suspect. There's fashion to catch up on."

He half smiled, his lips cracking a little. "You okay?"

"*Moi?*" She held a hand to her breast as if surprised. "I'm perfectly okay, now we've found you. Plus they're going to give us a medal, don't you know? We're now fully fledged heroes, so you better start treating us with some respect!" She smiled. "Hey, your parents rang earlier, tried to come and see you but we put them off. Said you needed more time to rest."

"Thank God."

"Thank Caroline, actually. I think she's grown up a lot this past week."

"Yeah right," he said, this time managing to smile.

And there it was, his full-throttle, melt-your-heart smile and she felt herself exhale as she soaked it up.

"I'm so sorry, Max," she said eventually, but he held a finger up.

"No ... nothing to be sorry for."

"Oh there's plenty. I won't go on about it, I promise, but I do need to say this before your bloody sister comes back and takes over again." She hesitated, took a deep breath. "I'm so sorry, Max, that I behaved so badly when you first told me about the Mercedes job, and I'm sorry that I let you go without so much as a congratulations or a good-bye. But mostly I'm sorry that I could never quite step up when we were going out." She sniffed back a small tear. "Can you ever forgive me?"

He smiled again and reached a hand to brush her tear away. "You saved my life, Roxy. I think I can forgive you. It's the least I can do. Now ... can you do one thing for me?"

She gave him a sideways look. "What, saving your life wasn't enough?!" She smiled but he wasn't smiling back.

"It's about us," he began and she went to say something but he held a hand up to stall her. "Can you please be my best mate again?"

She looked crestfallen. "I never stopped."

"Oh yes you did, for a while there. When we started going out." His voice was croaky with emotion. "I lost you, Parker, you changed."

She bowed her head. "I'm so sorry—"

"It's okay, it's fine, really. But I want my buddy back." He waited until she looked into his eyes and said, "Can we forget this whole relationship crap, we're so bad at it and I miss you, I just want to be mates again."

"Best mates?" she asked.

"Best mates for life."

Roxy threw herself across Max's chest causing him to groan. "Oooh, sorry, sorry." She looked into his eyes again. "I do love you, you know?"

"I know, that's why we have to stay friends, so you keep that up."

"Can I ask just one small favour?"

"What?! Now I have to do something for *you*?" It was his turn to smile. "Of course, Parker, I'll do anything. I owe you my life."

"No, just this." She slowly leaned in towards him and placed her lips very gently on his. They kissed then, just softly, just for a few seconds, but slowly the sadness of the past three months dissolved and the terror of the past week subsided, and she knew he was absolutely right. She had struggled to call him her boyfriend because that hat had never quite fit, despite their best efforts. He was her best friend and there was no denying it.

"Oh get a room!" came Caroline's voice from the doorway where she had been watching them, several magazines in one hand, a tray of plastic cups in the other. She glanced around. "Oh, this *is* a room. Well, then, go right ahead."

"We're done," Roxy said, laughing as she stepped back.

Caroline placed her things down then handed Roxy a cup. "Latté with two sugars, right?"

"Yes, thank you." Roxy and Max shared an impressed glance but Caroline wasn't watching, she was reaching for the iPhone in her handbag.

"Okay, I have more messages to report." Max groaned. "No, no, this won't take long." She began tapping at the screen. "Okay, so, Mum says, make sure the hospital feeds you plenty of nutritious raw vegies, none of that overcooked mush, Dad says the Australian embassy has called and wish you a speedy recovery—fat lot of use they were. Umm, Oliver left a quick message, sending his best to you, Max, and telling you, Roxy, to stay out here for a while and I quote, 'work is as slow as a snail's plop'." She paused so Roxy could groan this time. "Oh, and Gunter called from Berlin, Max, to say take as long as you need, your job will be waiting for you when you return."

"That's good to know," Roxy said and Caroline's eyebrows shot up.

"I thought you'd demand Max return to Sydney pronto."

Roxy shook her head. "Why would I do that? Max is my best mate and I only want the best for him." She turned to look at him. "You love your job so you'd be crazy to come home now. I'll miss you and I'll e-mail you every single day."

"E-mail? That's so passé," scoffed Caroline but Roxy ignored her.

"And I'll be sure to keep the beer on ice for when you return. In fact, I'll keep a running reservation at Pico's wine bar, just in case."

Then she swooped in and gave him another kiss, but this time it was on his cheek, while Caroline rolled her eyes then immersed herself in the latest issue of *Italian Vogue*.

ABOUT THE AUTHOR

C.A. Larmer is a journalist, editor, teacher and author of multiple crime series, stand-alone novels and a non-fiction book about pioneering surveyors in Papua New Guinea. Christina grew up in PNG, was educated in Australia, and spent many years working in Sydney, London, Los Angeles and New York. She now lives with her musician husband, boomerang sons and their very cheeky Bluey on the east coast of Australia.

Sign up for news, views and giveaways:
calarmer.com